2011

FICTION uncovered

GREAT WRITING TO DISCOVER
by eight of the UK's best fiction writers

THE WATER THEATRE
LINDSAY CLARKE
ALMA BOOKS

NIMROD'S SHADOW
CHRIS PALING
PORTOBELLO BOOKS

THE ENGLISH GERMAN GIRL
JAKE WALLIS SIMONS
POLYGON (BIRLINN)

FORGETTING ZOË
RAY ROBINSON
WILLIAM HEINEMANN (RANDOM HOUSE)

NIGHT WAKING
SARAH MOSS
GRANTA

THE LONDON SATYR
ROBERT EDRIC
DOUBLEDAY (TRANSWORLD)

THE PROOF OF LOVE
CATHERINE HALL
PORTOBELLO BOOKS

DISPUTED LAND
TIM PEARS
WILLIAM HEINEMANN (RANDOM HOUSE)

AVAILABLE FROM BOOKSTORES NOW

SELECTED BY OUR JUDGING PANEL

CHAIRED BY Giles Foden   WITH   Damian Barr   Simon Burke   Sarah Crown

fictionuncovered.co.uk
DOWNLOAD OUR FREE IPHONE APP NOW

LOTTERY FUNDED

GRANTA

12 Addison Avenue, London W11 4QR
email editorial@granta.com
To subscribe go to www.granta.com
Or call 845-267-3031 (toll-free 866-438-6150) in the United States, 020 8955 7011 in the United Kingdom

ISSUE 116: SUMMER 2011

LITERATURE & SPOKEN WORD

SEPTEMBER – DECEMBER 2011 HIGHLIGHTS

HAL FOSTER
Wednesday 7 September

Hal Foster explores his theory of a new international style in architecture marked by the cult of the 'starchitect'.

PETER ACKROYD
Thursday 8 September

Peter Ackroyd takes us on an epic journey from England's primeval forests to its first Tudor king to mark the publication of the first volume of his history of England, *Foundation*.

AMIN MAALOUF
Saturday 10 September

On the tenth anniversary of 9/11, Lebanese author Amin Maalouf dissects the world that emerged following the attack on the Twin Towers.

JIMMY CARTER
Wednesday 5 October

Former President of the United States Jimmy Carter talks about his career as president and shares his views of global politics today.

CLAIRE TOMALIN
Tuesday 18 October

Claire Tomalin's new biography of Charles Dickens illuminates the life one of Britain's most revered and popular novelists.

MOURID BARGHOUTI
Thursday 3 November

Mourid Barghouti reads and reflects upon life in Palestine to mark the publication, the second volume of his memoir, *I Was Born There, I Was Here*.

BRIAN COX & JEFF FORSHAW
Sunday 11 December

Brian Cox and Jeff Forshaw take us on a journey deep into the universe as they discuss their new book, *The Quantum Universe*, followed by a book signing.

TICKETS FROM £10
0844 847 9910
SOUTHBANKCENTRE.CO.UK

Image from Amin Maalouf's *Disordered World*

SOUTHBANK CENTRE

CONTENTS

Space
to Imagine

Study Creative Writing at Bath Spa

The Creative Writing Centre at Bath Spa University has been helping
people get published for over three decades. We are now accepting
applications for Autumn 2011 entry on the following programmes of study:

MA Creative Writing

MA Writing for Young People

MA Scriptwriting

MA in Travel & Nature Writing

PhD in Creative Writing

www.bathspa.ac.uk/schools/humanities-and-cultural-industries/creative-writing

GRANTA

REDEPLOYMENT

Phil Klay

We shot dogs. Not by accident. We did it on purpose and we called it 'Operation Scooby'. I'm a dog person, so I thought about that a lot.

First time was instinct. I hear O'Leary go, 'Jesus,' and there's a skinny brown dog lapping up blood the same way he'd lap up water from a bowl. It wasn't American blood, but still, there's that dog, lapping it up. And that's the last straw, I guess, and then it's open season on dogs.

At the time you don't think about it. You're thinking about who's in that house, what's he armed with, how's he gonna kill you, your buddies. You're going block by block, fighting with rifles good to 550 metres and you're killing people at five in a concrete box.

The thinking comes later, when they give you the time. See, it's not a straight shot back, from war to the Jacksonville mall. When our deployment was up, they put us on TQ, this logistics base out in the desert, let us decompress a bit. I'm not sure what they meant by that. Decompress. We took it to mean jerk off a lot in the showers. Smoke a lot of cigarettes and play a lot of cards. And then they took us to Kuwait and put us on a commercial airliner to go home.

So there you are. You've been in a no-shit war zone and then you're sitting in a plush chair looking up at a little nozzle shooting air conditioning, thinking, what the fuck? You've got a rifle between your knees, and so does everyone else. Some Marines got M9 pistols, but they take away your bayonets because you aren't allowed to have knives on an airplane. Even though you've showered, you all look grimy and lean. Everybody's hollow-eyed and their cammies are beat to shit. And you sit there, and close your eyes, and think.

The problem is, your thoughts don't come out in any kind of straight order. You don't think, oh, I did A, then B, then C, then D. You try to think about home, then you're in the torture house. You see the body parts in the locker and the retarded guy in the cage. He squawked like a chicken. His head was shrunk down to a coconut. It takes you a while to remember Doc saying they'd shot mercury into his skull, and then it still doesn't make any sense.

You see the things you saw the times you nearly died. The broken television and the haji corpse. Eicholtz covered in blood. The lieutenant on the radio.

You see the little girl, the photographs Curtis found in a desk. First had a beautiful Iraqi kid, maybe seven or eight years old, in bare feet and a pretty white dress like it's First Communion. Next she's in a red dress, high heels, heavy make-up. Next photo, same dress but her face is smudged and she's holding a gun to her head.

I tried to think of other things, like my wife Cheryl. She's got pale skin and fine dark hairs on her arms. She's ashamed of them but they're soft. Delicate.

But thinking of Cheryl made me feel guilty, and I'd think about Lance Corporal Hernandez, Corporal Smith, and Eicholtz. We were like brothers, Eicholtz and me. The two of us saved this Marine's life one time. A few weeks later Eicholtz is climbing over a wall. Insurgent pops out a window, shoots him in the back when he's halfway over.

So I'm thinking about that. And I'm seeing the retard, and the girl, and the wall Eicholtz died on. But here's the thing. I'm thinking a lot, and I mean, a lot, about those fucking dogs.

And I'm thinking about my dog. Vicar. About the shelter we'd got him from, where Cheryl said we had to get an older dog because nobody takes older dogs. How we could never teach him anything. How he'd throw up shit he shouldn't have eaten in the first place. How he'd slink away all guilty, tail down and head low and back legs crouched. How his fur started turning grey two years after we got him, and he had so many white hairs on his face it looked like a moustache.

So there it was. Vicar and Operation Scooby, all the way home.

Maybe, I don't know, you're prepared to kill people. You practise on man-shaped targets so you're ready. Of course, we got targets they call 'dog targets'. Target shape Delta. But they don't look like fucking dogs.

And it's not easy to kill people, either. Out of boot camp, Marines act like they're gonna play Rambo, but it's fucking serious, it's professional. Usually. We found this one insurgent doing the death rattle, foaming and shaking, fucked up, you know? He's hit with a 7.62 in the chest and pelvic girdle; he'll be gone in a second but the company XO walks up, pulls out his KA-BAR, and slits his throat. Says, 'It's good to kill a man with a knife.' All the Marines look at each other like, 'What the fuck?' Didn't expect that from the XO. That's some Pfc. bullshit.

On the flight, I thought about that too.

It's so funny. You're sitting there with your rifle in your hands but no ammo in sight. And then you touch down in Ireland to refuel. And it's so foggy you can't see shit but, you know, this is Ireland, there's got to be beer. And the plane's captain, a fucking civilian, reads off some message about how general orders stay in effect until you reach the States, and you're still considered on duty. So no alcohol.

Well, our CO jumped up and said, 'That makes about as much sense as a goddamn football bat. Alright, Marines, you've got three hours. I hear they serve Guinness.' Ooh-fucking-rah. Corporal Weissert ordered five beers at once and had them laid out in front of him. He didn't even drink for a while, just sat there looking at 'em all, happy. O'Leary said, 'Look at you, smiling like a faggot in a dick tree,' which is a DI expression Curtis loves. So Curtis laughs and says, 'What a horrible fucking tree,' and we all start cracking up, happy just knowing we can get fucked up, let our guard down.

We got crazy quick. Most of us had lost about twenty pounds and it'd been seven months since we'd had a drop of alcohol. MacManigan, Second Award Pfc., was rolling around the bar with his nuts hanging out of his cammies telling Marines, 'Stop looking at my balls, faggot.' Lance Corporal Slaughter was there all of a half-hour before he puked in the bathroom, with Corporal Craig, the sober Mormon, helping him out and Lance Corporal Greeley, the drunk Mormon, puking in the stall next to him. Even the Company Guns got wrecked.

It was good. We got back on the plane and passed the fuck out. Woke up in America.

Except, when we touched down in Cherry Point there was nobody there. It was zero dark and cold and half of us were rocking the first hangover we'd had in months, which at that point was a kind of shitty that felt pretty fucking good. And we got off the plane and there's a big empty landing strip, maybe a half-dozen red patchers and a bunch of seven tonnes lined up. No families.

The Company Guns said that they were waiting for us at Lejeune. The sooner we get the gear loaded on the trucks, the sooner we see 'em.

Roger that. We set up working parties, tossed our rucks and seabags into the seven tonnes. Heavy work and it got the blood flowing in the cold. Sweat a little of the alcohol out too.

Then they pulled up a bunch of buses and we all got on, packed in, M16s sticking everywhere, muzzle awareness gone to shit but it didn't matter.

Cherry Point to Lejeune's an hour. First bit's through trees. You don't see much in the dark. Not much when you get on 24 either. Stores that haven't opened yet. Neon lights off at the gas stations and bars. Looking out, I sort of knew where I was but I didn't feel home. I figured I'd be home when I kissed my wife and pet my dog.

We went in through Lejeune's side gate, which is about ten minutes away from our battalion area. Fifteen, I told myself, way this fucker is driving. When we got to McHugh, everybody got a little excited. And then the driver turned on A Street. Battalion area's on A, and I saw the barracks and I thought, there it is. And then they stopped about four hundred metres short. Right in front of the armoury.

I could've jogged down to where the families were. I could see there was an area behind one of the barracks where they'd set up lights. And there were cars parked everywhere. I could hear the crowd down the way. The families were there. But we all got in line, thinking about them just down the way. Me thinking about Cheryl and Vicar. And we waited.

When I got to the window and handed in my rifle, though, it

brought me up short. That was the first time I'd been separated from it in months. I didn't know where to rest my hands. First I put them in my pockets, then I took them out and crossed my arms, and then I just let them hang, useless, at my sides.

After all the rifles were turned in, First Sergeant had us get into a no-shit parade formation. We had a fucking guidon waving out front, and we marched down A Street. When we got to the edge of the first barracks, people started cheering. I couldn't see them until we turned the corner, and then there they were, a big wall of people holding signs under a bunch of outdoor lights, and the lights were bright and pointed straight at us so it was hard to look into the crowd and tell who was who. Off to the side there were picnic tables and a Marine in woodlands grilling hot dogs. And there was a bouncy castle. A fucking bouncy castle.

We kept marching. A couple more Marines in woodlands were holding the crowd back in a line, and we marched until we were straight alongside the crowd and then First Sergeant called us to a halt.

I saw some TV cameras. There were a lot of US flags. The whole MacManigan clan was up front, right in the middle, holding a banner that read: OO-RAH PRIVATE FIRST CLASS BRADLEY MACMANIGAN. WE ARE SO PROUD.

I scanned the crowd back and forth. I'd talked to Cheryl on the phone in Kuwait, not for very long, just, 'Hey, I'm good,' and, 'Yeah within forty-eight hours, talk to the FRO, he'll tell you when to be there.' And she said she'd be there, but it was strange, on the phone. I hadn't heard her voice in a while.

Then I saw Eicholtz's dad. He had a sign too. It said: WELCOME BACK HEROES OF BRAVO COMPANY. I looked right at him and remembered him from when we left and I thought, 'That's Eicholtz's dad.' And that's when they released us. And they released the crowd too.

I was standing still and the Marines around me, Curtis and O'Leary and MacManigan and Craig and Weissert, they were rushing out to the crowd. And the crowd was coming forward. Eicholtz's dad was coming forward.

He was shaking the hand of every Marine he passed. I don't think a lot of guys recognized him, and I knew I should say something but I didn't. I backed off. I looked around for my wife. And I saw my name on a sign: SGT PRICE, it said. But the rest was blocked by the crowd and I couldn't see who was holding it. And then I was moving toward it, away from Eicholtz's dad, who was hugging Curtis, and I saw the rest of the sign. It said: SGT PRICE, NOW THAT YOU'RE HOME YOU CAN DO SOME CHORES. HERE'S YOUR TO-DO LIST. 1) ME. 2) REPEAT NUMBER 1.

And there, holding the sign, was Cheryl.

She was wearing cammie shorts and a tank top, even though it was cold. She must have worn them for me. She was skinnier than I remembered. More make-up too. I was nervous and tired and she looked a bit different. But it was her.

All around us were families and big smiles and worn-out Marines. I walked up to her and she saw me and her face lit. No woman had smiled at me like that in a long time. I moved in and kissed her. I figured that was what I was supposed to do. But it'd been too long and we were both too nervous and it felt like just lip on lip pushed together, I don't know. She pulled back and looked at me and put her hands on my shoulders and started to cry. She reached up and rubbed her eyes and then she put her arms around me and pulled me into her.

Her body was soft and it fit into mine. All deployment I'd slept on the ground, or on canvas cots. I'd worn body armour and kept a rifle slung across my body. I hadn't felt anything like her in seven months. It was almost like I'd forgotten how she felt, or never really known it, and now here was this new feeling that made everything else black and white fading before colour. Then she let me go and I took her by the hand and we got my gear and got out of there.

She asked me if I wanted to drive and hell yeah I did, so I got behind the wheel. A long time since I'd done that too. I put the car in reverse, pulled out and started driving home. I was thinking I wanted to park somewhere dark and curl up with her in the back seat like high school. But I got the car out of the lot and down McHugh. And driving down McHugh it felt different from the bus. Like, this is Lejeune. This is the way I used to get to work. And it was so dark. And quiet.

Cheryl said, 'How are you?' which meant, How was it? Are you crazy now?

I said, 'Good. I'm fine.'

And then it was quiet again and we turned down Holcomb. I was glad I was driving. It gave me something to focus on. Go down this street, turn the wheel, go down another. One step at a time. You can get through anything, one step at a time.

She said, 'I'm so happy you're home.'

Then she said, 'I love you so much.'

Then she said, 'I'm proud of you.'

I said, 'I love you too.'

When we got home she opened the door for me. I didn't even know where my house keys were. Vicar wasn't at the door to greet me. I stepped in and scanned around and there he was on the couch. When he saw me he got up slow.

His fur was greyer than before, and there were weird clumps of fat on his legs, these little tumours that Labs get but that Vicar's got a lot of now. He wagged his tail. He stepped down off the couch real careful, like he was hurting. And Cheryl said, 'He remembers you.'

'Why's he so skinny?' I said, and I bent down and scratched him behind the ears.

'The vet said we had to keep him on weight control. And he doesn't keep a lot of food down these days.'

Cheryl was pulling on my arm. Pulling me away from Vicar. And I let her.

She said, 'Isn't it good to be home?'

Her voice was shaky, like she wasn't sure of the answer. And I said, 'Yeah, yeah it is.' And she kissed me hard. I grabbed her in my arms and lifted her up and carried her to the bedroom. I put a big grin on my face, but it didn't help. She looked a bit scared of me, then. I guess all the wives were probably a little bit scared.

And that was my homecoming. It was fine, I guess. Getting back feels like your first breath after nearly drowning. Even if it hurts, it's good.

I can't complain. Cheryl handled it well. I saw Lance Corporal Curtis's wife back in Jacksonville. She spent all his combat pay before he got back, and she was five months pregnant, which, for a Marine coming back from a seven-month deployment, is not pregnant enough.

Corporal Weissert's wife wasn't there at all when we got back. He laughed, said she probably got the time wrong, and O'Leary gave him a ride to his house. They get there and it's empty. Not just of people, of everything: furniture, wall hangings, everything. Weissert looks at this shit and shakes his head, starts laughing. They went out, bought some whiskey and got fucked up right there in his empty house. Weissert drank himself to sleep and when he woke up, MacManigan was right next to him, sitting on the floor. And MacManigan, of all people, was the one who cleaned him up and got him into base on time for the classes they make you take about, don't kill yourself, don't beat your wife. And Weissert was like, 'I can't beat my wife. I don't know where the fuck she is.'

That weekend they gave us a 96, and I took on Weissert duty for Friday. He was in the middle of a three-day drunk, and hanging with him was a carnival freak show filled with whiskey and lap dances. Didn't get home until four, after I dropped him off at Slaughter's barracks room, and I woke Cheryl coming in. She didn't say a word. I figured she'd be mad and she looked it, but when I got in bed she rolled over to me and gave me a little hug, even though I was stinking of booze.

Slaughter passed Weissert to Addis, Addis passed him to Greeley, and so on. We had somebody with him the whole weekend until we were sure he was good.

When I wasn't with Weissert and the rest of the squad, I sat on the couch with Vicar, watching the baseball games Cheryl'd taped for me. Sometimes Cheryl and I talked about her seven months, about the wives left behind, about her family, her job, her boss. Sometimes she'd ask little questions. Sometimes I'd answer. And glad as I was to be in the States, and even though I hated the past seven months and the only thing that kept me going was the Marines I served with and the thought of coming home, I started feeling like I wanted to go back. Because fuck all this.

The next week at work was all half-days and bullshit. Medical appointments to deal with injuries guys had been hiding or sucking up. Dental appointments. Admin. And every evening, me and Vicar watching TV on the couch, waiting for Cheryl to get back from her shift at Texas Roadhouse.

Vicar'd sleep with his head in my lap, waking up whenever I'd reach down to feed him bits of salami. The vet told Cheryl that's bad, but he deserved something good. Half the time when I pet him I'd rub up against one of his tumours and that had to hurt. It looked like it hurt him to do everything, wag his tail, eat his chow. Walk. Sit. And when he'd vomit, which was every other day, he'd hack like he was choking, revving up for a good twenty seconds before anything came out. It was the noise that bothered me. I didn't mind cleaning the carpet.

And then Cheryl'd come home and look at us and shake her head and smile and say, 'Well, you're a sorry bunch.'

I wanted Vicar around, but I couldn't bear to look at him. I guess that's why I let Cheryl drag me out of the house that weekend. We took my combat pay and did a lot of shopping. Which is how America fights back against the terrorists.

So here's an experience. Your wife takes you shopping in Wilmington. Last time you walked down a city street, your Marine on point went down the side of the road, checking ahead and scanning the roofs across from him. The Marine behind him checks the windows on the top levels of the buildings, the Marine behind him gets the windows a little lower, and so on down until your guys have the street level covered, and the Marine in back has the rear. In a city there's a million places they can kill you from. It freaks you out at first. But you go through like you were trained and it works.

In Wilmington, you don't have a squad, you don't have a battle buddy, you don't even have a weapon. You startle ten times checking for it and it's not there. You're safe, so your alertness should be at white, but it's not.

Instead, you're stuck in an American Eagle Outfitters. Your wife gives you some clothes to try on and you walk into the tiny dressing room. You close the door, and you don't want to open it again.

Outside, there're people walking around by the windows like it's no big deal. People who have no idea where Fallujah is, where three members of your platoon died. People who've spent their whole lives at white.

They'll never get even close to orange. You can't, until the first time you're in a firefight, or the first time an IED goes off that you missed, and you realize that everybody's life, everybody's life, depends on you not fucking up. And you depend on them.

Some guys go straight to red. They stay like that for a while and then they crash, go down past white, down to whatever is lower than 'I don't fucking care if I die'. Most everybody else stays orange, all the time.

Here's what orange is. You don't see or hear like you used to. Your brain chemistry changes. You take in every piece of the environment, everything. I could spot a dime in the street twenty yards away. I had antennae out that stretched down the block. It's hard to even remember exactly what that felt like. I think you take in too much information to store so you just forget, free up brain space to take in everything about the next moment that might keep you alive. And then you forget that moment too, and focus on the next. And the next. And the next. For seven months.

So that's orange. And then you go shopping in Wilmington, unarmed, and you think you can get back down to white? It'll be a long fucking time before you get down to white.

By the end of it I was amped up. Cheryl didn't let me drive home. I would have gone a hundred miles per hour. And when we got back we saw Vicar had thrown up again, right by the door. I looked for him and he was there on the couch, trying to stand on shaky legs. And I said, 'Goddamn it, Cheryl. It's fucking time.'

She said, 'You think I don't know?'

I looked at Vicar.

She said, 'I'll take him to the vet tomorrow.'

I said, 'No.'

She shook her head. She said, 'I'll take care of it.'

I said, 'You mean you'll pay some asshole a hundred bucks to kill my dog.'

She didn't say anything.

I said, 'That's not how you do it. It's on me.'

She was looking at me in this way I couldn't deal with. Soft. I looked out the window at nothing.

She said, 'You want me to go with you?'

I said, 'No. No.'

'OK,' she said. 'But it'd be better.'

She walked over to Vicar, leaned down and hugged him. Her hair fell over her face and I couldn't see if she was crying. Then she stood up, walked to the bedroom and gently closed the door.

I sat down on the couch and scratched Vicar behind the ears and I came up with a plan. Not a good plan, but a plan. Sometimes that's enough.

There's a dirt road near where I live and a stream off the road where the light filters in around sunset. It's pretty. I used to go running there sometimes. I figured it'd be a good spot for it.

It's not a far drive. We got there right at sunset. I parked just off the road, got out, pulled my rifle out of the trunk, slung it over my shoulders, and moved to the passenger side. I opened the door and lifted Vicar up in my arms and carried him down to the stream. He was heavy and warm, and he licked my face as I carried him, slow lazy licks from a dog that's been happy all his life. When I put him down and stepped back he looked up at me. He wagged his tail. And I froze.

Only one other time I hesitated like that. Midway through Fallujah an insurgent snuck through our perimeter. When we raised the alarm he disappeared. We freaked, scanning everywhere, until Curtis looked down in this water cistern that'd been used as a cesspit, basically a big round container filled a quarter way with liquid shit.

The insurgent was floating in it, hiding beneath the liquid and only coming up for air. It was like a fish rising up to grab a fly sitting on the top of the water. His mouth would break the surface, open for a breath and then snap shut, and he'd submerge. I couldn't imagine it. Just smelling it was bad enough. About four or five Marines aimed straight down, fired into the shit. Except me.

Staring at Vicar it was the same thing. This feeling, like, something in me is going to break if I do this. And I thought of Cheryl bringing Vicar to the vet, of some stranger putting his hands on my dog, and I thought, I have to do this.

I didn't have a shotgun, I had an AR-15. Same, basically, as an M16, what I'd been trained on, and I'd been trained to do it right. Sight alignment, trigger control, breath control. Focus on the iron sights, not the target. The target should be blurry.

I focused on Vicar, then on the sights. Vicar disappeared into a grey blur. I switched off the safety.

There had to be three shots. It's not just pull the trigger and you're done. Got to do it right. Hammer pair to the body. A final well-aimed shot to the head.

The first two have to be fired quick, that's important. Your body is mostly water, so a bullet striking through is like a stone thrown in a pond. It creates ripples. Throw in a second stone soon after the first, and in between where they hit the water gets choppy. That happens in your body, especially when it's two 5.56 rounds travelling at supersonic speeds. Those ripples can tear organs apart.

If I were to shoot you on either side of your heart, one shot . . . and then another, you'd have two punctured lungs, two sucking chest wounds. Now you're good and fucked. But you'll still be alive long enough to feel your lungs fill up with blood.

If I shoot you there with the shots coming fast, it's no problem. The ripples tear up your heart and lungs and you don't do the death rattle, you just die. There's shock, but no pain.

I pulled the trigger, felt the recoil, and focused on the sights, not on Vicar, three times. Two bullets tore through his chest, one through his skull, and the bullets came fast, too fast to feel. That's how it should be done, each shot coming quick after the last so you can't even try to recover, which is when it hurts.

I stayed there staring at the sights for a while. Vicar was a blur of grey and black. The light was dimming. I couldn't remember what I was going to do with the body. ■

GRANTA

A TALE OF
TWO MARTYRS

Tahar Ben Jelloun

TRANSLATED FROM THE FRENCH BY LINDA COVERDALE

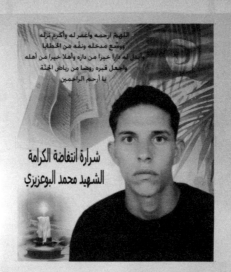

The Spark

I had never heard of the little Tunisian town of Sidi Bouzid. And yet, that's where it all began. With an ordinary incident, one that happens frequently, but so frequently that it finally started something unstoppable.

Once upon a time there was a young man of twenty-eight, with some education but no job, who lived with his mother and brothers and sisters. To earn a bit of money, he'd managed to get himself a market stall, a sort of cart to display fruit and vegetables. A street pedlar: one sees them just about everywhere in the cities of the Maghreb. Cars often pull up alongside them, double-parking, for last-minute purchases of fruit for dessert at lunch. Too poor to set themselves up in a shop, such vendors live from hand to mouth. Their carts sometimes impede the flow of traffic, but everyone carries on. And if a vendor 'buys' the goodwill of the policeman on the corner, he can relax and sell his produce without fear of harassment. On occasion, that same policeman may make a show of zeal to impress his boss by sternly forcing the vendor to go elsewhere. Well, some spots are more strategically situated than others, and places with a lot of traffic are clearly the best for business. Such spots must be 'purchased', of course, with one or two bills slipped to a policeman, establishing between the police and the pedlars a dominance hierarchy that resembles the petty neighbourhood mafias in Italy. You want to work? Then you must pay. If the vendor protests, he'll see his cart suddenly tipped over, or confiscated for 'causing a disturbance on the public thoroughfare'.

A street vendor doesn't make a stupendous profit, just barely enough to feed his little family. You'll never see a pedlar get rich. Mohamed Bouazizi was one of those people who work hard every day and try to live with dignity. He refused to beg, steal, compromise with corruption, or do anything illegal. He was well aware of how President Ben Ali and his wife – née Trabelsi – and their extended families shamelessly plundered the country. Like all Tunisian citizens, Mohamed knew about the banditry of the Ben Ali brothers, brothers-in-law, sons-in-law, cousins and friends, that clique busily stashing away millions right out in plain sight. Every big business, major firm and foreign investment in the country was subject to the 'Ben Ali–Trabelsi Law'. This was common knowledge, people talked about it, adding, 'We close our eyes, because Tunisia has got rid of the Islamists.' The solid middle classes of Tunis and the tourist towns like La Marsa, Sidi Bou-Saïd and Hammamet prided themselves on living in a country with 'impeccable security': 'No break-ins, no muggings – the police do a wonderful job.' People who collaborated with the regime lived in remarkable comfort and were grateful to Ben Ali, that former soldier who had learned so well how to turn his country's riches to advantage. French and Italian politicians often held up Tunisia as a model state in the Arab Muslim world. After the activist Rachid Ghannouchi was driven into exile, seeking refuge in London, no one heard any more talk about him and his Islamist movement, Ennahda. Islamism was dead.

When Mohamed's stepfather, a farm labourer, falls ill and cannot work, the young man must abandon his studies and become the sole support of his family. So, intending to sell fruit and vegetables in the street, he buys a cart. He has no permit, however, and is targeted by the local police officers. He refuses to bribe them, and anyway, where would he get the money? The officers are relentless: whenever they see him, they chase him away, threatening to confiscate his cart and weighing scales. On the morning of 17 December 2010, Mohamed has a run-in with some particularly unpleasant municipal officials who confiscate his cart and everything in it. One of his tormentors, a woman, slaps him, and her colleague spits on him. Complete humiliation! Mohamed tries to get his scales back, explaining that he has seven people to feed, that he's done nothing wrong. The officials get really nasty. Furious, Mohamed decides to try the town hall . . . Nobody will listen to him. He goes to the provincial headquarters . . .

No one is aware, yet, that this humiliation is the spark that will ignite a revolt with incalculable consequences.

You spend your life swallowing insults, trying to be reasonable, to accept your destiny, telling yourself over and over that a bright morning will dawn some day and that life isn't just one long mess of disasters. You don't lose hope. You pray, you look around at the loveliness of trees, a bird in flight, a passing butterfly, a smile on a child's face, and with sudden confidence in humanity you assure yourself that you're only having a bad spell, it will pass, for God is great and will open some doors. On that particular day, however, Mohamed runs head first into a concrete wall. He can't see a single way to escape his fate. He finds no help in the eyes of passers-by, sees no hand held out to him, hears not one word of encouragement, of justice. Mohamed is the universal citizen who runs out of patience. At that point, he could have remembered Ayub – Job, in the Quran – and the patience he must have shown to endure all the afflictions God sent him. But that thought never occurs to Mohamed. Job is far away. Everyone is far away. There is no one left around him. He doesn't even see his mother, or his sister Leïla, whom he loves deeply. He feels alone, abandoned. Abandoned by God. Mohamed is sure of that. He looks up at the sky on that cold December morning. Nobody makes the slightest gesture towards him. His solitude is absolute, intensified by the cruel feeling of an injustice he cannot bear. Slapped, and then spat on. No one should do that, not even to a dog. His humanity has been erased, the way make-up is wiped off a face. Mohamed has no more face, no more pride, no way to look anyone in the eye any more. His dignity has been crushed, trampled beneath the dirty shoes of the police. 'It's insane,' he thinks, 'how mean the poor are to other poor people, those even poorer than they are.' Because those officers are pathetic, they live off corruption, cringing, running like the governor calls for them to bring him a coffee or come repaint his villa. They obey, bending over backwards to serve authority. They bow and scrape, toadying to those to whom they owe their jobs. Everyone knows this. Being beholden is a modern form of slavery. So these sycophants do more than their jobs: they take initiatives, think of themselves as bosses, small ones, but bosses all the same. Mimicking their superiors, they give orders with the same arrogance, the same violence. A street pedlar is an ideal poor man. You can despise him because he's in your power, you can confiscate his cart, and if he doesn't like it, he can just croak. 'Ah! Let him croak!' That's what President Zine al-Abidine Ben Ali supposedly said when told of the pedlar who'd set himself on fire.

Mohamed Bouazizi lingered for eighteen days and nights in atrocious suffering before croaking like a dog, a nothing-at-all, anonymous, like a ghost. Like a poor man. And to be poor in Tunisia, in Egypt, in Yemen and many other countries is to be destined to croak like a dog, either because a local police officer will drive you to suicide or because when you get sick, you can't afford any care and will die for want of medicine and assistance.

Mohamed Bouazizi resolved to make an end of it. But whatever made him burn himself to death? Such a thing is definitely not part of the tradition and culture of the Maghreb, and it is explicitly forbidden by Islam. Anyone who decides to defy God by going willingly to certain death must go on committing this suicide throughout all eternity. Mohamed must have seen some pictures of Buddhist monks sacrificing themselves by fire, or perhaps he'd heard about them. This action is spectacular; it is immediately significant and unambiguous. Fire leaves nothing behind. It takes everything away. It causes horrible agony. Mohamed sacrificed himself in public, in front of the provincial headquarters, before the administration that had refused to listen to him and give him justice. He knew that he had lost his property forever, that the police would not give it back to him, and that their superiors were not going to take his side to help him.

He knew that in his country, the poor man is guilty simply because he is poor. And his despair must therefore lead to something that might impress other people, those who have been indifferent, unjust, who had no other choice but to ignore him, because the fate of a street vendor is of no interest to anyone.

Hang himself at home? That would be useless . . . Slit his wrists? No good either . . . Stuff himself with sleeping pills? He couldn't afford to buy any and, besides, that would be a silent suicide and people would say, 'The poor soul, he died a good death: in his sleep!' No, Mohamed wanted to die and to make his death useful in some way to others, to the poor, to the country. Perhaps he wasn't thinking of everyone in the country, but as he poured petrol over himself and struck that match, he must have had time to think of his mother, his brothers and sisters, and maybe his father, who had died when Mohamed was only three. Mohamed must have thought that it was better to join his father than to live humiliated, without dignity, without money, victimized by the whims of little bastards whose venom is just as terrible as that of the big bastards.

The fire blazed up immediately. Mohamed kept perfectly still. When people ran up to save him, it was too late: the flames, too quick for them, had finished their work. Mohamed was still breathing, but he was breathing in a burned-up body whose soul was already fragrant with the perfume of paradise – or perhaps the smoky inferno of hell. Mohamed was rushed to a hospital in the city of Sfax, then on to the Burn and Trauma Centre in Ben Arous, near Tunis. The body was fissuring into a mass of cracks, but the soul, trapped within the ashes, could not manage to free itself, imprisoned within a body that was no longer a body, simply proof of what humiliation can do.

In his hospital bed, Mohamed was swathed in bandages, which we hoped would suddenly unwrap themselves magically before our eyes and the TV cameras of the world, so that a frail new body would gradually appear, as if through the agency of an angel or a God who would have taken pity on this poor man who had just sacrificed his life for some 11,000,000 citizens.

On 19 December, the townspeople of Sidi Bouzid took to the streets. This was the beginning of what has since been called the Jasmine Revolution.

On 28 December, visiting Mohamed lying prostrate in his hospital bed, Ben Ali presented a grotesque image: a president trying to appear paternal but looking as if he might be privately cursing this damned penniless pedlar whose desperation had inspired the first street protests. And Mohamed, transformed into a mummy, well, he was running out of time. He died on 4 January 2011. Ten days later, it was Ben Ali's regime that gave up the ghost: after hunting around for a haven, the ex-president wound up in Jeddah, because Saudi Arabia, land of Islam, cannot refuse hospitality to a Muslim. As for Ben Ali's wife and family, they had already decamped.

That's how Mohamed Bouazizi became a hero, in self-defence, over his own dead body. And his sacrifice was not in vain. Which is doubtless what he'd hoped for, but neither he nor anyone else could have foreseen what would happen next. And what did happen was, quite simply, historic. Not only did Tunisia rise up peacefully and with dignity (for the violence was caused by the police, whose brutality left dozens of people dead and hundreds wounded), but this people who had suffered under a stealthy dictatorship for twenty-three years managed to get rid of Ben Ali, his family and his entire unscrupulous clan of criminal thugs.

Sayed Bilal

Alexandria, Egypt: His name was Sayed Bilal, he was thirty years old, married, and his wife was pregnant. He was a practising Muslim, neither an activist nor an agitator. He had a job and did not stand out from the crowd in any way. He lived near the Thahereyya train station. On the evening of 5 January 2011, he received a phone call from state security agents telling him to report to the local police station in the Al Raml District at 10 p.m. to help with an inquiry.

'Bring a blanket with you,' he was told. 'You might need one.'

Sayed Bilal is poor. A simple, unpretentious man, an average citizen. No one is happy to be summoned to the police station in such countries. But since he has nothing to reproach himself for, Sayed takes a taxi with a clear conscience and shows up at the appointed time. No one has come with him. He does not know that his last hour is fast approaching. And how could anyone have known that? Sayed Bilal has no criminal record at all and has never had to deal with his country's police force. In fact, that is why he has been singled out: he is a perfectly ordinary man.

The interrogation begins with the verification of his identity; a completely normal procedure. Sayed is calm. He doesn't dare ask what's on the tip of his tongue: 'Why am I here? What complaint do you have against me? What are you going to do with me? What have I done wrong?'

Sayed says nothing, answers their questions as best he can and waits to see how things go.

All of a sudden, the men move him to another room. They push him along and take him down to the basement; soundproofed, it is a place where no sound can get in or out, a place for torture. The police have thought of everything. The neighbours must not be disturbed. No noise, nothing shocking, because it seems that certain citizens cry out when they're hit too hard. They scream. That hurts the torturer's ears and might split the cork glued to the walls to absorb noise.

Sayed has never gone down into one of these basements. He has heard about them. He knows that they are torture chambers. But him, he's done nothing to be punished for . . . His conscience, so relaxed an hour ago, begins to panic. He thinks back on the events of the last few days and wonders, 'Perhaps I met someone I shouldn't have? Maybe I was seen with somebody involved in a plot, a horrible terrorist trying to destabilize the country? No, I went to school, I did my job, then I came home – my wife needs me, she's in her seventh month, I don't want her getting tired, so my parents often come over to help us. I place my life in the hands of God. Oh, could it be *that's* what is antagonizing them? God? They must be suspicious of anyone who seeks guidance from his greatness!'

'What were you doing last Saturday at about midnight?'

'I was asleep at home.'

First slap. They ask him the question again. Then they tell him that he was seen in the vicinity of a Coptic church, the Church of Two Saints, where a man blew himself up on the night of 31 December, killing twenty-three people and injuring more than ninety.

Sayed has heard about that tragedy, of course, and replies that 'as a Muslim', he does not kill human beings.

That's when the torture really begins. A confession must be torn out of him, even if it isn't true; those are the orders. The police want a culprit. If torture doesn't work, they'll invent a guilty man out of thin air. That is what will happen to Sayed Bilal. He does admit to being a Salafist, a member of a sect that promotes a strict observance of Islam, but that doesn't mean he's a terrorist, especially since Salafists believe in the literal application of divine laws, and nowhere in the Quran is it said that one must plant bombs in a church during a Mass. But the police pay no attention. He must confess. A devout Muslim, Sayed gives himself over to martyrdom and puts his trust in God. If God wants to call him home through this ordeal, if such is the will of Allah, then what can he do? Sayed confesses nothing, since he has done nothing, and thus has nothing to confess. The executioners labour over him, subjecting him to ever more excruciating torments; they learned such things at the police academy, and the old-timers even attended training courses in East Germany. To torture properly requires real skill. The Egyptian police have often distinguished themselves in this field, even as far back as Nasser's time.

Sayed is the ideal culprit for the 31 December bombing. He's innocent, but his captors couldn't care less. The minister of the interior wants prompt results, wants to be able, the next morning, to parade the terrorist before the media. The Al Raml district chief of police urges his torturers on. Too bad: despite all the suffering endured and the sophistication of the techniques applied, Sayed Bilal – for the good reason that he has nothing to admit – admits nothing. He dies of a heart attack, his body studded with bruises, haematomas, wounds, black and blue from beatings. It's been a long night for everyone. For the unfortunate Sayed Bilal and for the executioners, who were tired of torturing and wanted to go home to their wives and children. A long night for the chief of police, who won't be able to announce any good news to his superiors. And for the minister, who must deliver a report to his government in the morning and admit that the suspect died under torture.

On the evening of Thursday 6 January, the body is left in front of the local hospital. The police keep watch. A male nurse notices the corpse and has it brought inside. Finding identity documents on the dead man, he calls the family. Meanwhile, the police have arrested Sayed Bilal's brother Ibrahim in an attempt to keep him quiet. The parents arrive at the hospital, identify their son and take pictures of the obvious signs of torture on his body. Distraught and grieving, they decide to file a complaint, but the police immediately intervene, making it clear that they have Ibrahim in custody and that if the family causes trouble, another son will meet the same fate as his brother did.

Nothing is left for the parents but tears and prayer. The police order them to bury their son that same night, to avoid a disturbance on Friday, the holiest day of the Muslim week. The parents try to negotiate, but it's no use: unless they drop their demands, Ibrahim will not be released. The parents know the officers will not hesitate to kill him. Sayed Bilal is finally buried just before midnight.

That's how the police operate under Hosni Mubarak. ∎

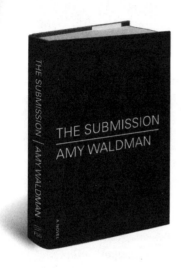

CROSSBONES

Nuruddin Farah

Ahl heads for his room to make sure that his personal effects, including his cash and passports, are safely locked away before going off to Guri-Maroodi, the village where groups of young men congregate – would-be illegal migrants bracing for a sea trip to Yemen and then Europe. He puts the key in the door, but the lock won't engage. The TV in the room is blaring, but he doesn't recall turning it on before going down earlier. He pulls the key out and inserts it a second time, and a third. Still, it won't turn. He is about to go down to the reception desk to ask for help when the door opens a crack. He sees that a young man with a familiar face – the TV programmer – is in the room.

Ahl asks, 'What are you doing in my room?'

As soon as the words leave his mouth, he asks himself if one can say 'my room' when one has only temporary access to it.

'I am programming the TV. For you.'

'With the door locked?'

'Does it matter whether the door is or isn't locked when I am in the room, programming your TV?' the young fellow says with incorrigible cheekiness.

Ahl stares in silence at the young man – the door open, the key in the clutch of his hand, his eyes washing over his suitcase and shoulder bag, uncertain if they are where he left them. Do they seem a little disorderly, as if someone has tampered with them? Ahl recalls opening the computer bag before he went down to breakfast. But did he leave the bag unlocked? No point asking the young man anything. People out here are jittery, their tetchiness priming them to jump to the wrong conclusions.

He says to the young man, 'Get out!'

Alone in the room, the door securely latched from the inside, he unplugs the TV. The sealed envelopes with Taxliil's photograph and the cash are still in the computer bag – there is no time to make sure that nothing else is missing. He decides to carry these valuables on his person, unable to think of a better way of keeping them safe. He wears the cash belt and carries the laptop with him. But for the sake of form, he locks his suitcase, in which there is nothing but his dirty clothes.

Back outside, his eyes clap on a pack of young crows with feathers so shiny they look as if they've been dipped in black oil. Some strut around, as if daring him to chase them; others take off as he approaches, then alight on the tree branches and descend to the patch of garden. They make a racket, clucking and pecking at one another.

Ahl goes to reception to complain about the TV programmer. An unfamiliar middle-aged man who is missing one eye is at the front desk. He hesitates, not sure if he wants to discuss his grievance with this man, whom he assumes doesn't work here.

'Where is the manager?' Ahl asks.

'What do you want?' the one-eyed man demands.

'I'd like to submit a complaint about the young man who has made a habit of locking my room from the inside, and rummaging in my stuff. He claims he's the TV programmer,' Ahl says.

The one-eyed man scratches his stubbled chin. He says, 'I am afraid we do not have a TV programmer in our employ. We fired the last one who worked here three days ago precisely because he was found rooting about in a guest's room.'

'But he was in my room just now,' Ahl says.

'He has no business being in your room.'

Ahl asks, 'How does he gain access unless he has a master key, or collects one from reception? I chased him out a few minutes ago.'

'He has no business being in your room, or collecting a master key from here,' the one-eyed man insists. 'I'll report him to the management. Action will be taken against him soon.'

'Please do that,' Ahl says, although he doesn't believe for a moment that the man will take any such action.

A car horn honks, and the outside gate opens to admit a battered jalopy. Fidno is at the wheel. Ahl wonders whether it makes sense for him to carry all his cash and his computer with him when Fidno evidently thinks the village they are driving to rates no better than the bucket of bolts he is driving rather than his usual posh car. But what else can he do? He puts his faith in his good fortune, trusting that all will be well for now. Maybe he will check out of the hotel at the first opportunity and move in with Xalan and Warsame, if the offer still stands.

Barely has Ahl clambered into the four-wheel wreck, placed his laptop at his feet and put on the seat belt when Fidno squeals out of the gate and steps on the gas, as if eager to be clear of the place. Within half a kilometre they are in a poor neighbourhood on the outskirts of the city, where the huts are built of coarse matting reinforced here and there with zinc, or from packing material bearing the names of its manufacturers, although they are moving too fast for Ahl to make out the letters. The doors to the dwellings, which are improvised out of cloth, blow in the wind. Everything about these huts and the lean-tos that serve as their kitchens has an air of the temporary about it. The residents are those displaced by the fighting in the south of the country. They have come to Bosaso because there is peace here.

Fidno climbs through the gears in quick succession, the clunker rattling so loudly that neither man talks, not even when Fidno nearly runs over a couple of pedestrians loitering in the centre of the road. At the last second, they scatter and Fidno roars on, like a race-car driver participating in an autocross relay through an uninhabited countryside. The ride is as disagreeable as mounting a bad-tempered young male camel that spits, kicks and foams furiously at the mouth.

Straining to be heard over the ruckus, Ahl asks, 'Why the rush? Are we late?'

'Our man is restless,' Fidno says. 'We may not find him still there if we delay.'

'What's his name?'

Fidno responds irritably, 'If you really must know, he is known by his nickname, Magac-Laawe. A no-name man.'

'Have you spoken to No-Name yourself, then?'

'I've spoken to his henchman.'

Ahl wishes Malik were here. Malik who knows how to deal with this specimen of humanity, the dirt no one dare clean up, in a land with no laws; a country where brute force earns high dividends. If warlords have deputies, and presidents their vice presidents, then it follows that, in a world in which coercion is the norm, a human trafficker must have underlings as well.

'What have you told No-Name about me?'

'That you are my friend.'

What does that make him? Ahl wonders. An associate of a known criminal? Is this what children do to you, knowingly or unwittingly, make you into an accomplice of outlaws? He prays that Fidno does not run foul of the authorities while they are together, especially not with so much cash and his laptop on him, in this beat-up vehicle on the way to Guri-Maroodi, a hot spot with few equals in notoriety, even within Puntland.

'What else did you tell him?'

'That you are looking for your runaway nephew.'

'My nephew – why nephew? He is my son.'

'Makes no difference. Nephew, son, stepson!'

Of course it does make a difference; but Ahl says nothing.

Fidno says, 'I was worried that No-Name might think you would become too emotional, irrational, or hard to please if things do not go the way you want them to. "My son" is different from "my nephew". I don't know if this makes sense to you, but that is what I thought. I did it for your sake. To make things happen.'

Again, Ahl thinks that he is not suited for this kind of assignment the way Malik is, having interviewed Afghani drug lords as well as Pakistani Taliban warlords. It requires a familiarity with the criminal mind that is beyond his experience. Ahl worries that once he's endorsed a lie, he will be open to telling more, and there will be no end to it.

He says, 'I'll set No-Name right on this. A lie does not run off my tongue easily, and I'll have to beware of what I say all the time.'

'Do what suits you,' Fidno concedes.

They go through a drab-looking hamlet that boasts only a few low shops built of stone, atop wood foundations, the zinc roofing painted in different colours, mainly blue. Billboards advertise cigarettes, soda, milk and other products, Ahl guesses more for decoration than because they are actually available. They have slowed to a snail's pace, and Ahl can see people in clusters of three and four, with their curious eyes trained on the jalopy. He can even hear them: they are speaking a babble of Swahili, Oromo, Tigrinya, broken Yemeni Arabic and Somali. A microcosm of the Horn, a cosmopolitan misery marked with unforgiving poverty.

Minibuses ply the road to Bosaso, and young men and women walk along the road, hitching a ride or footing it; almost everyone here is young, and there are more men than women.

'I could hear Amharic, Swahili and Tigrinya as we passed,' Ahl says. 'How on earth do they all get here?'

'The Ethiopians, Eritreans and Somalis from the south of the country walk for several days to get here,' Fidno responds. 'Some of the Kenyans and the Tanzanians arrive by plane or by boat. But only a few make it to Yemen. The owners of the fishing boats have been known to throw three-quarters of their passengers overboard before they make it ashore to avoid the possible confiscation of their boats.'

There is a group of young men gathered around a pickup with its boot open. A woman has set up a stall close by, selling *qaat*. Ahl sees one of the youths carrying a bundle and a number of his mates following, some clearly asking him to give them a share.

'Tell me how you described Taxliil,' asks Ahl.

Fidno says, 'A bright young fellow with excellent language skills, impeccable manners, assigned to welcome foreign Shabaab recruits here to join the insurgency in Somalia.'

'In what capacity does No-Name enter the scene?'

'It makes business sense for the boat owners not to return empty after transporting the migrants to the shores of Yemen,' Fidno explains. Ahl considers how this works to the advantage of several groups operating outside the law. Likewise, it makes sense for the pirates and the religionists to work together, not only for profit but also for mutual security.

They have reached the outskirts of the village. As they continue south, the landscape turns desolate, burned. Then there is sudden change in the wind, which picks up and brings along with it a cooler breeze from the sea. The vegetation is sparse, much of it of the thorny sort, with a few trees to provide shade to humans and fodder for camels. A young boy, shirtless and in a sarong, with a chewing stick in his mouth, looks lost as his camels chomp away at one of the treetops. Ahl says, 'There is a world of difference between the young Somali nomad looking after his beasts and the migrants wanting to cross the sea, isn't there?'

'Do you suppose the young nomad is content, because he knows no better life?' asks Fidno.

'I would imagine that many of the migrants, being city-born and city-bred, are unhappy with their lot and eager to seek adventure elsewhere,' Ahl observes. 'Perhaps because they've seen too much TV and believe that life elsewhere is more comfortable.'

'What about your son? He had the possibility of a successful future ahead of him. Do you know what made him leave Minneapolis to return to this desolate place?'

'I wish I knew,' Ahl mumbles.

They enter another enclave. The sea breeze is now stronger as they pass men sitting around or lying in the scanty shade of the trees, chewing *qaat*.

'Who are they?' asks Ahl, pointing out a group of young migrants, half lying and half sitting, as if they are too tired even to sit all the way up.

'Migrants exhausted from waiting.'

'What are they waiting for?'

But Fidno does not answer Ahl's question. 'We're here,' he says instead, and he turns in and stops at a metal gate guarded by armed men in khaki uniforms. A young man with large eyes and a thin, half-trimmed moustache comes forward. Fidno waves his hand in greeting, and the youth acknowledges him with a broad smile.

One side of the gate opens and the young man steps out, just as another youth with a small head and wearing huge spectacles emerges from the gatehouse and stands by a second barrier that needs to be removed

manually. The first young man approaches the car to check out Ahl.
'We're expected,' Fidno says.
The gate opens and Fidno drives in.

The grounds on which the villa is built are extensive and surrounded in all directions by a high fence. The house itself, set far back, is two storeys high, with French windows and a glassed-in balcony large enough for a sumptuous party. The sea is visible behind the house. An awning extends almost to the gates providing shade as they drive in. Fidno parks, and Ahl picks up his laptop and follows him towards the pair of uniformed young men who wait in front of the awning. The entire structure looks new and well made; the railing on the upper storey is shiny with fresh paint. The loud humming of a heavy-duty generator comes from the back.

There is order here, the order of a corrupt autocrat imposed through coercion, Ahl thinks. One of the liveried men leads them up to the house, his pace measured. He knocks on the door in a rhythmic knock, presumably a code. The door opens. Fidno and Ahl enter; the liveried youth stays behind, bowing.

'Welcome, AhlulKhair. I am your host.'

The voice Ahl hears has something magisterial about it: distant, assertive. He identifies it as belonging to a little lean man of advanced years sitting in what looks like a child's high chair, with a full, greying beard and penetrating eyes. How very odd that such a small man, almost a midget, can produce such a commanding voice, Ahl thinks. He can't be more than four feet tall. He reminds Ahl of pictures he has seen of Emperor Haile Selassie, and because of this, he somehow expects a chihuahua to be imperiously perched on No-Name's lap. Ahl wonders if No-Name is a cripple.

'How have things been?' he says to Ahl, in a tone of surprising familiarity.

'Everything has been good so far,' Ahl says, although this is not what he feels inside.

'What about you, Fidno?' No-Name asks, his voice sounding a

notch more authoritative, its timbre more full-bodied.

Fidno says, 'Everything is according to plan.'

'Excellent.'

'How have you been yourself?' Fidno asks.

No-Name appears a little offended. He says to Fidno, 'Give us a few minutes, will you? You may join the others outside. You know your way around here.'

The caller of tunes, No-Name expects to be obeyed, and Fidno takes his leave. 'Thank you for seeing my friend,' he says.

'We'll see you later.' Ahl notes the royal 'we'.

When Fidno opens the door to leave, the hall is awash in the intense brightness of the midday sun. And once again Ahl wonders if he is doing the right thing, liaising with criminals.

As Ahl approaches, No-Name frowns, like someone used to wearing spectacles. It's plain he's not accustomed to anyone doing anything without his say-so. The closer Ahl gets to the high chair No-Name is sitting in, the weirder it all looks. Almost hilarious.

No-Name says, 'Please sit.'

But there is nowhere to sit, save a lounge area at the other end of the hall, furnished with an ottoman and a plush carpet dotted with cushions propped up against the walls. Is this where No-Name chews *qaat* with his pals? Does an emperor have pals?

What a day and what humiliation! Ahl crouches down, knees creaking, wondering if children have any notion what troubles one goes through for them.

With a trace of a grin around his lips, No-Name says, 'Tell me everything about your nephew.'

'My son, actually.'

'I am sure Fidno described him as your nephew,' No-Name says.

'That may be so, but he is my son.'

'That changes my perspective on things.'

'I am not his father. His mother is my wife. But I raised him.'

No-Name takes all this in. His right foot shakes as though it has its own mind.

'What else did Fidno get wrong, before we move on?'
Ahl shrugs his shoulders in a search-me gesture.
'Tell me about your son, all that I need to know.'
Ahl tells him.
'Have you a photo of the runaway youth?'
Ahl produces it.
'What's his date and place of birth?'
Ahl tells him.
'What are his mother's and your full three names?'
Ahl supplies him with these, wondering how No-Name can possibly remember such details without taking notes or having a secretary do so. Is he being made a fool of, or does No-Name already know where and who Taxliil is?

'Any other particulars that may help locate him?'
'He broke his spectacles recently and I hear his minders in Kismayo got him a pair too big and too clumsy for his face,' Ahl says. 'I've brought along a spare pair, which I mean to give him if and when I see him.'
'What is the name of the imam at the mosque in Minnesota who recruited him?'
Ahl answers the question fully, with details.
'Do you know the names of his fellow jihadis?'
Ahl shakes his head.
'He didn't know the twenty other recruits from Minnesota and nearby?'
Ahl says, 'I don't know; we don't know.'
'How do we reach you if we wish to do so?' No-Name asks and Ahl provides him with a host of phone numbers.
'How long have you been here?'
Ahl tells him.
'When do you leave?'
Ahl shrugs. 'It all depends on my success.'
'Or lack of it,' No-Name says. Then, 'Fidno has mentioned that Malik, a journalist, is in Mogadiscio.'

'What about Malik?'

'Is he likely to come here?'

'Why do you ask?'

'Because I'd like to meet him.'

'He hasn't said he will come and visit here, but I will make sure to introduce you to him if he does.'

'I look forward to that.'

Ahl finds himself sitting uncomfortably forward, supporting his body on his knees, like a devotee at an ashram.

He says, 'If I may ask a question, please?'

'Go ahead.'

A current of worry goes through his body, lodging for a moment or so in his heart, then in his head. One indiscreet question from him might jeopardize everything. Nonetheless, he asks it. 'Why did you agree to see me?'

No-Name presses his forehead and winces, as if thinking of the reasons or sharing them with Ahl is causing him pain. His eyes closed, he says, 'One, because I am doing Fidno, my pal, a favour.'

'That's very good of you.'

'Two, because sometime in the past few days someone spoke three names in my presence – I cannot recall in what context. But Taxliil's name was one of them, and the name stuck, as I have never known anyone else with it. So when Fidno came to me, I agreed to step in and to assist. I'll do all I am able to help you find Taxliil.'

As if on cue, a mobile phone rings in another room. No-Name shifts in his high chair in a manner that suggests to Ahl that their conversation is at an end. The liveried young man enters from the back, and offers Ahl a hand to help him straighten up. Then he leads him out to where Fidno is waiting in the jalopy.

Fidno takes off in the direction of Bosaso, driving even faster than before and appearing agitated. He wants to hear Ahl's impression of No-Name. Ahl thinks that extortionists, like whores attempting to collect up front the fee for services not yet rendered, and then to render them speedily, are prone to presenting their bills much too fast.

'I don't know what answer to give,' he says.

Fidno says, 'No-Name has extensive connections among top people in Puntland and beyond – insurgents, pirates; the lot.'

Ahl feels a little reassured by this, but he is not at all certain that he is any closer to locating Taxliil than before. Partners in crime: Fidno, No-Name, and all their associates! Then he adds, 'Let's say I am more optimistic than before.'

'All will work out well, you'll see.'

Ahl senses that Fidno is now softening him for a hit; he can't wait to hear it.

Fidno says, 'Please ring Malik and let him know.'

'Don't worry. I will. Later.'

'Now, please. Ring him now.'

'What do I tell him?'

'Ask him if he'll see me, when and where.'

'I'll call him later.'

Fidno's voice takes on a threatening tone. 'Please call him. Now.'

Ahl opens his window to a blast of wind and sand. The land they are driving through is more desolate than he remembers from the journey down. The truth is, he has been hesitant to call Malik since they disagreed about the wisdom of his interviewing the sheikh, with Ahl insisting that family trumps career. Given the choice, Ahl would prefer to make the call in the privacy of his hotel room, alone, but he feels he has no choice but to telephone Malik now.

He dials and lets it ring. The line is busy and he disconnects, promising Fidno that he'll try again shortly. Then he switches on the car radio, and they catch the tail end of a news bulletin. There has been fierce fighting between the Ethiopian occupying army and the insurgents, with high civilian casualties. He tries again, and this time Malik answers on the fourth ring. Ahl puts him on speakerphone so that Fidno can hear the exchange. He tells his brother about the meeting with No-Name and assures him that it has made him feel optimistic. Then he asks, 'Have you thought when you might have time to meet up with Fidno? You could interview him here in

Puntland. If you are unable to fly out here, he is willing to come down to Mogadiscio.'

But Malik is in no mood at the moment. He's just learned about the death of yet another journalist, thanks to yet another roadside bomb. 'Why don't we speak later in the evening,' he says, 'and we'll figure it out then? Looks like he'll have to come to Mogadiscio, as I won't be able to come to Puntland.'

'Good.'

'I'm delighted things are working out.'

'But tell me about yourself, Malik,' Ahl says anxiously. 'Are you hurt or anything?'

'Just shocked, traumatized – out of sync.'

They agree to talk more in the evening, and say goodbye. After he hangs up, there is silence for long enough that Ahl assumes Fidno isn't going to speak. But just then Fidno says, 'It'll give me joy to go to Mogadiscio. Because I am so eager, maybe I'll take the first available flight. But I won't book it until I hear from you. And there is a small possibility I'll want to bring along a friend to the interview.'

'That's the first I've heard of a friend going with you.'

'We'll talk, you and I,' Fidno promises. 'There is time yet.'

Ahl stares at Fidno in anger and mistrust. Of course, Malik will be upset at this development. But Malik is family, and he will do what is best for Taxliil in the end. Or, at least, Ahl hopes he will.

As before, the door to Ahl's room is locked from the inside. After he knocks on it repeatedly, the TV programmer lets him in. Ahl can't help but feel amused at this point, especially once he has reflexively checked that he still has his money belt, and felt the weight of the laptop he is carrying. Then, as if to prove a point, he pretends to check on the state of his suitcase, which has had its lock torn off. Without waiting for the TV programmer to leave, he telephones his wife's cousin, Xalan, to ask her to please come for him as soon as she can. He doesn't explain why, he just wants to leave. *Basta!*

He moves about the room, picking up a towel, running the tap and, with the luxury of a man who has a lot of time to kill, washing his hands and his face. Seemingly unperturbed and unflustered, the TV programmer stays in the room, fiddling with the knobs and taking no notice of Ahl's presence or his need for some privacy. Maybe the never-ending conflict in this country won't tail off until its burglars master their art, Ahl thinks. Maybe the foolishness displayed by the nation's politicians, its so-called intellectuals, its clan elders and imams, and its rudderless youths is contagious; everyone in the land seems somehow lacking in horse sense.

His mobile rings: Xalan is downstairs, waiting. Ahl awkwardly picks up his suitcase with the broken lock, not bothering to check if any of his shirts, pairs of trousers, underwear or sandals are missing. He leaves the door to the room open, the TV man still tinkering with the set, the volume high, then low.

Xalan is a joy to behold: she is dressed in a kaftan, arms showing, her figure handsome, and her smile beautiful. She meets him halfway and they both laugh when their attempt at a hug fails and they both stumble. She carries his laptop down and leaves him to struggle with the suitcase with the broken lock.

There is no one at the reception, so they decide to put the suitcase in the boot and wait by the vehicle, in the hope that one of the receptionists will show up and alert the manager to bring Ahl the bill. As they wait, Ahl tells Xalan all that has transpired so far.

'It's shocking,' she says. 'He's still in the room? In any event, I am delighted you are moving in with us.'

Then they have a laugh about it.

'I don't look forward to having further altercations with the hotel staff, including the hotel manager. Most likely, he won't believe me if I tell him: it's my word against the TV tinkerer's. And I suppose his co-workers will gang up against me, an alien guest, never mind that I speak Somali.'

When the manager arrives with the bill, Xalan studies the squiggly figures, frowning; among other things, Ahl is being charged for

TV repair, along with the use of sheets and towels and meals he did not order. The combined shakedown comes to a lot, but Ahl knows that you do not negotiate with extortionists, and this price is par for the course for a diaspora Somali visiting home from the 'dollar countries'. If he refuses to pay and reports the rip-off to the authorities, he stands little chance of success. Later, he'll be made to pay at gunpoint, possibly with his life. Woe betide the man who denies his bodyguard's request for a loan, or the journalist whose newspaper refuses the ransom asked when his kidnapping happens to occur on the day he is scheduled to leave for home.

But Xalan won't be cowed. 'What if he says he won't pay?' she asks.

'I'd advise him not to take that route,' the manager says, in a tone meant to intimidate.

An argument ensues when Ahl points out that he had already reported the programmer's misdemeanour to a one-eyed man at the reception and the manager denies that any such person works in the hotel.

'Well, that's something,' Ahl says with a sigh.

Inevitably, Xalan and the manager exchange harsh words, after the manager accuses Ahl of lying. She threatens to call the police and the manager retorts that the police are in his pocket and, in fact, he'll have her arrested if they don't pay up and leave.

Meanwhile, the heat has grown unbearable. Ahl's shirt sticks to his back; even his hair is damp with sweat. He hasn't the proper hardiness for this situation. He remembers hearing of an incident in which armed youths, too weak to carry their loot home, forced their victims to load the plunder into their own vehicles and, since the thieves did not know how to drive, to chauffeur them home with it. He doesn't want to lose sight of why he is here, and to him the sum demanded is paltry. He insists on paying it in full, in dollars, and adds a tip for good measure. At last they are free. ∎

GRANTA

STONES AND ARTICHOKES

Nicole Krauss

I

Sitting in the Closerie des Lilas in Montparnasse, my friend tells me two stories. The first is about her grandfather, who arrived at Gare de l'Est after the Shoah, in which all forty-two members of his family were killed. He was hungry, maybe even starving, and took a seat in the restaurant of the station. The waiter handed him a menu and, speaking only Yiddish, my friend's grandfather pointed to an item at random. The waiter went away and returned with an artichoke. My friend's grandfather looked at it helplessly. He had never seen an artichoke before, that strangest, most stubbornly hermetic of all things humans have deemed edible. A mute and mutual incomprehension settled between the artichoke and the man who was the sole survivor. The waiter saw all of this and understood something. Tenderly, careful not to insult the dignity of my friend's grandfather, the waiter sat down across from him and taught him how to eat the artichoke. *A people willing to teach a Jew how to eat,* my friend's grandfather thought, and at that moment he decided to spend the rest of his life in France.

The second story my friend told me was as follows: when she was seventeen, fat and unhappy, a boy who belonged to a very chic group of young and beautiful people invited her to a dinner party. My friend had always been in awe of this group, having watched them drink champagne many nights at the Closerie des Lilas, where her father brought her along with his model girlfriends. She was overwhelmed by the invitation. When she arrived at the dinner party, there was a large round table set with eight places, and she, it turned out, was the ninth guest. The host suggested she pull up a chair behind the others, outside the circle. That night my friend – who until then had lacked ambition – swore silently that she would make something of herself and have her revenge. She became the most famous artist in France. Most of the people at that dinner table are now dead.

II

M y three-year-old son is standing on a chair, looking out of the window of our apartment on Boulevard Saint-Michel. Am I going to die in Paris or Brooklyn? he asks. I'm afraid to tell him that there is not one but an infinite number of places he might die; that as we get older, the world grows to fit our fear of death.

III

M y son and I spend every afternoon in the Jardin du Luxembourg where he collects stones from the gravel paths. I love you, he tells me, so I want to give you a present, and he hands me all the stones he can carry. I don't know what to do with so many stones. The airline only allows us fifty pounds each. But I can't throw them away.

I bring my son to the cemetery in Montparnasse to visit Beckett. After some difficulty, we find him. I don't tell my son that we're in a cemetery and that this is a grave for fear of further encouraging his preoccupation with death. On the slab of granite marked simply with Beckett's name, someone has left a circle of pebbles. I tell my son that this place makes me remember a writer I love, and when a place reminds a Jew of someone, we pick a stone and leave it on that spot. He accepts this with the same plain trust with which he accepts everything I tell him. He wanders off, returns with a small speckled pebble and places it at the centre of the circle of stones. We stand looking at it in appreciation. Then, with one swipe, he sends all of the pebbles rolling.

Walking across the Pont Neuf, my husband wonders aloud how Paul Celan managed to kill himself in such a mild-looking river, even with stones in his pockets. I make a mental note to add one more to my list of uses the Jew has for stones.

Back in Montparnasse, my son begins to cry. What's wrong? I ask him. I died an ant, he says, pointing at one he has accidentally crushed under his shoe.

IV

Like many apartment buildings in Paris, the one we live in has an old and very small elevator, only slightly larger than a coffin. When it is called, the motor gasps and with enormous effort groans to life. To enter it, you must first pull open the wrought-iron door, then push aside the metal gate that folds like an accordion, then close the door and the gate again behind you, and – if you happen to be unlucky enough to be sharing it with another passenger – take your place pressed up against one of its walls. It ascends the hollow centre of the circular staircase around which all of the apartments are laid out. It rises slowly, with terrifying ambivalence, as if at any moment it might give up and plummet into a free fall. A light sleeper, during the night I'm awakened each time it lurches out of its inertia and begins to drag its weight up through the floors.

The other sound that wakes me is the rumble, like the sound of an approaching earthquake, of the RER train as it runs underground between Luxembourg and Port Royal. The trains run every quarter of an hour until the line closes at midnight, but, even on nights when I go to sleep early, the rumble can only be heard twice, or at most three times. Depending on the night of the week, the elevator can be heard three or four times, five or six at most. Not once in all of our nights in Paris has the elevator risen and the train passed at exactly the same moment. ■

So Where Are We?

So where were we? The fiery
avalanche headed right at us – falling,

flailing bodies in mid-air –
the neighborhood under thick gray powder –

on every screen. I don't know
where you are, I don't know what

I'm going to do, I heard a man say;
the man who had spoken was myself.

What year? Which Southwest Asian war?
Smoke from infants' brains

on fire from the phosphorus hours
after they're killed, killers

reveling in the horror. The more obscene
the better it works. The point

at which a hundred thousand massacred
is only a detail. Asset and credit bubbles

about to burst. Too much consciousness
of too much at once, a tangle of tenses

and parallel thoughts, a series of feelings
overlapping a sudden sensation

felt and known, those chains of small facts
repeated endlessly, in the depths

of silent time. So where are we?
My ear turns, like an animal's. I listen.

Like it or not, a digital you is out there.
Half of that city's buildings aren't there.

Who was there when something was, and a witness
to it? The rich boy general conducts the Pakistani

heroin trade on a satellite phone from his cave.
On the top floor of the Federal Reserve

in an office looking out onto Liberty
at the South Tower's onetime space,

the Secretary of the Treasury concedes
they got killed in terms of perceptions.

Ten blocks away is the Church of the Transfiguration,
in the back is a Byzantine Madonna –

there is a God, a God who fits the drama
in a very particular sense. What you said –

the memory of a memory of a remembered
memory, the color of a memory, violet and black.

The lunar eclipse on the winter solstice,
the moon a red and black and copper hue.

The streets, the harbor, the light, the sky.
The blue and cloudless intense and blue morning sky.

PUNNU'S JIHAD

Nadeem Aslam

By the charging stallions of war, snorting!
— QURAN, I00:I

I

Adam was pardoned in winter.
The thought comes to Punnu as he stands in the cold air, his
breath appearing and disappearing before him. In the palm of his
right hand he holds the small dried flowers he has kept hidden in
his pocket. He looks at them, faded and torn, but with all the grey
around him they are still the brightest things in his gaze. He shields
the blossoms as he would a candle flame, as though preventing their
colours from being extinguished.

He turns and goes back into the building. The chain at his ankles
is long enough for him to walk at a slow pace but not to run. He goes
through the kitchen without pausing and slowly climbs the staircase
and then continues along a dark corridor, towards a room filled with
voices at the other end. This is the mountain house owned by the
Afghan warlord who is holding him captive and Punnu was brought
here the previous week. The house is surrounded by towering pines
and snow-covered peaks, most of its rooms locked, the only human
presence being a retinue of six of the warlord's men.

Punnu saw the meteor shower Quadrantids three nights ago so he
knows what month it is. Meteor showers occur at approximately the
same time every year, and the Quadrantids means it is the beginning
of January.

Four months ago, on the first day of September 2001, Punnu's
father was at work in the ice factory when a rectangular block of
ice slid down a ramp and shattered. Temporarily as sharp as glass,
a foot-long splinter flew up and pierced his diaphragm from below.
It continued through the left lung and entered his heart. He fell

backwards on to the floor and that was where he was discovered half an hour later. By then the ice fragment inside him had melted away.

The neighbourhood women insisted he had been killed with a ghost dagger by Punnu's mother, who had died the previous year and who had known nothing but contempt and ruthlessness from her husband while she was alive.

After the funeral, Punnu went to live with his uncle on the other side of the city, carrying a suitcase in one hand and his book of constellations in the other, the large pages full of heroes and beasts caught in diamond-studded nets. His uncle worked behind the counter at a gun shop on the Grand Trunk Road; his aunt was a servant in someone's house. They had sent their only child away to a seminary at the age of seven to learn the entire Quran by heart.

On 11 September, Punnu's cousin, now fourteen years old, returned home from the seminary, having completed his blessed endeavour. He and Punnu didn't know each other but he embraced Punnu affectionately nevertheless, smiling with happiness at having returned. Eagerly, he ate the food his mother had cooked before she went to work that morning, and spent the rest of the day courteously receiving the neighbours who came to congratulate him. When his parents returned home in the evening, he produced a revolver from his waistband and shot them both dead at point-blank range.

Satan prevented children from learning the Quran by heart, and so those who found it difficult were kept in chains at the seminary. Every single one of the Quran's thousands of words had to be committed to memory in perfect sequence, and over the seven years Punnu's cousin had received regular beatings, the bruises fading in one place only to appear in another. To drive off Satan, a child could be made to go hungry for days or be deprived of sleep, made to stand out in the burning summer sun or the winter cold, or be held below water for entire minutes until he almost drowned. Parents were firmly discouraged from visiting – and they stayed away because a child memorizing the Quran meant that the sins of seven generations were erased by Allah.

In October, when the armies of the West arrived to punish neighbouring Afghanistan, Punnu joined the jihad and travelled towards Kabul with thousands of other Pakistanis – boys and young men dazzled by themselves, by the role they were about to play in one of the pivotal moments in Islam's history. Within hours of entering Afghanistan, Punnu found himself on the front line. He was sixteen years old.

Terror gripped him when the carnage began, a cold darkness suddenly opening up within when he saw men screaming with half their skulls or jaws blown off, the men on fire thrashing in agony, and the men who died quietly as though nothing important had befallen them. 'I am not a soldier,' Punnu pleaded in desperate horror. 'I came here to help the wounded. My mother was a nurse.' But the mullah who had brought him to Afghanistan said to him that the soil of the grave lies lightly on a martyr, that one moment of jihad is worth one hundred years of prayer, and also that he would cut Punnu's throat and wipe the floor with his blood if he did not fight. 'Baghdad was destroyed in 1258,' the mullah said in a rage. 'Spain was lost in 1492, India in 1857 and Turkey in 1922. Is "Afghanistan 2001" to be the next date in this sequence, you accursed coward?' He thrust a Kalashnikov into Punnu's hands. Gun sellers across Pakistan had lowered the prices of weapons as soon as Afghanistan was invaded, an act of piety encouraging people to join the holy war.

II

The chain rattling between his feet, Punnu walks in out of the cold corridor to find the warlord's men huddled around a coal brazier. He was trying to escape from here the night he saw the meteor shower. Never away from his mind, not even for a single second, is the thought of flight.

The last thing he remembers of the fighting on that October day is the battle-torn smoke and a bright burst of poppy before his face. They tied him with a length of barbed wire while he was insentient, and when he opened his eyes he couldn't move and near him a pack of dogs was eating the blood-soaked earth. He caught a brief glimpse of the group of American soldiers who had coordinated the warlord's battle against the Taliban. The Americans were now confronted with the corpses of almost two hundred enemy men, and they told their Afghan allies to dispose of them as quickly as possible before they were filmed by a passing satellite, making Punnu wonder if the world's dead exceeded the number of graves in the world.

The American soldiers disappeared and Punnu became a prisoner of the warlord, who cut off the trigger finger on each of Punnu's hands and nailed the two pieces to a door frame along with those taken from dozens of other captives. Fearing gangrene, Punnu begged them to extract the bullets from his body, to no avail. But then, two nights later, while he slept, a large group of them came at him with scalpels and blades. A rumour had circulated that the Americans had used solid-gold bullets.

Punnu lifts a pomegranate from a basket and squats in the far corner of the room, listening to the men as he opens the fruit with his teeth and fingernails, inhaling the scent with its insistence of sunlight, manipulating the fruit carefully because the wounds from the missing fingers are still tender these months later. The warlord is a bandit and the son of bandits, and Punnu has heard stories of how much he is feared. Once, having received word that he was about to mount a raid, the inhabitants of a village had left their jewellery and valuables out in the streets at night, thousands of banknotes blowing about in the air as he rode in.

Punnu's eyes search constantly for the invisible path that exists between him and his one objective – escape. The warlord has told him that he would have to be ransomed, but Punnu has no one who would pay for him. The only way his captor can gain financially from him is to send him to work on various construction sites every day – a school being built, a prison for women being expanded – and he labours while still in chains, becoming thinner with each week, his clothes hanging on him in rags. He still wears the boots he was wearing back

YOUR GATEWAY
TO GOOD WRITING

Have *Granta* delivered to your door four times a year and save up to 42% on the cover price.

'AN INDISPENSABLE PART OF THE INTELLECTUAL LANDSCAPE'
– *OBSERVER*

```
*******************************
*                             *
*  UK                         *
*  £34.95                     *
*  (£29.95 by Direct Debit)   *
*                             *
*  EUROPE                     *
*  £39.95                     *
*                             *
*  REST OF THE WORLD*         *
*  £45.95                     *
*                             *
*******************************
```

Subscribe now by completing the form overleaf, visiting granta.com or calling free phone 0500 004 033

*Not for people in America, Canada or Latin America – there's one of these cards just for you a bit further on . . .

GRANTA

THE MAGAZINE OF NEW WRITING

SUBSCRIPTION FORM FOR UK, EUROPE AND REST OF THE WORLD

Yes, I would like to take out a subscription to *Granta*.

GUARANTEE: If I am ever dissatisfied with my *Granta* subscription, I will simply notify you, and you will send me a complete refund or credit my credit card, as applicable, for all un-mailed issues.

YOUR DETAILS

MR / MISS / MRS / DR ....

NAME ....

ADDRESS ....

....

POSTCODE ....

EMAIL ....
(Only provide your email if you are happy for Granta *to communicate with you this way)*

☐ Please tick this box if you do not wish to receive special offers from *Granta*
☐ Please tick this box if you do not wish to receive offers from organizations selected by *Granta*

YOUR PAYMENT DETAILS

1) ☐ Pay £29.95 (saving £22) by Direct Debit
   To pay by Direct Debit please complete the mandate below and return to the address shown above.

2) Pay by cheque or credit/debit card. Please complete below:

   1 year subscription: ☐ UK: £34.95   ☐ Europe: £39.95   ☐ Rest of World: £45.95

   3 year subscription: ☐ UK: £89.95   ☐ Europe: £99   ☐ Rest of World: £122

   I wish to pay by   ☐ CHEQUE   ☐ CREDIT/DEBIT CARD
   Cheque enclosed for £_____ made payable to *Granta*.

   Please charge £ _____ to my: ☐ Visa   ☐ Mastercard   ☐ Amex   ☐ Switch/Maestro   ☐ Issue No.
   Card No. ☐☐☐☐☐☐☐☐☐☐☐☐☐☐☐☐☐☐

   Valid from *(if applicable)* ☐☐☐☐   Expiry Date ☐☐☐☐
   Security No. ☐☐☐☐

SIGNATURE .... DATE ....

Instructions to your Bank or Building Society to pay by Direct Debit
BANK NAME ....
BANK ADDRESS ....
POSTCODE ....
ACCOUNT IN THE NAMES(S) OF: ....
SIGNED ....
DATE ....

Bank/building society account number
☐☐☐☐☐☐☐☐

Sort Code
☐☐☐☐☐☐

Originator's Identification
9 1 3 1 3 3

Please mail this order form with payment instructions to:

Granta Publications
12 Addison Avenue
London, W11 4QR
Or call 0500 004 033
or visit GRANTA.COM

in October, having washed the blood out of them, and he works as hard as he can because he fears they would otherwise shoot him for being just another mouth to feed.

The seeds are packed under the pomegranate's rind in crystal-tight arrays. He chews them and drips the red liquid from his mouth on to the bandaged areas of his hands, knowing it is a potent healer. His combat-seamed body remains a little raw elsewhere too, where the bullets had gone in, where the bullets had been taken out. The left arm, which was torn open by a dagger in search of gold, is restricted in its functions – he can touch the right shoulder with it but not the left one.

He has been brought here to the mountain house to assist in a mission, a theft. Around the coal fire the men are finalizing the details of the plan. The Prophet Muhammad's 1,400-year-old cloak has been kept at the mosque in Kandahar since 1768. But when the American bombing started back in October, the cloak was brought into the mountains for safe keeping, and it hasn't been sent back to Kandahar yet. It is still there in a high-altitude mosque a distance of fifty miles from this house, and the warlord wishes to acquire it to increase his prestige, to benefit from its miraculous powers.

The warlord's most expert thief will go with Punnu to steal the cloak, and he is bringing along his son, a boy the same age as Punnu. The sacred garment is no doubt guarded and if they are discovered during the crime a fight will ensue. Punnu would rather not take part in the theft but he has to obey. In addition, the warlord has said he will consider granting Punnu his freedom if the cloak is successfully brought to him. Punnu doesn't believe the man would keep his word, and so he resolves to remain alert to every possibility of escape during the journey.

They stand up when they are ready to go, everyone beginning to walk out to the front courtyard to see them off. Punnu lingers in the room and is the last one through its door; with as much swiftness as his chained legs allow him, he picks up the bullet he had seen lying under a chair the moment he came in. He works it into the waistband of his trousers as he walks behind the others in the dark corridor, the metal cold as ice against his skin even through the fabric.

Outside, as they walk towards the van, minute specks of frozen moisture float in the otherwise dry air. It glitters in the late-morning sun like shining sand or a dust of glass. The mansion has high walls of stone with lookout posts and five large Alsatians roam the compound at night. In spite of this Punnu had made three attempts at escape, getting further on each successive occasion, and it was only the sub-zero temperatures that had forced him back. He had wrapped his ankle chain in rags to muffle it but in the end he couldn't walk fast enough to generate the necessary heat, the mountainside locked in the white iron of winter.

The thief gets behind the steering wheel, and he and his son utter in unison the Arabic phrase all good Muslims are meant to invoke before setting out on travel: 'I hope Allah has written a safe journey for us.'

Punnu climbs into the second row of seats. He has known for two days that something is wrong with the vehicle, that it could break down during the journey. The day before yesterday they had gone hunting for deer in the woods, and when they came back the Alsatians had not recognized their approach, had barked as they would at the noise of an unfamiliar vehicle. Some mechanism inside the engine is about to fail, a fracture spreading in the chassis.

He touches the painful arm as they drive off. For a while his wounds had made him manically alert to bees, following the progress of each one in the air with the hope of being led to the hive, coveting the yellow colour sealed inside the cellular wax, knowing from his mother that honey can mend flesh as nothing else can, healing wounds that have remained open for a decade.

III

The air inside the van becomes colder as they climb towards the snowline, moving through the rocks and the immense boulders, the landscape ripped to pieces by its own elemental energies. Punnu falls asleep and enters the nightmare of the battlefield yet again, the

place where he'd learned what two hundred corpses look like. He had
had to dig his way out from under them after the guns and rockets
and missiles had fallen silent, emerging into the light that revealed
the futility of war to him – he who had already learned the futility
of peace – the bodies full of insect scribble, the mouths that would
ignite their red lament for him in the sunrise every morning from
then on, the eyes ruined but still dreaming of returning to whatever
Egypts, Algerias, Yemens, Pakistans and Saudi Arabias they had
known, rotting men who were true believers and read the Quran as
ravenously as they devoured meat and sugar and milk, and men who
came to the jihad because, well, to be honest, Punnu, there wasn't
much else to do, and men who thought that the holy had its abode
only in denial and who thought of death to the exclusion of all matters
so that in the end life was easy to give up. They lay all around him
then, slain, slaughtered, stinking, cleansed at last of the burden of
being who they were on earth, the souls pulled clean out of them,
the arms twisted, the heads decapitated, the feet separated from legs
that had been separated from torsos, and the dark decaying mulch
of the names OmarFareedAbdulYusufKhalidSalmanFaisalShakeel-
MusharafAnwarImranRashidSaleemHusseinNomanIbrahim-
MansoorIkramMushtaqNaimAsimTaha, and he stood above their
corpses, puffing out wide flowers of breath into the Afghanistani air, a
dawn light so pure and undeceiving it might have been the dawn that
Adam saw. For an instant he wanted Allah to appear and explain it
all to him, not just watch from His high distance through unappalled
eyes. Punnu hadn't known he could summon such deep feelings, and
was this earth nothing more than a toy with six billion moving parts
for Him? And he was enraged at the peace that reigned at that very
moment on other parts of the planet, and in grief he had cursed the
lives that were continuing uninterrupted elsewhere.

The van coming to a halt brings him out of sleep: the journey has
been broken for the afternoon prayers. Getting out, they spread
a blanket on the rock-strewn ground while the wind howls in a gorge

to the left of them. Standing next to each other on the blanket, the three of them begin to bend and bow towards Mecca hundreds of miles away; the divine magnet is upon that city and the metal in them responds.

Punnu finishes earlier than the thief and his son and hurries back into the vehicle, his hand working the bullet out of his waistband as he goes. It's a .22 calibre, and working as fast as he can he replaces the fuse of the van's headlights with it. The procedure requires about thirty seconds and all through it he fears the father and son will conclude their prayers and look towards him, but his luck holds. The bullet is a perfect fit in the fuse box located next to the steering-wheel column: after about fifteen miles the bullet should overheat, explode and discharge, and enter the driver's leg. It'd be as though he has been shot with a gun.

Afterwards Punnu sits looking out, waiting for them to finish praying, the sky composed of horizontal pink, yellow and grey bands repeated in Allah's strict order above them. When they come back the thief scolds him for rushing his communion with Allah, and then they move on. The headlights – they have been in use since before they stopped to pray in the afternoon gloom – illuminate giant slabs of stone thrust out at all angles as though the place had been attacked from below with pickaxes and sledgehammers, resulting in entire zones of star-shaped fractures.

The days are short in the mountains and the greyness intensifies as one hour passes and another begins. While they are making a narrow turn, Punnu notices that the soles of several boots have left deep imprints on the muddy ground of the bend. America is everywhere. The boots are large, as if saying, 'This is how you make an impression in the world.' The war has devolved into a series of raids and manhunts for terrorist leaders and lieutenants, and these must be Special Forces soldiers looking for a possible Osama bin Laden hideout or gravesite, that gangster with a Quran, the deluded criminal who thinks a person is allowed to sin in praise of Allah.

Punnu sits leaning forward, his head between the two front seats.

When the bullet enters the thief's body it will cause an accident: the damage to the vehicle could mean that the son would not to be able to drive them to safety, that Punnu too could bleed to death here in the wilds. A part of him wants to cancel the plot he has set in motion, and after a while that is exactly what he tries to do.

'Stop the van,' he says.

'What?' the boy asks, turning round to look at him.

'We must say the evening prayers.'

'It's a little early for that,' the thief says, and the van keeps moving, the headlights burning into the mountainside. Punnu reaches out and grabs the steering wheel and it swings violently to the left for a moment. The son takes hold of Punnu at the collar and pushes him backwards and shouts for him to be still. Punnu sits back and the thief strikes his face hard without turning round, the back of his fingers paved with coloured gems. The vehicle continues to move beyond any hope of influence, and again Punnu says, 'We have to stop.'

A second later there is a sound as deafening as a gunshot, followed by the loud tearing of steel against granite, and then the van enters the sky above the gorge. Twenty feet below is a river overhung with weeping trees, and as they begin their plunge towards it everything out there becomes darker because the bullet leaving the fuse box has broken the electric connection to the headlights, the voices from the two boys loud, abject, almost animal in their fear.

It's a bullet wound,' says the thief with a mixture of shock and confusion, turning his back to the two of them and opening his trousers and looking down at his thigh. 'I have been shot.'

They've splashed ashore, the man limping badly, barely able to stand upright. Every pain in Punnu's body has been awakened, a jolt to the spine when the vehicle landed in the shallow river.

'Shot? How is that possible?' the son says, going round to look at the wound. 'Maybe a part of the van pierced you.'

'I know what a bullet wound looks like,' the thief says. He is a large man but at this moment just the effort to raise his voice seems too much for him.

Beyond them in the glacial water a thick rope of blood emerges from the driver's side of the wrecked van and goes swaying down the slow current. It is as though the metal itself is bleeding.

'We need to bring it out,' says the thief, gesturing towards the van. Punnu can see that apart from everything else both father and son are terrified at having ruined their master's property.

'It's not going to move now,' Punnu says. He looks under his shirt for any injuries. There is a pause while everyone reflects on what has happened, the drenched bodies shivering in the terrible cold, the thief's son wincing as he touches the two-inch cut on his forehead. 'It's a warning from Allah,' the boy says quietly. 'This is a wicked and sinful thing we are attempting, stealing the blessed cloak. I think we should turn back . . . '

His father looks at him sharply. 'You have no knowledge of this matter. Stop talking nonsense.'

The boy shakes his head. 'We have to turn back. You've been shot with an invisible pistol. It's a warning from Allah . . .'

'Be quiet,' the man says, attempting to remain in control, and the son looks away, torn between who he fears more, Allah or his father. The man is losing blood very fast, the red-black liquid spreading on the pebbles at his feet. It seems to be something seeping up from the earth due to the weight of his body. 'We can't stay here,' he says. 'We have to walk the five miles to the mosque.'

'Go and see if you can rip out the seat belts,' Punnu says to the boy. 'We need to bind your father's leg.' And he asks the thief, 'Are the keys to my chain in the van?'

'I didn't bring them.'

Punnu is aghast. 'How did you think I would help you steal?' He doesn't believe the man is telling the truth. 'What if I'd had to run?'

The thief lifts his gun and, with shivering hands, aims it unsteadily at Punnu. The pain is making his eyes murderous. 'I don't have them. And don't think you can run away from me. Now go and get the seat belts.'

After applying the tourniquet they begin to walk, finding a path that leads them back up to the level from which they fell, the thief leaving a glistening trail. Moving through freezing air in wet clothes, the footsteps of all three soon become less sure but they continue, wordlessly, Punnu's chain the only sound. Two years ago he had gone hunting with his father in Pakistan at the same latitude as this, and they had prevented frostbite by duct-taping their faces entirely, leaving just a half-inch slot for the eyes and another for the nose. Now he watches the thief and his son as they weaken. He knows they'll fail sooner than him, the father leaning on the son as they stagger along. He must summon the last bit of warmth inside him.

As if all bones in his body have instantly vanished, the thief is the first to collapse among the grey rocks, just as they are approaching a ridge. The son succumbs a moment later as though he had needed permission. From where he lies, the man swipes at Punnu's shirt in sudden desperation, to hold on to him, but the mountains have sucked out all his strength, the slopes and summits that stand around them like solidified silence – time made visible in a different way, ancient and on an elongated scale.

In a trance of liberty Punnu keeps walking towards the ridge. In another half-hour the darkness will be complete. He looks over his shoulder and sees that the injured man, lying on the ground, is attempting to aim his gun at him, the barrel fluttering as though he is trying to shoot a butterfly that won't settle.

He goes over the ridge and stops in his tracks, seeing what lies on the other side. 'What the hell?' And only after a long moment does he take another step forward.

He is facing a graveyard of planes and helicopter gunships, Russian MiGs and Hinds, all resting at odd angles with cockpits slung open and glass smashed, the tyres ripped and rotting. There are several dozen of them, a swathe of hulks stretching all the way to another ridge half a mile away.

He moves towards a helicopter gunship and looks inside. There is graffiti scratched on to the tarnished walls by soldiers in Russian.

Names, sentences, and hearts that enclose initials. The interiors have been stripped of everything, from the seats to the instrument dials, so that what's left is little more than a pod or shell, a coffin meant for a giant, and the metal of each must weigh thousands of kilograms. At some point every aircraft had a growth of lichen on it, layer upon thick layer dried now to a crust. He continues to walk in an almost straight line through and between them, climbing in and out of the doors, speaking quietly to himself as he goes, to stop from losing focus. 'Punnu is free at last. Punnu keeps walking. Punnu wants to go home. Punnu hears the sound of his chains. Punnu cannot feel *any* of his fingers. Punnu has probably caused the death of a man. Punnu is not going to die in this metal cemetery . . .' After a while he stops and turns round.

He arrives back at the first helicopter gunship and sees that the thief and his son had attempted to follow him – they'd made it over the ridge but have collapsed once again, one prone, the other supine. He approaches and astonishingly the father raises his wildly trembling arm with the gun towards him once again. The son's eyes remain closed but even in the state of unconsciousness his body is shaking. Punnu, shivering almost as much as them, frees the weapon from the father's grip and, standing with his feet as wide apart as possible, points the barrel at the taut chain. The action is stiff from the cold, the equivalent of his own bone-deep chill, and since he is having to use a hand that has no trigger finger, there is little precision in his aim. He fires into the hard ground twice, powdered granite and the blue smoke of the gun rising very slowly towards his face.

He looks up as though for help. Some Muslim astronomers saw a woman's hand dyed with henna in the constellations Cassiopeia and Perseus, while others said that it was the hand of Fatima stained with drops of blood – Fatima, the daughter of Muhammad, from whom Punnu is descended.

He puts the gun in his pocket and prises loose the one from the son's rigid fingers too. From the father's pocket he takes out the brass cigarette lighter. The man stares up at him helplessly, too far gone.

Under the darkening blue sky and the already-countless stars, and with his feet still bound in chains, Punnu walks up to a MiG.

The MiG is fifteen feet high. He stands under the wing coated densely with the black lichen and raises his hand and snaps the lighter. The lichen catches on the sixth try and an area of it glows indigo for a moment, then the glimmer spreads sideways and becomes a sheet of scarlet combustion. *Fffff!* He steps back: at first it's only the wing, but then the entire plane is sheathed in the bright flame, the tinder-dry lichen flaring abruptly with an explosion of heat. There is a brilliant upwards suck, a one-moment-long vacuum. The machine is on fire from top to bottom, back to front, in about twenty seconds, a burning transparency rushing over the fifty-foot metal shape, a bird made of flames.

He is still cold, his clothing wet, but his hand has become a little steadier and he takes the gun from his pocket and shoots into his chain, shattering the seventh of the thirteen links.

Though they are still lying where they fell, the blood of the other two is beginning to revive also, life returning to their limbs. A great roaring fills the air. Brought out of sleep to find itself in flames, the metal is screaming, and it is as though the plane might take off with the blaze.

'Come closer,' he calls over his shoulder.

The thief and his son rise and slowly walk towards the source of heat, a blast of August temperature in January. Hand's-breadth pieces of lichen are separating to float up as flakes of blinding light. And then, as suddenly as it began, the blaze completes itself and the plane starts to creak emptily and smoulders here and there. Fragments of charcoal lie on the ground with bright crimson points worming along their edges. The smoke disappears into the darkness like unravelling lace.

The scorched metal continues to give off heat and the father and son stand as close to it as they can tolerate. With a wave of the gun Punnu tells them to follow him as he walks over to another plane, flicking open the lighter once again.

They move from hulk to hulk, from one bright roaring platform to the next, the rotor blades of the Hind helicopters burning like fifty-foot-wide gold stars above them, bathing them in light. They leave a crooked wandering path behind them through that necropolis of steel, their clothes steaming.

When it begins to snow, the snowflakes hiss upon encountering the heated metal.

Eventually both Punnu and the thief's son stop shivering, the released river-grit falling away from their dry clothes, but the thief himself has lost too much blood and his condition deteriorates, his face pallid, the lips dark.

'He'll be fine when we get to the mosque,' says the son.

Punnu looks at him. 'I hope so. But I am not coming with you. I have to go my own way.'

'Please don't run away,' the boy says softly. 'We'll be punished by the master.'

Punnu shakes his head. 'I have to go. Release that tourniquet every fifteen minutes.'

'We will be beaten if you run away. Already there is the matter of the ruined van.'

'I can't help you. I have to go.'

'He will kill us.'

'Then don't go back,' Punnu says, suddenly full of fury at the world. 'You disappear too.'

'We *have* to go back,' the boy shouts. There is an edge of desolation to the voice. 'Our family is where the master is. If we run away he'll torture them to find out where we are, to force us out of hiding.'

Punnu looks to the ground, then shakes his head. 'I can't.'

Sitting in a half-faint, the thief opens his eyes for an instant and points to Punnu's fingers. 'Maybe when you touch the Prophet's cloak, the pain in your wounds will stop.'

Punnu begins to walk away, still shaking his head.

'How can you abandon fellow Muslims like this? Just help me carry him to the mosque. After that you can leave.'

Punnu stops and looks back.

'I can't carry him on my own, you can see that,' the boy says, on the verge of tears. 'He'll bleed to death.'

'All right. You and I will take him to the mosque and then I will leave. And we are not stealing anything.'

IV

It's past midnight when they see the mosque in the far distance, a glass moon shining above it. The sacred building stands on the expanse of blue and white snow, appearing separate and singular like something presented on the palm of the hand.

The thief has been babbling, hallucinating as he begins to die.

'Run to the mosque and get help,' the son tells Punnu when the man falls silent; then he lowers his father on to his back and, brushing the snow away from his chest, listens for a heartbeat. In his other hand he holds the torch they'd made with a branch and a torn turban. Although it has stopped snowing, the snowflakes lie so thickly on them that almost half of their bodies are invisible.

Punnu shakes the whiteness off his face and clothing, patting himself into visibility, and sets off towards the mosque, his mind retaining very few impressions during the distance to the giant door. Now and then his two pieces of broken chain catch on something behind him, and thin plates of ice break under his feet when he encounters frozen puddles. He arrives at the mosque door but instead of knocking he convinces himself that there is no harm in lying down for a few minutes of rest. How long he lies there at the foot of the door, he doesn't know, but at one point when he tries to turn his head he discovers that his hair has become locked in ice, and later that the two sections of the ankle chain are also fused with the ground.

He lies looking up at the mosque that has the entire Quran inscribed on its exterior walls, domes and balconies. The calligraphy is said to be there on the interior walls and ceilings too. He watches the facade in the moonlight through half-open eyes and it is as though there has been a rain of ink – every drop that had landed on a surface had formed a word instead of a splash. When his cousin was sent away to the seminary to become a vessel for the holy words, Punnu had thought that the boy's brain and heart, muscles and bones, would slowly become inscribed with the verses over the years, that when he came back the sacred script packed tightly inside him would be visible through the skin.

He looks at the sky as he sinks into sleep. Arabic is written up there in the cosmos too, he knows. Of the 6,000 stars visible to the naked eye, 210 have Arabic names. Aldebaran, the follower. Algol, the ghoul. Arrakis, the dancer. Folmalhaut, the mouth of the fish. Altair, the bird . . . He falls asleep and there is a city under the stars in an undiscovered country, no lamp in any window. The only light is the constellations and the city's minarets, each one of which is burning, a tall plume of fire, the flames streaming in the wind now and then. He enters the deserted city knowing that a group of black-clad figures is following him. Though he cannot see them, he somehow knows that they have the natural fighting power of mountain lions, and he passes under several burning minarets before pushing open a door and entering a house and some time later he hears his pursuers come in. They spread out through the rooms and they make no attempt to lower their voices, to conceal their search for him. He climbs over the wall into the mosque next door. He picks up a book from a niche and removes a page and crumples it in his hand and then straightens it and places it on the floor. He does this with another page – introducing wrinkles into it and then putting it on the floor beside the first one – and then with another and then another, and eventually with all of them, lit by the light of the burning minaret, moving backwards as he leaves the paper on the floor. If anyone steps on them, he'll hear it. When the floor around him is lined with the pages, he lies down at the centre of them and closes his eyes – a rectangular clearing, the exact dimensions of a grave.

V

There are moments of faint awareness through the dark. People moving near him. Hands that touch. Candlelight. Eventually he is able to awaken fully and things are called into being. He is on a sheet spread out on the bare floor, no pillow, and he is wearing a dry set of clothes. An aged man is tending to him with a gentle pensiveness, his beard falling to his stomach in two silver divisions.

'Did you get them out of the snow?'

'Who?'

'I left two people outside.' Punnu sits up slowly and looks around.

'There's no one out there.'

'Maybe you can't see them because it's dark.'

'It's no longer night. It's morning.'

The mosque is a ruin, and the man is burning a reed prayer mat and a heap of straw prayer caps to keep him warm. Propped up against the pillars are words that have fallen away from the walls, lines of calligraphy that curve and knot purposefully, collecting force and delight and aura as they go.

He stands up, wrapping the sheet around him as he rises. 'In which room is the Prophet's cloak kept?'

The man offers him a piece of bread. 'The Prophet's cloak is in Kandahar. What would it be doing here?'

'I was told it was brought here.'

'No. It's always been in Kandahar.' The man touches his forehead. 'You are tired. Lie down and rest.'

'I dreamed I tore pages out of a book of hymns to protect myself.'

The man thinks for a moment. 'There is a kind of tree whose leaves do not fall,' he says, 'and in that it is like an ideal Muslim. But Allah understands if we don't succeed in being perfect in this imperfect world.' He smiles at Punnu.

Punnu begins to eat the bread, its core humid and porous. The man tells him that he is from Yemen, a foreigner trapped in Afghanistan. Scattered in various areas of the mosque, there are others like him, smelling more like wild animals than humans, entire families from Arab countries, destroyed-looking women and children, their eyes dark as though tormented by dreams of justice on earth. They have been on the run since October, making various journeys towards places of safety, to find some path back to their homelands. One little girl stands apart from other children, not participating in their activities, and he realizes only after a while that she has no arms.

Though still very tired and weak, he opens the door to the south minaret and begins to climb up, looking out through the small recessed windows as he goes, the landscape altering with every turn of the spiral. Emerging into open air at the top, he examines his surroundings, the sky a water stain on paper. He is unable to understand why he had been told the mosque contained the cloak, why he had been sent on this trip.

Beside him on the facade, an ant is wandering in the shallow trough that forms the word 'Allah', carrying a wheat grain in its mouth, trying to climb out of the word but falling back into it again and again.

He turns round to leave and everything slides into place when he notices the large boot print in the snow next to his feet, a quick ray of recognition: the warlord sent him here to be picked up by the Americans. The thief was *delivering* him.

The Americans pay $5,000 for each suspected terrorist.

He rushes down the spiral – as fast as he is able, the two pieces of chain falling ahead of him and getting under his feet – and asks if they know the warlord who'd been holding him prisoner.

'Yes,' the bearded man answers. 'He was the one who sent all of us to the mosque. He told us to gather here and wait to be taken out of Afghanistan.'

Punnu counts the men and they are twenty-two including him. $5,000 x 22 = $110,000. They are all followers of Islam, as is the warlord, but that much money cuts a lot of religious ties.

And now his hearing picks up the outermost ring of a wave of sounds, something just on the limit of being audible. Everyone gives a questioning stir and then they too catch the reverberation of American Chinooks arriving overhead, his heart giving a great leap and then seeming to go still in recoil. Cautiously, Punnu moves towards the mosque door and reaches out his hand to part the panels, but the door is opened suddenly from the other side just then and blinding snowlight fills his eyes and there is a confusion of shouts. Several figures overpower him and he watches the aged gentleman begin to run to the other side of the prayer hall, watches as an American soldier picks up a chair and launches it towards the man across the long space: a clean, effortless arc is described and then the chair arrives and connects with the fleeing man's shoulders and he falls with a sharp cry. Punnu's hands and feet are fastened with zip-locks and he is carried outside to the big bird with the twin propellers. He hears gunfire from the building and the screams of women and children. They leave him on his stomach beside the machine and go back inside for the other men, and before closing his eyes Punnu casts a spell on the world, telling it to last until he awakens. ∎

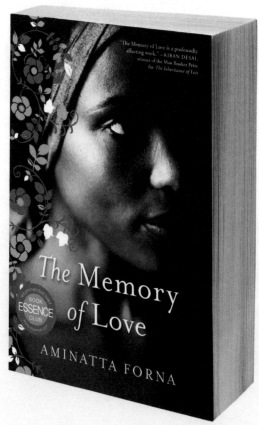

GRANTA

A HANDFUL OF WALNUTS

Ahmed Errachidi

INTRODUCTION BY CLIVE STAFFORD SMITH

EDMUND CLARK
Camp One, Isolation Unit
From the book *Guantanamo: If The Light Goes Out*
© Edmund Clark

Introduction

We brought the original litigation against the lawlessness of Guantánamo Bay in February 2002, shortly after it opened for its sordid business. By mid-2004, the Supreme Court had ordered that lawyers be allowed access and I was able to visit for the first time. Soon, I was requested to represent Ahmed Errachidi. When I first went to see him, in early 2005, the soldiers at Guantánamo warned me that he was one of the very worst: a bitter terrorist; Osama bin Laden's general, his main man. I was intrigued.

He didn't seem bitter. He laughed: a deep-chested laugh. He told me that he was a chef who had worked in London for eighteen years. I was not sure I believed him, but Ahmed's story – stranger than fiction – turned out to be entirely true. I took the Tube from one restaurant to another on his list, and each manager described his cooking. He said he was bipolar, and I obtained the medical records of his first mental breakdown, following the death of his father. I spoke with the immigration lawyers who had been trying to secure him permanent leave to remain in the UK. I obtained copies of his plane tickets from London to Morocco and Pakistan. At the time he was meant to have been at the al-Farouq terrorist-training camp, in July 2001, he was temping on the King's Road in Chelsea.

On 18 September 2001, Ahmed Errachidi left his home in England to visit his wife and children in Morocco. He was particularly keen to see his youngest son, one-year-old Imran, who needed an urgent heart operation to repair a blocked artery. This condition is often fatal without surgery, and Ahmed saw his young son struggling to breathe, his face turning blue. But he could not afford to pay for treatment. So he hatched a plan and sank all his savings into a new business venture, flying out to Pakistan to buy silver jewellery – the profit from sales back in Morocco would pay for the medical care. It was during his stay in Pakistan that Ahmed watched CNN news footage – on a television at a nearby mosque – of the US bombings and found himself moved by the plight of the Afghan refugees.

The interrogators in Guantánamo didn't believe him, but the story made sense to me. The bombs that were about to fall on Afghanistan were thousands of miles away to Ahmed, and his grandiose plans were all explained by the statement he made early on, openly, without the stigma common in the West: he is bipolar. My father, too, was bipolar and while his dreams might have landed him in jail for fraud many times, they were very real to him. Likewise, to Ahmed, anything was possible, even this dangerous mission: 'I entered Afghanistan to help the poor children and the women and to partake in their calamity, to taste what they tasted, to fear as they feared, and to be hungry as they were hungry.'

He told me that the Pakistanis had sold him to the Americans. I obtained copies of the American bounty leaflets promising $5,000 for 'terrorists', with a photograph of a bearded Arab, looking very similar to my client. 'I am a traded commodity,' said Ahmed. 'No matter how long it takes, the dust will settle and the buyer and the seller will be known, and only the anecdotes and the memories will remain.'

Ahmed was taken from Pakistan to Bagram air base where he spent nineteen consecutive days being tortured and interrogated before he was sent to Guantánamo Bay. There, he became a leading force in the intermittent prisoner protests against the abusive Guantánamo regime. As a result he was held in punitive isolation in Camp Delta for almost three years – the longest period served in isolation by any Guantánamo prisoner.

At a certain point, Ahmed had another breakdown. The military, seemingly oblivious to his condition, continued interrogating him through his psychotic haze. When asked whether he knew bin Laden, Ahmed indignantly assured them that he was bin Laden's superior officer. The interrogators wrote it down, and passed it on. They omitted, however, the next thing he said – that there was a large snowball that was about to envelop the earth, and that the officers should warn their families to make their peace with God.

A s with most people who have been liberated so far – 562 of the 601 who have been sent home – Ahmed was set free due to public pressure rather than the court of law. We showed how risible the allegations against him were, and embarrassed the authorities into returning him to Morocco. Guantánamo itself remains open. President Obama has rejuvenated the tainted military commissions and this year put forward a law that justifies detaining prisoners indefinitely without trial, subject to regular reviews by so-called periodic Administrative Review Boards. Forty-eight prisoners have been labelled 'too dangerous to transfer but not feasible for prosecution', partly because their confessions have been obtained under duress. As things stand, they are fated to remain in Cuba indefinitely, without trial and without judgment. ∎

A HANDFUL
OF WALNUTS

Ahmed Errachidi

This is how life in Guantánamo was, being moved from prison to prison, from camp to camp.

After the deaths of the three brothers, they moved me to Camp 5, where the cells were made of concrete and completely sealed. In the middle of the rear wall there was a window of opaque glass that allowed some light to come through. I had found a clear area about the size of the head of a matchstick in the top corner of this window. From this tiny spot, I could see out. I would stand on the concrete bed and watch the sun, the blue sky, the clouds and even the birds, trees and hills. After spending three years in segregation, I felt lucky at this good fortune.

This is how it began. When the events of 11 September took place, I was sat with a colleague in a cafe opposite our restaurant in north-west London. We watched – with horror and shock – the events unfold before our eyes. Soon afterwards, I travelled to Islamabad, to scout the silver markets. Everybody was talking about the human catastrophe that would follow should America bomb Afghanistan. When I returned to my lodgings I would watch the news, and see the refugees; most of them women, children and old people.

After ten days I decided I had to help, somehow. I caught a taxi in Peshawar and asked the driver to take me to Torkham, a border crossing between Pakistan and Afghanistan. Throughout the journey we saw trucks and buses full beyond capacity travelling in the opposite direction. Even the roofs were crammed with refugees. We reached Torkham – a few small houses surrounded by mountains – just before sunset. The driver showed me a man who could get me into Afghanistan. We decided to have dinner in Torkham, and then cross the borders at night.

The night had cast sheer darkness across the mountains surrounding us, adding to their enormity and vastness. We set out walking through the valley of stones. The man was carrying my bag and after about ten minutes we reached the main road. There were some small shops by the road, and he said, 'You are now in Afghanistan.' I looked around and saw those huge dark mountains, like giant creatures surrounding me. I never felt that I was in danger. On the contrary, I felt full of life because I had crossed the borders and valleys to save lives.

I stayed for some two weeks, cooking for the refugees. One sunny morning I heard the sound of an American F-16 skimming the skies. I saw the missile before hearing an enormous explosion. The target was a bus carrying civilian passengers. The bus was hardly recognizable – imagine a can crushed by the wheels of a car. Inside and around it were the torn limbs of men, women and children. I saw a woman whose skull had been smashed. Her brain and hair were burning. Shoes and belongings were thrown everywhere. It was a scene that time will not erase from my memory.

I came back to Pakistan across those mountains and valleys with the mass exodus from Afghanistan. Every time we came to a village we would stay for a few days because we faced the twin dangers of bombardment and the Pakistani Army, who were handing over people escaping Afghanistan to the Americans in exchange for money, especially the Arabs among us. We reached a place called Bannu, and I, together with four other refugees, got into a car headed for Lahore. I wanted to reach a Pakistani city so that I could call my family and check on them. But we had a traffic accident on the way. The driver and his friend jumped out of the car and fled. Some policemen climbed into our car and took us to the police station. I couldn't digest all the events that were taking place in quick succession. I remember that moment – it was as if the scorpions of time had momentarily left their path; the sun was high in the sky, and an inescapable fate had befallen me.

The police brought us, blindfolded, to the intelligence services prison in Lahore. They promised that they would send me home after making the necessary travel arrangements with the embassy. Three weeks later, an FBI team arrived and interrogated me inside the prison. They took my fingerprints and photograph, to ensure, they said, that I was not on the FBI's wanted list. The Pakistanis told me the checks would only take two or three days. Forty-four days later they took seven of us to the airport. Even then, the Pakistanis claimed that they were taking me home.

We waited at Islamabad airport shackled in handcuffs and leg irons, with black hoods over our heads. Hours later, I heard American accents. I heard the sound of money changing hands, and I knew that we were being bought and sold in the Diplomatic Lounge at Islamabad airport. The soldiers took us out one by one, replacing our Pakistani hoods and chains with American ones.

In the plane they shackled us even tighter, until we were like insects in a spider's web. When we arrived, they pulled us down the runway, the soldiers singing and cheering. The only word I remember from their song is: 'Taliban, Taliban.' They beat us. I heard one of them laughing and saying to another, 'Leave this short one for me, he is my share.' This was Bagram.

They ordered us to lie on the floor, beat us and threw liquid at us. It was cold and noisy from aircraft turbines. I bumped into one of the soldiers, and instinctively said sorry, in English.

'Who speaks English?' one of them asked.

'Me,' I replied.

'We have someone who speaks English with us,' he said to his friends. Then he came close and asked, 'Are you scared?'

At about two in the morning I was finally put into a barbed-wire cage. It was hard to hear anything because of the generators. By day and by night they would generate electricity and drown our screams. There were seven of us in the cage. Our hands and feet were shackled throughout our entire nineteen-day stay in Bagram.

I started to cooperate with people from the FBI, CIA, the US military intelligence and the British intelligence services: MI5 and MI6.

We arrived at Kandahar in the same manner as we arrived at Bagram, except that it was even harsher. We were left lying on the cold runway for a long time, while the soldiers walked on our heads with their boots on, saying, 'Are you the ones who came to fight us?' There were dogs everywhere, barking. They cut my clothes off with scissors while I was face down. They took us away, one by one. When my turn came, they took me inside a tent and sat me on a chair. They took off my hood. I saw my friends naked, tied to chairs. They had already finished shaving their heads and beards and were replacing the black hoods over their heads. I started crying when I saw them, naked and shackled, with black hoods. The soldiers were laughing and taking photos. The floor of the tent was covered with hair. They started to shave me.

When they finished, they threw me to the ground and put some blue prison clothes on me. They could not find shoes my size, so they forced on a pair of shoes that were too small. They dragged me away to an old hangar, threw me on the sandy floor and took off my hood and handcuffs. They tried to take off my leg irons too, but they were too tight against my feet and they couldn't remove them. So they left me in my leg irons and said, 'Don't talk,' before leaving. I looked around me. There were about ten cages and two guard towers. It was dawn, and some of the prisoners were walking in their cages. Some were looking at me, but no one talked. I prayed the dawn prayer in my leg irons. When I finished I found a blanket and an iron bucket, which was the toilet. I got under the blanket to sleep.

I woke to the shouts of soldiers coming with saws to cut off my leg irons. They still couldn't remove them as they were attached to my skin, and had to stop cutting when they saw blood. They came back with pliers to cut them, which didn't work either. I was rolling on the ground, screaming with pain.

I stayed in Kandahar for nearly two months. That whole time they did not allow us to use water for washing our hands or faces. Despite sanctions, prisoners, concealed by their friends, would from time to time pour a bottle of water on their bodies to wash.

Finally, my interrogator told me that soon I would travel to a distant place by the sea. I would be offered Arabic bread and good food. There are people there, he said, who want to ask you some questions. You will stay there for three months, then they will give you $500, and a bus ticket to travel back to your country and family.

Guantánamo

My block was made of metal, like a giant shipping container. The area of each cell was approximately seven by nine feet, and there were forty-eight cells in the block, enclosed with steel mesh. There was a mesh window in the metal wall. By the window, there was an open Turkish-style lavatory. To the right there was a small metal washbasin, to the left, a metal bed. The floor was metal too and so was the ceiling. If the bed had been a bath, the cell would have been a medium-sized bathroom. There was a slot in the middle of the door from where the prisoner would collect his food, clothes and medicine. From there, also, he was shackled before any contact with the guards. There was another opening at the bottom of the door from which they shackled the prisoner's feet.

Every six months or so, the soldiers and interrogators would change, and fresh rounds of interrogations would begin. After some time I came to believe that the purpose of the interrogations was not to determine innocence or guilt, but rather to train the interrogators. Guantánamo had become a training school for new interrogators. I was asked the same questions again and again for a period of five years, by a succession of interrogators. If a prisoner refused to speak, the interrogators would tempt him with good food, or chocolates, or books. If that didn't work, they used methods of coercion: sleep deprivation and exposure to extreme cold.

We were in the Oskar punishments block when Farooq's turn came. The interrogators strapped him to a chair in the cold room for thirty-six hours, and kept him awake. Then they returned him to his cell. Every hour, just as he fell asleep, they took him to another cell. Then he was moved back to the interrogation room to remain there for another thirty-six hours. We saw our friend in torment, and decided to put an end to his suffering. As was the custom whenever the prisoners wanted to fend off injustice, we resorted to a protest to put pressure on the camp administration. We decided, therefore, to refrain from returning the paper plates and plastic spoons after dinner. We told the soldiers that we would not return them until Farooq was returned to us, and was allowed to sleep.

Inevitably, a confrontation ensued. Two divisions of the emergency reaction force entered the ward wearing black protective gear. They walked with a dance rhythm to cast fear into us – all of them raised their feet at once and then struck the metal floor of the ward hard with their military boots. This terrifying dance shook every prisoner, telling him that now there was no escape.

At the time we were collectively engaged in the evening prayer. They stormed the cells as we prayed. They began with cell number 1. I was in cell number 19, and when my turn came the officer gave me a last warning. I said, 'No, I am one of them.' As they opened the door, however, by luck I was able to push them away and get out of the cell. I ran out into the corridor without shackles or chains, while they surrounded me and tried to drop me to the ground. The scene was like a match of American football: one side in military kit against one man in an orange kit. The prisoners watched in amazement and cheered by beating on the doors of their cells. It only lasted a few seconds; they dropped me in the middle of the corridor and rained beatings down on me.

That night they used gas, and dogs, and the noise of ventilation fans and mechanical vacuums to drown the screams of the prisoners. Many of the prisoners suffered injury, and one of us was bitten by dogs. When they finished taking the spoons and plates from the prisoners' cells, they still wanted to punish us, so that we would not protest again. But in the ward of punishments we did not have anything left to be deprived of, except our daily ten sheets of toilet paper each. Those were taken away, as a collective punishment.

I loved to entertain the other prisoners, particularly in the isolation wards where we would spend months. Whenever circumstances permitted and we were able to hear each other, I would ask them to sit down in their cells and listen to me as I described to them some delicious meals, to imagine that they were guests in my house in Morocco sitting around a large dining table. I would describe different types of delicious seafood. There was fish – fried, grilled or roasted – in all, an array of seven different types of fish, surrounded by smaller dishes filled with all types of salads, chips and various salsas. I described roast chicken and oven-roasted lamb, fruit, juices and desserts. After describing all the food, I would say, 'Why don't we take a short siesta now and sleep a little?' After a few hours I would hear the prisoners calling out to me, 'Oh Abu Imran, this siesta has been a long one, now can we come back to your dining table?' And then we would laugh.

The Visitors

Visitors would come three times a day after every meal. They would come by the dozen and I would wait eagerly for them. I would sit with them, thoroughly enjoying their company. I spent long hours with them, and yet did not get bored. They would come and give us hope that life had not come to a halt. Every time I saw them, I felt comfortable. They walked so quietly that the guards didn't know they were there, otherwise they would be eliminated.

I am talking about the wonderful nation of ants. These beautiful creatures would visit me in my steel prison, bringing hope and life. I secretly saved food for them in a corner. If the guards saw them they would either spray them with pesticide or crush them beneath their military boots. I would get angry, and shout at them, 'Do not the ants have a right to life? They do not trouble you so why do you have to kill them?' When the soldiers found out that we fed the ants, they punished us by cutting our rations. That didn't stop me from keeping ants in my cell. I observed them and studied their way of life every day.

I would sometimes leave them a peanut, whenever available. I split the bean into halves and left each half on the floor with the flat side down. The ants would come and eat the entire bean from the inside, leaving the skin as it had been left for them. If you saw it you wouldn't know that the inside had been eaten until you turned it over to find it empty. I found it amusing. Whenever I put food in the corner, one of the ants would come to search. If it found food it would return to its friends and inform them, and show them the way. The ants all varied in their contribution to the work; some carried small pieces, and others carried pieces bigger than themselves back to their homes. I didn't know that ants drank before, but now I would save them a few drops of sweet tea, which they would drink until they swelled up.

When the ants came to visit, life would creep back into my dead cell. I would feel hope instead of despair. Their presence in my company, however, was not free of danger, as the soldiers would come to inspect the cells, so I always feared for them. Before inspections I would blow towards them, which made them disperse, while I got rid of the food. They soon became accustomed to this puff of air, which became their warning signal, so that each time they felt it they realized danger was close and ran away. When the soldiers would return me back to my cell after the search, the first thing I would look for were ant bodies. When I didn't find any I felt relieved, knowing that the ants had safely escaped.

After spending excessive periods of time in the solitary cells, I felt that I was secluded from the rest of the world. Life and the beauty of nature began to fade from my memory. I was not able to take more than three medium steps in my cell until I stopped at the steel wall. When I turned, I found myself in front of the steel door. Steel surrounded me and captivated me. There was no horizon, no life and nothing to see. So I began to fly out of the cell with my thoughts and my imagination into the vast world of existence. I would put myself on the horizon, imagining that I was looking at this sun and its rays; I would travel to see birds and trees, imagine bees collecting nectar from flowers, and long for their honey. I would imagine the colours and scents of roses so that I wouldn't forget them. I travelled into the scenery of clouds as they moved through the sky, as if they were ships sailing in the still blue sky, before breaking up and dispersing. I travelled to the moon, enjoying its quiet beautiful light, which did not disturb those who wanted to sleep. I imagined the stars sailing through the darkness of night, and felt their beauty and presence. I remembered every beautiful thing that I had known or experienced in the universe. I imagined the sunrise, a ray of light drawing a line on the horizon, slowly expelling the dark of the long night. I imagined newborn plants splitting the ground, fruits emerging from their skins. I imagined leaves falling to the ground, the sea and the fish, the rocks and corals. I imagined cattle and sheep as they grazed, and wondered how their milk could be such a brilliant white even though the grass they ate was green. Thoughts were not restricted, even though hands and feet were shackled. I wandered in my thoughts every morning and every evening. I woke at dawn, prayed, and then escaped from my cell, my thoughts transcending the guarded doors, the razor wire, into the vast universe. I did it so I wouldn't forget. ∎

THE THIRD MATE

Adam Johnson

Jun Do was down in the *Junma*'s aft hold, a steel room big enough for a table, chair, typewriter and a stack of receivers that had been pilfered from American tanks and planes in the war. The hold was lit only by the green glow of the listening equipment, which was reflected in the sheen of fish water that seeped under the bulkheads and constantly slicked the floor. When Jun Do looked at the walls, he could visualize what was on the other side: chambers of tightly packed fish sucking their last breath in the refrigerated dark.

They'd been in international waters for three days now, their North Korean flag lowered so as not to invite trouble. First they chased deep-running mackerel and then schools of jittery bonito that surfaced in brief patches of sun. Now they were after sharks. All night the *Junma* had longlined for them at the edge of the trench. At daybreak, Jun Do could hear above him the grinding of the winch and the slapping of sharks as they cleared the water and struck the hull.

From sunset to sunrise, Jun Do monitored the usual transmissions: fishing captains mostly, the ferry from Uichi to Chongjin, even the nightly check-in of two American women rowing around the world – one paddled all night, the other all day, ruining the crew's theory that they'd made their way to the East Sea for the purpose of having sex.

Hidden inside the *Junma*'s rigging and booms was a strong array antenna, and above the helm, disguised as a loudspeaker, was a directional antenna that could turn 360 degrees. The US and Japan and South Korea all encrypted their military transmissions, which sounded only like piercing squeals and bleats. But how much squeal and where and when seemed important to Pyongyang. As long as he documented that, he could listen to whatever else he liked.

Jun Do couldn't abide programmed broadcasts. Why was the world so obsessed by politics, news and religion? A speech is made, something crashed, God is still angry. The news couldn't tell you anything about people. He loved short-wave operators, strangers who spoke into transmitters like the sky was a diary. The lepers broadcast, as did the blind, and the families of inmates imprisoned in Manila – all day the families would line up to speak of report cards, baby teeth and new job prospects. There was Dr Rendezvous, a Brit who broadcast his erotic 'dreams' every day, along with the coordinates of where his sailing boat would be anchored tomorrow. There was a station in Okinawa that broadcast portraits of half-Japanese families that US servicemen had refused to claim. Once a day, the Chinese broadcast prisoner confessions, and it didn't matter that the confessions were forced, false and in a language he didn't understand – Jun Do could barely make it through them. And then there was the girl who rowed in the dark. Each night she paused to relay her coordinates, how her body was performing and the atmospheric conditions. Often she noted things – the outlines of birds migrating at night, a whale shark seining for krill off her bow. She had, she said, a growing ability to dream while she rowed.

If North Koreans spoke this way, maybe they'd make more sense to Jun Do. Maybe he'd understand why some people accepted their fates while others didn't. He might know why people sometimes scoured all the orphanages looking for one particular child when any child would do, when there were perfectly good children everywhere. He'd know why all the fishermen on the *Junma* had their wives' portraits tattooed on their chests, while he was a man who wore headphones in the dark of a fish hold on a boat that was twenty-seven days at sea a month.

Not that he envied those who rowed in the daylight. The light, the sky, the water, they were all things you looked *through* during the day. At night, they were things you looked *into*. You looked *into* the stars; you looked *into* dark rollers and the surprising platinum flash of their caps. No one ever stared at the tip of a cigarette in the daylight hours and, with the sun in the sky, who would ever post a 'watch'? At night on the *Junma*, there is acuity, quietude, pause. There is a look in the crew members' eyes that is both faraway and inward. Presumably there was another English linguist out there on a fishing boat, pointlessly listening to broadcasts from sunrise to sunset. But Jun Do couldn't imagine anyone from his language school living in such solitude, smelling of fish oil, let alone doing it at night. All the students in his school had been *yangbans* from Pyongyang, kids of the elite who were in the military as a prerequisite to advancing in the Party and then a life as a diplomat or a host for foreign dignitaries. All those *yangbans* were social, well spoken, born with simple, elegant names, and they spent their days practising dialogues about ordering coffees, enquiring about the weather and buying plane tickets to Zurich. They were the reason Jun Do had studied alone in the language lab at night, playing English cassette tapes into his baby-blue headphones.

Above, another shark flopped out its last little aria, and Jun Do decided to call it a night. As he was turning off his instruments, he heard the ghost broadcast: once a week or so, an English transmission came through that was powerful and brief, just a couple of minutes before it was gone. Today the speakers had American and Russian accents and, as usual, the broadcast was from the middle of a conversation. The two spoke about a trajectory and a docking manoeuvre and fuel. Last week, there'd been a Japanese speaker with them. Jun Do manned the crank that slowly turned the directional antenna, but no matter where he aimed it, the signal strength was the same, which was impossible. How could a signal come from everywhere?

Just like that, the broadcast seemed to end, but Jun Do grabbed his UHF receiver and a hand-held parabolic and headed above decks. The ship was an old Soviet steel-hulled vessel, made for cold water, and its sharp, tall bow made it plunge deep into waves and leap the troughs.

He held the rail and pointed the dish into the morning haze, sweeping the horizon. He picked up some chatter from container-vessel pilots and towards Japan he got all the craft advisories cross-cut with a VHF Christian broadcast. There was blood on the deck, and Jun Do's military boots left drunk-looking tracks all the way to the stern, where the only transmissions were the squawks and barks of US naval encryption. He did a quick sweep of the sky, dialling in a

Taiwan Air pilot who lamented the approach of DPRK airspace. But there was nothing, the signal was gone.

'Anything I should know about?' the captain asked.

'Steady as she goes,' Jun Do told him.

The captain nodded towards the directional antenna atop the helm, which was made to look like a loudspeaker. 'That one's a little more subtle,' he said. There was an agreement that Jun Do wouldn't do anything foolish, such as bringing spying equipment on deck. The captain was older. He'd been a big man, but he'd done some time aboard a Russian penal vessel and that had wasted his flesh so that now his skin hung loose. You could tell he'd once been an intense captain, giving clear-eyed commands, even if they were to fish in waters contested by Russia. And you could tell he'd been an intense prisoner, labouring carefully and without complaint under severe scrutiny. And now, it seemed, he was both.

The captain lit a cigarette, offered one to Jun Do, then returned to tallying sharks, using a hand-counter to click off each one the machinist winched aboard. The sharks had been hanging from lead lines in open water so they were in a low-oxygen stupor when they breached the water and slammed against the hull before being boomed up. On deck, they moved slowly, nosing around like blind puppies, their mouths opening and closing like there was something they were trying to say. The job of the second mate, because he was young and new to the ship, was to retrieve the hooks, while the first mate, in seven quick cuts, dorsal to anal, took the fins and rolled the shark back into the water, where, unable to manoeuvre, it could race nowhere but down, disappearing into the blackness, leaving only a thin contrail of blood behind.

Jun Do leaned over the side and watched one descend, following it down with his parabolic. The water crossing the shark's gills would revive its mind and perceptions. They were above the trench now, almost four kilometres deep, perhaps a half-hour of free fall, and through his headphones, the background hiss of the abyss sounded more like the creeping, spooky crackle of pressure death. There was nothing to hear down there – all the subs communicated with ultra-low-frequency bursts. Still, he pointed his parabolic towards the waves and slowly panned from bow to stern. The ghost broadcast had to come from somewhere. How could it seem to come from every direction if it didn't come from below? He could feel the eyes of the crew.

'Did you find something, Third Mate?' the machinist asked.

His name made them nervous, so as a joke, they sometimes called him that.

'The opposite,' Jun Do said. 'I lost something.'

Come first light, Jun Do slept, while the crew – the pilot, machinist, first mate, second mate and captain alike – spent the day crating the fins in layers of salt and ice. The Chinese paid in hard currency, and they were very particular about their shark fins.

Jun Do woke before dinner, which was his breakfast. He had reports to type before darkness fell. There had been a fire on the *Junma* which took the galley, the head and half of the bunks, leaving only the tin plates, a black mirror and a toilet that had cracked in two from the heat. But the stove still worked, and it was summer, so everyone ate sitting on the hatches, where it was possible for the men to view a rare sunset. On the horizon was a carrier group from the American fleet; ships so large they didn't look like they could move, let alone float. It looked like an island chain, so fixed and ancient as to have its own people and language and gods.

They took off their shirts and smoked, even as the sun fell. The *Junma* was pilotless, cantering in the waves, buoys rolling loose on the deck, and even the cables and booms glowed orange in the oven-coloured light. Except for the captain, the life of a fisherman was good – there were no endless factory quotas to fill, and on a ship there were no loudspeakers blaring propaganda all day. There was food. And even though the crew were leery about having a listening officer on board, it meant the *Junma* got all the fuel coupons it needed, and if Jun Do directed the ship in a way that lowered the catch, everyone got extra ration cards.

'So, Third Mate,' the pilot said, 'how are our girls?'

'They're nearing Hokkaido,' Jun Do told them. 'At least they were last night. They're rowing thirty kilometres a day.'

'Are they still naked?' the machinist asked.

'Only the girl who rows in the dark,' said Jun Do.

'To row around the world,' the second mate said, 'only an American would do that. It's so pointless and arrogant. They must be sexy.' The second mate couldn't have been more than twenty. The tattoo of his wife on his chest was new, and it was clear she was a beauty.

'Who said they were sexy?' Jun Do asked, though he pictured them that way, too.

'I know this,' the second mate said. 'A sexy girl thinks she can do anything. Trust me, I deal with it every day.'

'If your wife is so hot,' the machinist asked, 'how come they didn't sweep her up to be a hostess in Pyongyang?'

'It's easy,' the second mate said. 'Her father didn't want her ending up as a barmaid or a whore in Pyongyang, so he pulled some strings and got her assigned to the fish factory. A beautiful girl like that, and along comes me.'

'I'll believe it when I see it,' the first mate said. 'There's a reason she doesn't come to see you off.'

'Give it time,' the second mate said. 'She's still coping. I'll show her the light.'

'Hokkaido,' the pilot said. 'The ice up there is worse in the summer. The shelves break up, currents churn it. It's the ice you don't see, that's what gets you.'

The captain spoke. Shirtless, you could see all his Russian tattoos. They looked heavy in the sideways light, heavy enough to pull his skin loose. 'The winters up there,' he said. 'Everything freezes. The piss in your prick and the fish gore in your beard. You try to set a knife down and you can't let go of it. Once, we were on the cutting floor when the ship hit a growler. It shook the whole boat, knocked us down into the guts. From the floor, we watched that ice roll down the side of the ship, knuckling big dents in the hull.'

Jun Do thought he was done. He looked at the captain's chest, where there was a tattoo of his wife, blurred and faded as a watercolour. When the captain's ship didn't return, his wife had eventually been given a replacement husband, and now the captain was alone. Plus, they'd added the years he was in prison to the service he owed the state, so there'd be no retirement now. 'The cold can squeeze a ship,' the captain suddenly said. 'Make the whole thing contract, the metal door frames, the locks, trapping you down in the waste tanks, and nobody, nobody's coming with buckets of hot water to get you out.'

The captain didn't throw a look or anything, but Jun Do wondered if the prison talk was aimed at him, for bringing his listening equipment on deck, for raising the spectre that it could all happen again.

When darkness fell and the others went below, Jun Do offered the second mate three packs of cigarettes to see how fast he could climb atop the helm and shimmy the pole upon which the loudspeaker was mounted.

'I'll do it,' the second mate said. 'But instead of cigarettes, I want to listen to the rowers.'

The boy was always asking Jun Do what Seoul and Tokyo were like, and he wouldn't believe that Jun Do had never been to Pyongyang. The kid wasn't a fast climber, but he was curious about how the radios worked, and that was half of it. Jun Do had him practise pulling the cotter pin so that the directional antenna could be lifted and pointed towards the water.

'Those girls in the boat,' the second mate said. 'You think they're married?'

'I don't know,' Jun Do said. 'What's it matter?'

'What's it take to row around the world? A couple years? Even if they don't have husbands, what about everyone else, the people they left behind? Don't they give a shit about anybody?'

Jun Do picked some tobacco off his tongue and looked at the boy, who had his hands behind his head as he squinted at the stars. It was a good question – *What about the people left behind?* – but an odd one for the second mate to ask. 'Earlier tonight,' Jun Do said, 'you were all for sexy rowers. They do something to piss you off?'

'I'm just wondering what got into them, to just take off and paddle around the world.'

'Wouldn't you, if you could?'

'That's my point, you can't. Who could pull it off – all those waves and ice, in that tiny boat? Someone should have stopped them. Someone should have taken that stupid idea out of their heads.'

The kid sounded new to whatever heavy thinking was going on in his head. Jun Do decided to talk him down a bit. 'They're halfway there,' he pointed out. 'Plus, they have to be pretty serious athletes. They're trained for this; it's probably what they love. And when you say boat, you can't be thinking of this bucket. Those are American girls, their craft is space age, with comforts and electronics – you can't be picturing them like Party officials' wives rowing a tin can around.'

The second mate wasn't quite listening. 'And what if you do make it around the world – how do you wait in line for your dormitory toilet again, knowing that you've been to America? Maybe the millet tasted better in some other country and the loudspeakers weren't so tinny. Suddenly it's *your* water that smells not so good – then what do you do?'

Jun Do didn't answer him.

The moon was coming up. Above, they could see a jet rising out of Japan – slowly it began its great veer away from North Korean airspace.

After a while, the second mate said, 'The sharks will probably get them.' He flicked his cigarette away. 'So, what's this all about, pointing the antenna and all? What's down there?'

Jun Do wasn't sure how to answer. 'A voice,' he said.

'In the ocean? What is it? What's it say?'

'There are American voices and an English-speaking Russian. Once a Japanese guy. They talk about docking and manoeuvring. Stuff like that.'

'No offence, but that sounds like the conspiracy plots the old widows are always trading in my housing block.'

It did sound a little paranoid when the second mate said it out loud. But the truth was the idea of conspiracy appealed to Jun Do. That people were in communication, that things had a design, that there was intent, significance and purpose in what people did – he needed to believe this. Normal people, he understood, had no need for such thinking. The girl who rowed during the day had the horizon of where she came from, and when she turned to look, the horizon of where she was headed. But the girl who rowed in the dark had only the splash and pull of each stroke and the belief that they'd all add up to get her home.

Jun Do pointed up. 'The Americans and Russians are up there, aren't they? Those satellites are all fitted with lasers and surveillance gear. You ever hear of someone putting a satellite in the sky for peace and fucking harmony?'

The second mate leaned back on the winch house, the sky vast above them. 'No,' he said. 'I suppose not.'

The captain came out of the pilot house and told the second mate he had tin plates and shit buckets to clean. It was Jun Do's turn to offer the captain a smoke, but when the boy had gone below, the captain refused it. 'Don't put ideas in his head,' he said and walked deliberately across the dark gangway to the high-riding bow of the *Junma*. A large vessel was creeping by, its deck carpeted with new vehicles. As it passed, likely headed from South Korea to California, the moonlight flashed in rapid succession off a thousand new windscreens.

The next night, the moon was strong, and they were far north, on the shoals of Juljuksan, a disputed island chain of tortured volcanic reefs. All day, the captain had told Jun Do to listen for anything – 'anything or anybody, anywhere near us' – but as they approached the southernmost atoll, the captain ordered everything to be switched off so that all the batteries could power the spotlights.

Soon, they could hear patches of open break, and seeing the white water froth against the invisibility of black pumice was unnerving.

Even the moon didn't help when you couldn't see the rocks. The captain was with the pilot at the wheel, while the first mate was in the bow with the big spotlight. Using hand-helds, the second mate was to bow and Jun Do was to port, everyone lighting up the water in an effort to gauge the depth. Holds full, the *Junma* was low in the water and slow to respond, so the machinist was with the engine in case power was needed fast.

There was a single channel that wound through fields of frozen lava that even the tide was at pains to crawl over, and soon the tide began drawing them fast and almost sideways through the trough, the dark glitter of the bottom whirring by in Jun Do's light.

The captain seemed revived, with a wild, nothing-to-lose smile on his face. 'The Russians call this chute the Foxtrot,' he said.

Out there in the tide, Jun Do saw a vessel. He called to the first mate and together they lit it up. It was a patrol boat, broken up, sideways on against an oyster bar. There were no markings left, and it had been upon the rocks for some time. The antenna was small and spiralled, so he figured there was no radio worth salvaging.

'Bet they cracked up someplace else and the tide brought her here,' the captain said.

Jun Do wasn't so sure about that. The pilot said nothing.

'Look for her lifeboat,' the captain told them.

The second mate was upset to be on the wrong side of the ship. 'To see if there were survivors?' he asked.

'You just man that light,' the pilot told him.

'Anything?' the captain asked.

The first mate shook his head *no*.

Jun Do saw the red of a fire extinguisher strapped to the boat's stern, and much as he wished the *Junma* had an extinguisher, he kept his mouth shut, and with a *whoosh*, they flashed past the wreck and it was gone.

'I suppose no lifeboat's worth sinking for,' the captain lamented.

They'd used buckets to put out the fire on the *Junma*, so the moment of abandoning ship, the moment in which it would have been revealed to the second mate that they had no lifeboat, never came. The second mate asked, 'What's the deal with the lifeboat?' 'You just man that light,' the pilot told him. They cleared the offshore break and, as if cut from a tether, the *Junma* settled into calmer water. The craggy ass of the island was above them, and in its lee, finally, was a large lagoon that the outer currents kept in motion. Here was where the shrimp might congregate. They killed the lights, and then the engine, and entered the lagoon on inertia. Soon, they were slowly back-pedalling with the circular tide. The water was constant and calm and rising, and even when the hull touched sand, no one seemed to worry.

Below raked obsidian bluffs was a steep, glassy black beach whose glint looked sharp enough to bleed your feet. In the sand, dwarfed, gnarled trees had anchored themselves, and in the blue light, you could see the wind had curled even their needles. Upon the water, the moon revealed much detritus had been swept in from the straits.

The machinist extended the outriggers, then dipped the nets, soaking them so that they'd submerge on their skim runs. The mates secured the lines and the blocks, and then raised the nets to see if any shrimp had turned up. Out in the green nylon webbing, a few shrimp bounced towards the trap, but there was something else out there, too.

They spilled the nets, and on the deck, amid the flipping and phosphorescing of a few dozen shrimp was a pair of athletic shoes. They didn't match.

'These are American shoes,' the machinist said. 'Nikes.'

The second mate grabbed one. Jun Do could read the look in his eye. 'Don't worry,' Jun Do said. 'The rowers are far from here.'

'Read the label,' the second mate said. 'Is it a woman's shoe?'

The captain came over and examined a shoe. He smelled it, and then bent the sole to see how much water squished out. 'Don't bother,' the captain said. 'The thing's never even been worn.' He told the pilot to turn on the floodlights, which revealed hundreds of shoes bobbing out in the jade-grey water. Thousands, maybe.

The pilot scanned the waters. 'I hope there's no shipping container swirling round this bathtub with us,' he said. 'Waiting to take our bottom out.'

The captain turned to Jun Do. 'You pick up any distress calls?'

Jun Do said, 'You know the policy on that.'

The second mate asked, 'What's the policy on distress calls?'

'I know the policy,' the captain said. 'I'm just trying to find out if there are a bunch of vessels headed our way in response to a call.'

'I didn't hear anything,' Jun Do said. 'But people don't cry on the radio any more. They have emergency beacons now, things that automatically transmit GPS coordinates up to satellites. I can't pick up any of that. The pilot's right – a shipping container probably fell off a deck and washed up here.'

'Don't we answer distress calls?' the second mate asked.

'Not with him on board,' the captain said and handed Jun Do a shoe. 'OK, gentlemen, let's get those nets back in the water. It's going to be a long night.'

Jun Do found a general broadcast station, loud and clear out of Vladivostok, and played it through a speaker on deck. It was Strauss. They started skimming the black water, and there was little time to marvel at the American shoes that began to pile atop the hatches. Only once, years ago, had Jun Do seen shoes even close to these.

There was a programme when he was young to bring home Koreans who lived in Japan. Even though many were wealthy and powerful, they were second-class citizens in Japan, and Pyongyang played on this, promising them cars and apartments and high social standing if they returned. Once a month, a ship was chartered to bring them to North Korea via Chongjin, an industrial port city. When the ship docked, many of the Koreans from Japan would line the rail, staring down at Chongjin, and perhaps what they saw scared them because there was always a problem with people not getting off the ship.

That's when Jun Do's orphanage was recruited to meet the ship with singing and dancing. Seniors from the Glory Everlasting Elderly Home would make 'WELCOME BACK' banners and while the children beckoned, the old-timers would wave their canes like they were lost relatives, anything to get the families to step off the ships on to North Korean soil, where the trucks were waiting to take them away to the prison camps.

All it took was for one prideful family to come down the gangplank, and the rest would follow, the orphans lining up on either side to witness people who seemed to arrive from the future, with unknown fashions and clothes of an undreamed-of quality. The shoes on the boys' feet, right before Jun Do's eyes on the gangplank, were never to be forgotten. Once, a boy wore white leather shoes with green stripes and bright green bottoms. Another boy had red, white and blue shoes, with blue patterned soles. Jun Do remembered thinking, *Those boys are going to the camps, where they won't need those shoes any more. Why shouldn't I have those shoes?* Of course, those were a child's desires, back when such things could get inside a kid's head and kick around until they seemed to matter. Now it's the families that Jun Do thinks about, wishing he could recall the looks on their faces. All he could picture was the captain's face: now that he wouldn't be retiring, now that his wife had been given a replacement husband, the captain seemed newly sure in the knowledge that if you had to go, it was best to go together because what was the point in living if you were the one left behind?

While the crew seined for shoes above, Jun Do donned his headphones. There were lots of squawks and barks out there, and that would make someone, somewhere, happy. He'd missed the Chinese confessions just after sundown, which was for the best, as the voices always sounded hopelessly sad, and therefore guilty, to him. He did catch the Okinawan families making appeals to fathers listening on their ships, but it was hard to feel too bad for kids who had mothers and siblings. Plus the 'adopt us' good cheer was enough to make a person sick. When the Russian families broadcast nothing but good cheer for their inmate fathers, it was to give the men strength. But trying to plead a father into returning? Who would fall for that? Who would want to be around such a desperate, pathetic kid?

In the morning, they were headed south again, the seine net full and swinging wildly with its lightweight purse of shoes. There were hundreds of shoes across the deck, the first and second mates stringing them together by general design. These garlands hung from all the cleats to dry in the sun. It was clear they'd found only a few matches. Still, even without sleep, they seemed to be in high spirits.

The first mate decided that a boy's seven was the size for him. He found a single pair, blue and white, and stowed them under his bunk. The pilot was marvelling over a size fifteen, over what manner of human would take that size, and the machinist had created a tall pile of shoes he intended for his wife to try. The silvers and reds, the flashy accents and reflective strips, the whitest of whites, they were pure gold, these shoes: they equalled food, gifts, bribes and favours. The feeling of them on, like you weren't wearing anything on your feet. The shoes made the crew's socks look positively lousy, and their legs looked mottled and sun-worn amid such undiluted colour. The second mate sifted through every shoe until he found a pair of what he called his 'America shoes'. They were both women's shoes. One was red and white, the other blue. He threw his own shoes overboard then and he traversed the deck with a different Nike on each foot.

Ahead, a large cloud bank had formed to the east, with conicals of seabirds working the leading edge of it. It was an upwelling, with cold water from deep in the trench rising to the surface and condensing the air. This was the deep water that sperm whales hunted and frill sharks called home. Surfacing in that upwell would be black jellyfish, squid and deep-water shrimp, white and blind. Those shrimp, with their large, occluded eyes, it was said, were eaten still wriggling and peppered with caviar, by the Dear Leader himself.

The captain grabbed his binoculars and surveyed the site. Then he rang the bell, and the mates sprang up in their new shoes.

'Come on, lads,' the captain said. 'We'll be heroes of the revolution.'

The first take was successful. The shrimp were clear in the water, white when the net was raised, then clear again when they were pitching with the slosh of the livewell, their long antennae unfurling and retracting, almost as a mode of propulsion. When the captain ordered the nets out again, the birds had vanished, and the pilot began motoring through the fog to find them.

Everyone was needed at the livewell to land the catch, which might wing any direction once over the deck. The machinist was operating the winch, but at the last moment the captain shouted for him to hold fast, the net oscillating wildly. At the gunwale the captain stared into the fog. Everyone else paused as well, staring at what, they weren't sure, unsettled by such stillness amid the bucking of the ship and the gyration of the catch. The captain signalled the pilot to sound the horn, and they all attended the gloom for a response.

'Go below,' the captain told Jun Do, 'and tell me what you hear.'

But it was too late. A moment later, the fog flashing clear, the steady bow of an American frigate was visible. The *Junma* pitched for all it was worth, but there was barely any motion from the American ship, whose rail was lined with binocular-holding men. Suddenly, an inflatable boarding craft was upon them, and the Americans were throwing lines. Here were the men who wore size fifteen shoes.

For the first few minutes, the Americans were all business, following a procedure that involved the levelling and lifting of their black rifles. They made their way through the pilot house and galley into the quarters below. From the deck, you could hear them move through the ship, shouting 'clear-clear-clear' the whole way.

With them was a South Korean ROK officer who stayed up top while the Americans secured the ship. The ROK officer was crisp in his white uniform, the name 'PAK' embroidered above the pocket. His helmet was white with black and light blue bands, rimmed in polished silver. He demanded a manifest and registration of the ship's origin and the captain's licence, none of which they had. Where was their flag, Pak wanted to know, and why hadn't they answered when hailed?

The shrimp swung in the net. The captain told the first mate to dump it in the livewell.

'No,' Pak said. He pointed at Jun Do. 'That one will do it.'

Jun Do looked to the captain. The captain nodded. Jun Do went to the net and tried to steady it against the motion of the ship. Though he'd seen it done many times, he'd never actually dumped a haul. He found the release for the trap. He tried to time the swing of the net over the livewell, thinking the catch would burst out, but when he pulled the cord, the shrimp came out in a stream that poured into the barrel and, swinging away, dumped all along the deck, the gutter boards and finally his boots.

'You didn't look like a fisherman,' Pak said. 'Look at your skin, look at your hands. Take off your shirt,' he demanded.

'I give the orders around here,' the captain said.

'Take off your shirt, you spy, or I'll have the Americans take it off for you.'

It only took a couple of buttons for Pak to see Jun Do's chest was bare.

'I'm not married,' Jun Do said.

'You're not married,' Pak repeated.

'He said he's not married,' the captain said.

'The North Koreans would never let you out on the water if you weren't married. Who would there be to throw in prison if you defected?'

'Look,' the pilot said, 'we're fishermen and we're headed back to port. That's the whole story.'

Pak turned to the second mate. 'What's his name?' he asked, indicating Jun Do.

The second mate didn't say anything. He looked at the captain.

'Don't look at him,' Pak said and stepped closer. 'What's his position?'

'His position?'

'On the ship,' Pak said. 'OK, what's your position?'

'Second mate.'

'OK, Second Mate,' Pak said. He pointed at Jun Do. 'This nameless guy, here. What's his position?'

The second mate said, 'The third mate.'

Pak started laughing. 'Oh, yes, the third mate. That's great, that's a good one. I'm going to write a spy novel and call it *The Third Mate*. You lousy spies, you make me sick. These are free nations you're spying on, democracies you're trying to undermine.'

Some of the Americans came back up top. They had black smudges on their faces and shoulders from squeezing through tight, half-burned passages. Security sweep over, their rifles were on their backs, and they were relaxed and joking. It was surprising how young they were, this huge battleship in the hands of kids. Only now did they seem to notice all the shoes. One sailor picked up a shoe. 'Damn,' he said. 'These are the new Air Jordans – you can't even get these in Okinawa.'

'That's evidence,' Pak said. 'These guys are all spies and pirates and bandits and we're going to arrest them all.'

Two other sailors were shaking their heads at the condition of the ship, especially the way the bolts for the lifelines had rusted out. 'Spies?' one of them asked. 'They don't even have radar. They're using a fucking compass. There are no charts in the chart room. They're dead reckoning this bitch around.'

'You don't know how devious these North Koreans are,' Pak countered. 'Their whole society is based on deception. You wait, we'll tear this boat apart, and you'll know I'm right.' He bent down and opened the hatch to the forward hold. Inside were thousands of small mackerel, mouths open from being frozen alive.

Jun Do understood suddenly that they'd laugh at his equipment if they found it, that they'd tear it out and drag it into the bright lights and laugh at how he had it all rigged. And then he'd never hear an erotic tale from Dr Rendezvous again, he wouldn't know if the Russian prisoners got paroled, and it would be an eternal mystery if his rowers made it home; he had had enough of eternal mysteries.

A sailor came out of the pilot house wearing the DPRK flag as a cape.

'Motherfucker,' another sailor announced. 'How the fuck did you end up with that? You are the sorriest sailor in the navy, and I will be taking that from you, now.'

Another sailor came up from below. Spelled out across his

clipboard was the name 'Lt Jervis'. 'Do you have any life vests?' he asked the crew.

When Jun Do was in the military, they'd used life vests, but these fishermen had never seen one.

Jervis tried to mime a vest, but the crew of the *Junma* shook their heads. Jervis checked a box on his list. 'How about a flare gun?' he asked and mimed shooting in the air.

'Never,' the captain said. 'No guns on my ship.'

Jervis turned to Pak. 'Are you a translator or what?' he asked.

'I'm an intelligence officer,' he answered.

'Would you just fucking translate for once?'

'Didn't you hear me, they're spies!'

'Spies?' Jervis asked. 'Their ship is half burned. They don't even have a shitter on this thing. Just ask them if they've got a fire extinguisher.'

Jun Do's eyes lit up.

'Look,' Pak said. 'That one completely understood you. They probably all speak English.'

Jervis mimed a fire extinguisher, sound effects and all.

The machinist clasped his hands as if in prayer.

Even though he had a radio, Jervis yelled up to the ship,

'We need a fire extinguisher.'

There was some discussion up there. Then came the response,

'Is there a fire?'

'Jesus,' Jervis yelled. 'Just send one down.'

Pak said, 'They'll just sell it on the black market. They're bandits, a whole nation of them.'

When Jun Do saw a red fire extinguisher descend from that battleship on a rope, he suddenly understood that the Americans were going to let them go. He'd never spoken English before, it had never been part of his training, but he sounded out, 'Life raft.'

Jervis looked at him. 'You don't have a life raft?'

Jun Do shook his head *no*.

'And send down an inflatable,' Jervis yelled up to the ship.

Pak was at the edge of losing it. He took his helmet off and ran his fingers along the surface of his flat-top. 'Isn't it obvious why they're not allowed to have a raft?'

'I got to hand it to you,' Jervis said to Pak. 'I think you're right about that one understanding English.'

In the pilot house, some sailors were screwing around with the radio. You could hear them in there transmitting messages. One picked up the handset and said, 'This is a person-to-person message to Kim Jong-Il from Tom John-son. We have intercepted your primping boat, but can't locate your hairspray, jumpsuit or elevator shoes, over.'

Jun Do had been expecting a lifeboat, so when down the rope came a yellow inflatable, no bigger than a rice sack, he was confused. Jervis showed him the red deployment handle and mimed with large arms how it would expand.

All the Americans had little cameras, and when one started taking pictures, the rest of them did, too, of the piles of Nikes, of the brown sink where they shaved, of the turtle shell drying in the sun, of the notch the machinist cut in the rail so he could crap into the sea. One sailor got a hold of the captain's calendar of the actress Sun Moon, depicting movie stills from her latest films. They were laughing about how North Korean pin-up girls wore full-length dresses, but the captain was having none of it: he went over and snatched it back. Then one of the sailors came out of the pilot house with the ship's framed portrait of Kim Jong-Il, which he'd managed to prise off the wall.

'Get a load of this,' he said. 'It's the man himself.'

The crew of the *Junma* stood graven.

Pak was instantly in motion. 'No, no, no,' he said. 'This is very serious. You must put that back.'

The sailor wasn't giving up the portrait. 'You said they were spies, right? Finders fucking keepers, right, Lieutenant?'

Lieutenant Jervis tried to diffuse things. 'Let the boys have a couple tokens,' he said.

'But this is nothing to joke about,' Pak said. 'People go to prison over this. In North Korea, this could mean death.'

Another sailor came out of the pilot house, and he'd got loose the portrait of Kim Il-Sung. 'I got his brother,' he announced.

Pak held out his hands. 'Wait,' he said. 'You don't understand. You could be sending these men to their graves. They need to be detained and questioned, not condemned.'

'Look what I got,' another sailor said. He came out of the pilot house wearing the captain's hat, and in two short steps, the second mate had drawn his sharking knife and put it to the sailor's throat.

A half-dozen rifles were unslung, and they made a nearly instantaneous *click*. Above, on the deck of the frigate, all the sailors with their cups of coffee froze. In the quiet was the familiar clank of the rigging, and water sloshing out of the livewell. You could feel how the waves rebuffed from the frigate's bow double-rocked the *Junma*.

Very calmly, the captain called to the second mate. 'It's just a hat, son.'

The second mate answered the captain, though he didn't unlock eyes with the sailor. 'You can't go around the world doing whatever you want. There are rules and the rules have to be followed. You can't just up and steal people's hats.'

Jun Do said to him, 'Let's just let the sailor go.'

'I know where the line is,' the second mate said. 'I'm not crossing it – they are. Someone has to stop them; someone has to take those ideas out of their heads.'

Jervis had his side arm out. 'Pak,' he said, 'please translate that this man is about to get shot.'

Jun Do stepped forward. The second mate's eyes were cold and flashing with uncertainty, and the sailor looked to Jun Do for help. Jun Do carefully took the hat off the sailor's head, then put a hand on the second mate's shoulder. The second mate said, 'A guy has to be stopped before he does something stupid,' then took a step back and tossed his knife into the sea.

Rifles high, the sailors cast an eye towards Jervis. He approached Jun Do. 'Obliged for helping your man stand down,' he said and, with a handshake, slipped Jun Do a business card. 'If you're ever in the free world,' he said, then gave the *Junma* a last, long look. 'There's nothing here,' he announced to his men. 'Let's have a controlled withdrawal, gentlemen.'

And then in what was almost a ballet – rifle down, retreat, shift, replace, rifle up – the eight Americans left the *Junma* so that seven rifles were pointed at the crew at all times, and yet, in a brief series of silent moments, the deck was clear and the boarding craft was gone.

Right away, the pilot was at the helm to bring the *Junma* about, and already the fog was stealing the edges of the frigate's grey-coloured hull. Jun Do half closed his eyes, trying to peer inside of it, imagining its communications deck and the equipment there, how it could perceive anything, how it had power to apprehend everything that was uttered in the world. He looked at the card in his hand. It wasn't a frigate at all, but an interceptor, the USS *Fortitude*, and his boots, he realized, were crawling with shrimp. ∎

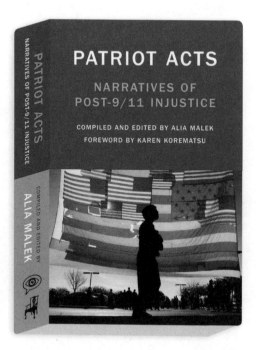

IN A LAND
OF SILENCE

Janine di Giovanni

The drive to Benghazi from the Egyptian border is long: hours through a stark undeveloped land, rapids over deep ravines, then barren desert. When we reach the city, it is something of a surprise – a decrepit, Mediterranean town cradled by a magnificent seafront, the blue-green coastline stretching to Tunisia. Not many people are swimming. Once or twice I see men wading in fully clothed, but never a woman. From the moment I arrive, I can see Kais al-Hilali's rage and isolation written on the city walls.

On 17 February – the 'Day of Rage' – Kais fought alongside the Shabaab (the angry Libyan youth whose protests sparked the rebellion) inside the Katiba army base. In the early days of the uprising, this impoverished thirty-four-year-old street artist and sign painter found his voice. Prowling Benghazi like a commando, along with other underground artists who had begun to taunt and torment their tormentor, Kais used his brushes and paint to boost the momentum of the revolution. His first political graffiti – a leering, buffoonish, venomous Gaddafi – was close to his apartment. He painted voraciously, and violently – attacking Gaddafi and his son Saif al-Islam, depicting them as monkeys, scratching lice. Gaddafi as a villain, Gaddafi as the devil.

By 21 February, anti-Gaddafi forces had taken the town, and people had begun painting flags of France and America all over the walls of the city's buildings as tributes to the Nato bombers. By mid-March, Kais's fame had spread. In an interview with the French channel TF1, he declared that Gaddafi was not the 'king of all kings of Africa but the monkey of all monkeys of Africa'. Even in the capital, Tripoli, there was talk of the skinny, bald street artist from Benghazi. On 19 March, Kais created his last mural. He was in a car with three other friends that night. Just after midnight, near what his mother later described to me as a 'fake checkpoint' on the western side of the city, the car was halted. Shots rang out and assassins, believed to be from the government secret service, hit Kais twice in the neck. No one else in the car was shot.

I visit Kais's mother on a sweltering afternoon in the middle of June. As I climb the four flights to his old bedroom in the flat where he lived with his family, she weeps silently, wiping her eyes with a dirty tissue. She had borne seven children before her husband abandoned the family. In 2004, her eldest son, who was only twenty-eight and the breadwinner of the family, died suddenly of a heart attack. Now her second eldest is dead.

Kais's mother shows me a photograph of him as a big-eared seven-year-old (the same age as my own son) with a pudding-bowl haircut, wearing a ridiculous clip-on bow tie. His younger brother Taha sits at an ancient PC and shows me pictures of Kais's artwork. Before the rebellion, he drew lonely images of fishermen in enormous, foreboding oceans, but after 17 February, his images were all caricatures of Gaddafi. His mother turns away. In Arabic, she tells me that he died because he refused to be silent. My translator, Mohammed, grimly repeats the words in English. *Refused to be silent.*

Then Taha clicks on a photograph I would rather not have seen: Kais dead in the morgue, his skin stretched purple like a bruised plum, the bullet holes visible in his neck.

Even though the city is now the rebel stronghold, one can still sense the fear. In the 1980s, Benghazi was a centre of dissent and then too the response was brutal. There were public hangings that have left an indelible mark. Once you have seen someone swinging from a rope, you learn to shut up.

One morning, I visit the oldest cafe in the city, situated behind the Corniche, the road that edges along the seafront. The Tiki Bar is dark, smoky and completely male. The barman makes me a strong Arabic coffee in a tiny cup and my friend, a young Libyan engineer, explains that until only very recently, people whispered over their cups in the morning – even saying a word about Gaddafi's family could get you imprisoned, tortured or killed.

Driving through the city, the walls of buildings are plastered with triumphant artwork and slogans: GAME OVER! WE HAVE A DREAM! THANK YOU, FRANCE! And finally, the powerful and politically outraged artwork, some of it by Kais but also, more recently, by one of his protégés, a silent and rather aggressive eighteen-year-old deaf mute called Radwan.

Kais signed his name in the New York-style tags of the type that you see on subways all over Europe and the United States. Radwan, deaf since birth and even more isolated than his compatriots – Libyans who were already separated from the rest of the world – signs with a crude drawing of an ear with a line slashed through it, depicting a world with no sound.

I wait to meet Radwan at the Media Centre of the courthouse. An exhibition of Kais's art is on display and I sit with Mohammed Atif, the young Libyan who runs the centre. When Radwan arrives, he is accompanied by another deaf mute, twenty-three-year-old Rafhi, his apprentice. Rafhi is calm, with a kind, gentle gaze, and struggles to communicate by making a high-pitched squeak from his useless vocal cords. Radwan, on the other hand, is like a lion trapped in a cage, with an energy that seems ready to explode. Both are grinning and dressed in what could easily be the uniform of urban youth around the world: low-slung Levi's that hang around their skinny hips, lots of silver rings and bracelets, tight black T-shirts and baseball caps.

Both young men are on their own, without families. Both were born poor. Communication is difficult as neither uses international sign language. Instead, they were taught an archaic form of signing that Gaddafi imposed on deaf mutes in Libya. Radwan and Rafhi sign in a desperate fashion to whoever is with me, my companions working out the meaning from their motions and translating into English.

We gather up spray paints and hit the streets: through winding alleys; bottleneck traffic; shops selling sneakers and T-shirts from Cairo; the old souk with its gold and silver vendors; and finally, the

Katiba, the former garrison of Gaddafi's forces. Radwan makes a painful, strangled noise as we approach. He was imprisoned here for three months last year and subjected to electric shocks. The garrison is a wreck now; it was one of the first symbols of the regime that the Shabaab attacked in the early days of the revolution. Kais was with them, and so was Radwan. Now Radwan searches for a wall that is empty and once he finds one that is suitable, he goes into a kind of trance. In less than thirty minutes he has created a mural of a giant disembodied fist punching Gaddafi in the jaw, blood spurting out of his eye. Rafhi goes next, climbing on a concrete block to reach the high parts of the walls. He is not as talented as Radwan – he draws Gaddafi as a devil. Radwan stands next to him, slapping him on the wrist to get his attention, trying to instruct him without the use of words.

If this rebellion is successful and a new Libya comes, the West will pour money into it as they have in Afghanistan and Iraq, appointing international bureaucrats and business-school graduates to transform the country, and building 'Green Zones' that separate them from the local population. I know these two won't be in that picture, nor will they share the benefits. Even though this revolution was all about the youth rising up, they will be as forgotten and isolated as they are now, in their own deaf-and-mute world.

That night, Radwan and Rafhi take me to their lair. It's a grim, depressing place – a former Mussolini-style monument with frescoes of silent fighters and patriotic mothers carrying babies. The building is neglected and has been destroyed by vagrants; there is sewer water inch-deep on the cracked concrete floor. This is where Radwan and an entire community of deaf mutes make their home. I try to ask if they sleep here at night – some say they do, others seem embarrassed. There are several dozen of them and they rise up from benches and slap Radwan and Rafhi on the back in greeting when we arrive.

There is a teacher with the youths on the night I visit, a heavyset, greying man called Mohammed who has a deep, rich voice. He is determined to teach them to sign. 'What is going to happen to them?' he asks. 'This whole generation? All they have known is Gaddafi.' The boys sit patiently in a circle and Mohammed and his assistant begin their lesson.

Most evenings, Radwan can be found near the makeshift tents in the area alongside the Corniche. This is where mothers display photographs of their dead and missing sons, hoping that someone will come forward with information; that they will find out that their children are not dead after all. The day I leave Benghazi, the rebels are still fighting outside Brega, on the Gulf of Sirte, in the direction of Tripoli. Someone tells me that Radwan has gone to Ajdabiya, about an hour away, to be with the rebel fighters there and to 'get inspiration'. Although he has told me that he 'likes to fight', and has knife marks up and down his tanned arms to prove it, Radwan is not fighting alongside the rebel army. I struggle to imagine him at the front line: seeing and absorbing but unable to hear the sound of rockets or bullets flying around him, lost in his silence.

Around the city, on various walls, there are scrawled tributes to Kais. I also see Radwan's drawings, his signature of a defunct ear. And there, near the tents along the Corniche, are the photographs and posters of those who have disappeared, staring out above the cellphone numbers of family members desperate to know their fate. ∎

GRANTA

FLEE

Nadia Shira Cohen

If the earth was flat, Ras Ajdir surely would mark the end. A sea of men had gathered here on the border between Tunisia and Libya: migrant workers, some still wearing hard hats or vests furnished by the companies that had employed them in the petroleum and construction industries of Libya. Now they waited for hours, maybe days, with everything they owned on top of their heads. They slept rough on the ground, about one hundred metres from the border fence, tying their synthetic blankets to tree branches. As another group was let across the border by the Tunisian authorities, they would join the wandering men. Eventually many were transported to a UNHCR-delegated refugee camp seven kilometres down the road in the middle of the desert.

This was the beginning of two weeks I would spend with the refugees. Every day I arrived at the camp by six in the morning. Every day the inhabitants seemed more worn down by the monotonous ritual of refugee life: the faded clothing strung along tent wires to dry; the queues at the feeding tents. At the passport handout, members of the UNHCR, together with Tunisian volunteers, called out the names of individuals whose passports had been processed in order for them to leave on planes or boats, whatever method of transportation their government or donor governments had provided. And then there were the Bangladeshis, all 30,000 of them, incessantly bathing, even in the coldest of temperatures. They would sometimes ask me curiously, 'My sister, how are you? Where are you from?' As I stopped to take pictures of them, there was that strange, familiar exchange between photographer and subject, an intimate moment in which both are engaged in each other's lives, even asking the most personal of questions and then parting ways, never knowing where the other is going, or where they would end up. It is an exchange that serves to put us at ease. At these times, although I rarely ask them if I can take their picture, I wait for the moment they sense what I am trying to do. And then it becomes a collaboration of sorts.

The refugees fleeing the unrest in Libya were all migrant workers, tens of thousands of them – Bangladeshis, Ghanaians, Filipinos, Somalis, Sudanese, Vietnamese. As the sun set, smoke from makeshift bonfires filled the chilly March air . . . they gathered around, wrapped in synthetic, flower-patterned blankets that had been handed out by Tunisian volunteers. Many had been robbed of their possessions either by Gaddafi's soldiers or the rebel militia. I suppose they didn't care much who the thieves were, as they found themselves refugees fleeing a war that was not their own, having moved heaven and earth to migrate to a new home. It seemed simple: one moves to another country seeking greater opportunity and pay, sending earnings back home to family members and saving for a better future. Many had already fled war; the Somalis found themselves two-time refugees. Others found themselves trapped. Queen, a young Nigerian woman, had escaped a forced arranged marriage in her home village, only to prostitute herself in Libya in order to pay off the man who had trafficked her. Queen was being sent home with the rest of the Nigerians as she did not qualify for asylum status. I wondered where she would end up, if she would leave again or if she would return to marry that old man from her village. ■

3.

4.

5.

6.

8.

9.

10.

11.

13.

14.

15.

16.

PICTURE CAPTIONS

1. Somali refugees at a UNHCR-constructed refugee camp. Ras Ajdir, Tunisia, on the border with Libya.

2. Over 10,000 Bangladeshi migrant workers fled Libya amid ensuing violence.

3. Waiting at the border, Ras Ajdir.

4. Refugees flood the western border of Libya after weeks of unrest and the threat of civil war.

5. A man sneaks on to a bus bound for the airport in Djerba, Tunisia.

6. The majority of Bangladeshi refugees remain just over the border from Libya, waiting for buses that are supposed to take them to the UNHCR camp. Instead, they will be made to walk the entire distance with all their belongings.

7. Bangladeshi refugees bathe at the UNHCR camp.

8. An Egyptian refugee on a bus headed to the airport waves to those left behind.

9. A diabetic Egyptian migrant worker collapses after crossing the border from Libya.

10. Refugees face extremely cold nights, sleeping outside with no more than blankets and home-made fires.

11. Sandra and her mother, from Nigeria, look out over the UNHCR camp.

12. A man prays among his fellow refugees from Ghana as they await their passports.

13. Libyans listen in on a meeting between Libyan Border Police and Khaled el-Hamadi, head of the NGO the International Organization For Peace, Care and Relief. The NGO is the only organization with access to migrant detention centres and works frequently on migration issues in the country. Mr el-Hamadi spoke to members of the press, proclaiming that Libya was quite peaceful and that the images on television had been taken from earlier footage of the war in Iraq from 2006.

14. Bangladeshi refugees wait for their passports.

15. Refugees wait for hours to be let through the border in Ras Ajdir.

16. Andwar Hoshem of Bangladesh clears the leaves from a tree branch in order to use it to plunge water from a hole in the ground.

17. Refugees bathing in the early morning.

18. A Somali refugee arriving at a camp. Somalis are now two-time refugees, having fled the violence in Libya, where they had originally found refuge from violence within their own country.

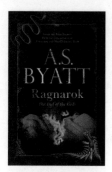

Ragnarok: The End of the Gods *A.S. Byatt*

The latest in Canongate's acclaimed Myths series is a retelling of the war that led to the downfall of the Norse gods. Natural disaster, reckless gods and the recognition of impermanence in the world are just some of the threads that A.S. Byatt weaves into this most timely of books. Linguistically stunning and imaginatively abundant, this is a landmark work of fiction from one of the world's truly great writers.

Canongate £14.99 | HB

Privacy is Dead *Index on Censorship*

International in outlook, outspoken in comment, the award-winning *Index on Censorship* is the only publication dedicated to freedom of expression. The new issue considers the impact of tabloid exposés, explores the world of Internet trolls and talks to the UK's leading privacy judge. Subscribe online now! For a 25% discount on a digital subscription, quote PRIVGRANTA at exacteditions.com/index_on_censorship

Index on Censorship £7.99 | Single copies

The Stranger's Child *Alan Hollinghurst*

From the Man Booker Prize-winning author comes a new masterpiece that draws an absorbing picture of an England constantly in flux. Spanning the last century through the story of two families, exploration of changing taste, class and social etiquette is conveyed in witty and observant prose that exposes our secret longings to the shocks and surprises of time. Read chapter one: Picador.com/strangerschild

Picador | HB

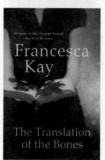

The Translation of the Bones *Francesca Kay*

When word gets out that a miracle may have occurred at the Church of the Sacred Heart, all hell breaks loose, but no one is prepared for the shocking outcome that ensues. The author of *An Equal Stillness*, winner of the 2009 Orange Award for New Writers, returns with a searingly powerful novel about belief, love and motherhood and a search for truth.

Weidenfeld & Nicolson £12.99 | HB

THE
TERMINAL
CHECK

Pico Iyer

I'm sitting in the expansive spaces of Renzo Piano's four-storey airport outside Osaka, sipping an Awake tea from Starbucks and waiting for my bus home. I've chosen to live in Japan for the past twenty years, and I know its rites as I know the way I need tea when feeling displaced, or to head for a right-hand window seat as soon as I enter a bus. A small, round-faced Japanese man in his early thirties, accompanied by a tall and somewhat cadaverous man of the same age, approaches me.

'Excuse me,' says the small, friendly-seeming one; they look like newborn salarymen in their not-quite-perfect suits. 'May I see your passport?'

When I look up, surprised, he flashes me a badge showing that he's a plain-clothes policeman. Dazed after crossing sixteen time zones (from California), I hand him my British passport.

'What are you doing in Japan?'

'I'm writing about it.' I pull out my business card with the red embossed logo of *Time* magazine.

'*Time* magazine?' says the smiling cop, strangely impressed. 'He works for *Time* magazine,' he explains to his lanky and impassive partner. 'Very famous magazine,' he assures me. 'High prestige!'

Then he asks for my address and phone number and where I plan to be for the next eighty-nine days. 'If there is some unfortunate incident,' he explains, 'some terrorist attack,' (he's sotto voce now) 'then we will know you did it.'

Six months later, I fly back to the country I love once more. This time I need to withdraw some yen from an ATM as I stumble out of my trans-Pacific plane, in order to pay for my bus home.

'You're getting some money?' says an attractive young Japanese woman, suddenly appearing beside me with a smile.

'I am. To go back to my apartment.'

'You live here?' Few Japanese women have ever come up to me in public, let alone without an introduction, and shown such interest.

'I do.'

'May I see your passport?' she asks sweetly, flashing a badge at me, much as the pair of questioners had done two seasons before.

'Just security,' she says, anxious not to put me out, as my Japanese neighbours stream, unconcerned, towards the Gakuenmae bus that's about to pull out of its bay.

I tell my friends back in California about these small disruptions and they look much too knowing. It's 9/11, they assure me. Over the past decade, security has tightened around the world, which means that insecurity has increased proportionally. Indeed, in recent years Japan has introduced fingerprinting for all foreign visitors arriving at its airports, and takes photographs of every outsider coming across its borders; a large banner on the wall behind the immigration officers in Osaka – as angry-looking with its red-and-black hand-lettering as a student banner – explains the need for heightened measures in the wake of threats to national order.

But the truth of the matter is that, for those of us with darker skins, and from nations not materially privileged, it was ever thus. When I was eighteen, I was held in custody in Panama's airport (because of the Indian passport I then carried) and denied formal entry to the nation, while the roguish English friend from high school with whom I was travelling was free to enter with impunity and savour all the dubious pleasures of the Canal Zone. On my way into Hong Kong – a transit lounge of a city if ever there was one, a duty-free zone whose only laws seem to be those of the marketplace – I was hauled into a special cabin for a lengthy interrogation because my face was deemed not to match my (by then British) passport. In Japan I was strip-searched every time I returned to the country, three or four times a year – my lifelong tan moving the authorities to assume that I must be either Saddam Hussein's cousin or an illegal Iranian (or, worst of all, what I really am, a wandering soul with Indian forebears). Once

I was sent to a small room in Tokyo reserved for anyone of South Asian ancestry (where bejewelled women in saris loudly complained in exaggerated Oxbridge accents about being taken for common criminals).

Another time, long before my Japanese neighbours had heard of Osama bin Laden, I was even detained on my way *out* of Osaka – and the British Embassy hastily faxed on a Sunday night – as if any male with brown skin, passable English and a look of shabby quasi-respectability must be doing something wrong if he's crossing a border.

But now, having learned over decades to accept such indignities or injustices, I walk into a chorus of complaints every time I return to California, from my pale-skinned, affluent neighbours. They're patting us down now, my friends object, and they're confiscating our contact-lens fluid. They're forcing us to travel with tiny tubes of toothpaste and moving us to wear loafers when usually we'd prefer lace-ups. They're taking away every bottle of water – but only after bottles of water have been shown to be weapons of mass destruction; they're feeling us up with blue gloves, even here in Santa Barbara, now that they know that underwear can be a lethal weapon.

I listen to their grousing and think that the one thing the 9/11 attacks have achieved, for those of us who spend too much time in airports, is to make suspicion universal; fear and discomfort are equal-opportunity employers now. The world is flat in ways the high-flying global theoreticians don't always acknowledge; these days, even someone from the materially fortunate parts of the world – a man with a ruddy complexion, a woman in a Prada suit – is pulled aside for what is quixotically known as 'random screening'.

It used to be that the rich corners of the world seemed relatively safe, protected, and the poor ones too dangerous to enter. Now, the logic of the terrorist attacks on New York and Washington has reversed all that. If anything, it's the rich places that feel unsettled. It used to be that officials would alight on people who look like me – from nations of need, in worn jeans, bearing the passports of more prosperous countries – as likely troublemakers; now they realize that even the well born and well dressed may not always be well-intentioned.

I understand why my friends feel aggrieved to be treated as if they came from Nigeria or Mexico or India. But I can't really mourn too much that airports, since 9/11, have become places where everyone may be taken to be guilty until proven innocent. The world is all mixed up these days, and America can no longer claim immunity. On 12 September 2001, *Le Monde* ran its now famous headline: WE ARE ALL AMERICANS. On 12 September 2011, it might more usefully announce: WE ARE ALL INDIANS. ∎

GRANTA

VETERANS OF A FOREIGN WAR

Elliott Woods

Sergeant Daniel Steciak

It's close to midnight when I cross the Mississippi River at Saint Louis. The soaring stainless-steel Gateway Arch gleams in the skyline light.

I'm driving west across the country from Pennsylvania to visit a couple of old veteran friends of mine, to see what their lives are like now that they're home, and to try to understand what the country makes of the continuing wars. After a dozen hours on the road, I pull over to sleep in my car at a rest area on the side of the freeway. In the morning, I drive south-west towards Fort Leonard Wood, where I attended US Army basic training and combat engineer school a decade ago. Rain hammers my windshield as I drive past dozens of billboards advertising tours of the caves where the James Gang hid from the law in the days when Missouri was still the Wild West, before it became part of the emblematically milquetoast Midwest.

Around lunchtime, I roll up to the same gatehouse where I arrived on a bus late one evening in October 2001, destined for fourteen weeks of trainee hell. Fort Leonard Wood seemed like a maximum-security prison back then – within hours I had my head shaved, civilian clothes confiscated and individual identity dismantled – but today I'm just another visitor. The guard looks at my ID and waves me through without a word.

A class of new combat engineer recruits graduated today. They shuffle around the Army Corps of Engineers museum with their families, wearing their red-and-gold engineer castles proudly over their right-breast pockets, looking barely old enough to shave. Beside a life-size diorama of a sapper exploring a Viet Cong tunnel, flashlight and pistol in hand, I meet a hefty man sporting a US Army Veteran hat and a much younger man in a blue dress uniform.

Preston Hutchins spent twenty years as a truck driver and infantryman in the Pennsylvania National Guard. Back during

Vietnam, he says, people 'figured the soldiers were all baby-killers'. He didn't serve in the war but says he's old enough to remember, and it's different now, he says, because today people know American soldiers are fighting for a cause. 'My oldest son was over in the second Gulf War,' he says, 'and people said we shouldn't have been there. And he said, "Yes, we should, because they freed people that were oppressed for hundreds of years and now they can do things that they couldn't do for a long time."'

For Hutchins, cushioned by geography from the world's complexity, belief in America's God-given mission to liberate the world from tyranny is an article of faith. Despite a disastrous decade of war, during which time tens of thousands of Afghan and Iraqi civilians have been killed and the populations of both countries have violently demonstrated against America's presence, Hutchins remains completely in earnest, still capable of seeing the facts through the lens of myth.

Tyler Hutchins, tall and thin, hovers at his father's side. Lingering patches of acne dot his cheeks. 'I think he's really grown since he joined,' Mrs Hutchins says of her nineteen-year-old stepson. 'His posture and everything, he looks like a regular gentleman now instead of a teenager.'

The younger Hutchins says he joined the army after high school because he didn't want to turn out like some of the older kids in his small town, wasting away in a dead economy, getting into trouble. 'I was seeing where people were going with it. It wasn't very good, so I wanted to do something to get out of there and move on,' he says with the caution of a student afraid of giving a wrong answer. 'I kind of like the idea of showing people what I can do and being there for people.'

Iraq has calmed considerably in recent years, but 100,000 American troops remain in Afghanistan, where they are dying at a higher rate than ever before in the war – nearly five hundred in 2010 alone. Tyler Hutchins will almost certainly go to war, but he says the prospect doesn't worry him. 'I'd like to go overseas,' he says with a boyish smile, searching my face for approval, 'whether it be

Afghanistan or wherever else – Libya if anything happens there.'

Tyler's nonchalant acceptance of a prospective ground war in Libya crushes me, but what else would I expect? The United States went to war when Tyler was nine years old; war in Islamic countries – much like the Internet – is an unquestioned fact of life for his generation.

There weren't any reporters around back in February 2002 when I visited the post museum with my dad. He drove from Pennsylvania to see me graduate and I made him proud – I was the top private of the class and received an award at the graduation ceremony, a rare moment of recognition in my life. In the glow of my father's approval, I felt I had been reborn. If someone had asked me then, I probably would've said I was eager to get to Afghanistan as soon as possible.

The flyer on my windshield promised free tuition at any state university and an $8,000 signing bonus in exchange for six years of part-time military service with the Virginia Army National Guard.

It was July 2001 and I was twenty years old, living with my mother in Richmond, Virginia, rotating between a job waiting tables and another folding clothes at a retail store. That May, I had received a letter explaining that I would not be eligible for re-enrolment at Fordham University in New York City in the fall because I'd failed every class but one in the spring term. The letter came as no surprise – I drank up the entire city that spring and rarely rose before noon. I passed American History only because it was at three o'clock in the afternoon and I already knew most of the answers.

When my father – a heart surgeon and Vietnam veteran – found out the news, he called to tell me that whatever I did henceforth, I would do without his financial support. By midsummer, my transformation to the loser of my nightmares was nearly complete. I had realized the immensity of my error and was desperate for a way out.

Sweltering in the afternoon heat, I read the recruiter's flyer over and over in my car. I'd been successful as a cadet at Valley Forge Military Academy and I thought I knew the drill well enough to skate through army training, so I dialled the number at the bottom of the page.

The recruiter explained a clause in the contract that said I could be called to active-duty service for up to two years in the event of a major foreign war, but I wasn't worried. The Soviet Union collapsed when I was in fifth grade, and we'd been the world's sole superpower ever since. The United States had contributed soldiers to peacekeeping missions in the Balkans and Africa but we had no enemies of real concern. The recruiter said he could get me a slot in basic training by October. He promised I could finish training and be back in school by the fall of 2002, with the army paying my way.

Five weeks after I raised my hand and swore the oath of enlistment, I was listening to the radio in the stockroom of Banana Republic, drowning in a new shipment of summer skirts and linen blouses. The DJ interrupted the music to say that a plane had crashed into one of the World Trade Center towers. When my shift ended, I raced home in time to see the North Tower swallowed up by a black hole of smoke and debris. Osama bin Laden's bearded face was all over the television by late afternoon, juxtaposed with the scenes of horror in New York, and I felt a surge of adrenalin mixed with a twinge of panic.

From Fort Leonard Wood, I drive west into the Ozarks, an expanse of watery wilderness spanning the border between Arkansas and Missouri. In a lakeside town called Warsaw, Travis, a gas-station attendant, is taking a smoke break on a bench outside. He wears big rhinestone studs in his ears, a black baseball cap and a neatly trimmed chinstrap beard. Travis was unemployed before his mother found him a job at the gas station here in Warsaw, and he blames the country's economic doldrums on the wars.

'It shouldn't have never happened,' he tells me. 'It's a good thing that we had troops that went in there and helped serve for our country and everything, but I don't think they shoulda been there so long. I think it's drawn out, too many people have lost their lives, really, after it's all done, for no reason.' I'm happy to find someone in the rural South with a level head, but it's hard for the former soldier in me to take Travis seriously, with his rhinestones and chinstrap beard and all.

While we talk, sunburned vacationers lug bags of ice and cases of cheap beer out to their cars. Travis watches, pulling on his cigarette. I think of Tyler Hutchins, standing next to his father like a shadow, eagerly edging toward the precipice. I didn't know him at all, but I want to keep him here, consumed with nothing more than chasing girls and the fluctuating price of gasoline. 'I better go back in now,' Travis says, stubbing out the cigarette. 'Break's over.'

Afghanistan receded from the headlines a few weeks after the invasion force ousted the Taliban and installed Hamid Karzai in Kabul in late 2001. There were only a few thousand troops in Afghanistan then, mostly special operations forces, and for a year or so after basic training it looked as if I would miss out on the war after all. Then, on my way home from class one day in the fall of 2002, I tuned in to National Public Radio and listened to a panel discussion on the Bush administration's case against Saddam Hussein. Suddenly an ultimatum was on the table and the next thing I knew, bombs were raining down on Baghdad and 150,000 American soldiers were rolling north through the Kuwaiti desert into Iraq. Nobody thought we'd get out of this one.

The alert order came eight months after the invasion, in November 2003, and by March I was living in a metal container on a former Iraqi airbase south of Mosul. My National Guard unit did whatever the active-duty units thought would be a waste of their time; we ran convoy security and route-clearance missions up and down Highway 1, pounded in hundreds of yards of razor-wire fences, guarded detainees and pulled watch at the gates to the base. The days passed like restless, sweaty sleep.

It was a different war back then in the north – the tail end of a tense lull before the Sunni insurgency exploded with terrifying ferocity. But the enemy was always out there – quietly taking our measure as we rolled through the villages, biding time. The war finally struck a few weeks before we were set to go home; on 21 December 2004, a suicide bomber blew himself up at lunchtime in a Mosul chow hall, killing nineteen people, including two men from my unit, David Ruhren and Nicholas Mason. Mostly quiet for an entire year, and then one day: *boom* – your friends are dead.

Omaha erupts from the dead-flat Nebraska plains like the Emerald City of Oz. Tall office buildings with reflective blue windows and the logos of banks and insurance companies flank wide, empty avenues. There are few people on the streets. I have plenty of fuel and no desire to stop, so I shoot west out of the city through a vast stretch of stubbly, rain-flooded cornfields.

A sign at the entrance to Scribner, Nebraska, a tiny grain-elevator town, says the population is 971. I stop for lunch at the Old Hotel Cafe and Saloon, where the waitress tells me I'm lucky: I ordered the last special – two meat-loaf slices on Wonder Bread, drenched in gravy, served with an ice-cream scoop of mashed potatoes. All around me, elderly locals chew quietly over plastic tablecloths to a muted symphony of silverware scraping ceramic plates.

Late-spring days are long on the high plains, and I still have another three hours before dark when I cross the state line into South Dakota at about 5.30 in the afternoon. Highway 83 takes me straight into Mission, the main crossroads on the Rosebud Indian Reservation, one of the arid parcels allotted to the Sioux as part of the US government's forced resettlement policy in the nineteenth century.

Mission is a downtrodden town with a couple of gas stations, a Subway and a motel that went bust last year. Asphalt is scarce here, and a fine layer of dust coats everything in sight. The place looks a lot like Afghanistan, though the mud-brick *qalats* in rural Afghanistan are tidier and more sophisticated than the jumbled clusters of weather-beaten trailers and rust-eaten mechanical junk on the outskirts of this town. At the Tree of Life Ministry – a sprawling, bland structure that looks more like an elementary school than a church – several games of basketball are going on in a large fenced-in recreation area. Sioux women sitting around a picnic bench eyeball me curiously as I walk through the gate.

Despite the cruel injustice of American history, the tribes have a strong tradition of military service. Some 24,000 Native Americans serve on active duty today – about 1 per cent of all Native Americans, double the service rate of the general population. If you ask, they might attribute their tradition of service to their common warrior values of strength, bravery and honour, just like anyone might tell you they joined out of patriotic obligation. On today's Indian reservations, however, youngsters have more dire cause to run off and join the army.

According to the US Census Bureau, the poverty level among Native Americans is double that of the general population, and in 2008, the Centers for Disease Control reported that nearly 12 per cent of all deaths among Native Americans between 2001 and 2005 – 1,514 in all – were alcohol-related, four times the national average. More than a third of all Sioux are under eighteen, a proportion partly explained by an average life expectancy of fewer than fifty years, about the same as life expectancy for Afghans.

For youth on particularly troubled reservations like Rosebud and nearby Pine Ridge, the war may seem like a safer alternative to the home front. Still, with chaos and decay on the 'Rez', coming home is no cakewalk. 'There's a lot of 'em that joined,' says John, a ponytailed twenty-two-year-old in jean shorts and a baggy T-shirt, a hint of a moustache on his upper lip. He draws on his cigarette and shrugs his heavy shoulders. 'I have some friends that headed out, and when they came back . . . you know, they came back kinda loony.'

Sitting on the ground near John's feet, an obese young woman coddles an infant. Nearby, thirty-nine-year-old Chad LaPointe takes a break from a game. He's the father of a happy-looking teenager with gelled hair and a cast on his arm who's playing basketball with a few of the older men.

Chad catches his breath and wipes the sweat off his pockmarked face with his T-shirt. He has only vague notions of why we're in Afghanistan, and he admits that America's wars do not rank highly on his list of priorities. His son is at the top of that list – more specifically, keeping him out of trouble. The kid is planning to join the military, Chad tells me, and I ask him how he feels about that. 'I support it all the way,' he says enthusiastically. When I mention the possibility that his son will fight in Afghanistan, his enthusiasm vanishes.

'No,' he says. 'Not while this war's going on.'

Roiling clouds follow me the next morning as I speed north-west across the wide-open ranch country of South Dakota and Wyoming. The rain is whipping across the plains in horizontal sheets as I pull into the parking lot of the Little Bighorn Battlefield National Monument, in eastern Montana.

In a room with panoramic windows overlooking the battlefield, I listen with a roomful of senior citizens as Ranger Steve Adelson describes the June day when Lieutenant Colonel George Custer fell with his entire command of 262 cavalry troops and scouts to an overwhelming force of some 1,500 Sioux and Cheyenne warriors. With a wood-shafted arrow, Adelson points out the windows to indicate the terrain features on the rolling plain where Custer's men died trying to fend off the Indians.

After his talk, I ask Adelson – who bears a striking resemblance to the actor Tommy Lee Jones – if he sees parallels between our westward expansion and our current wars in the Middle East and Central Asia. 'In the Middle East, we're trying to change a culture. We're trying to get them to adopt democracy. We're dealing with people who have their own values, their own belief system, their own sense of purpose, and I don't know what we're ever going to do to change that,' he says.

Fourteen years after Little Bighorn, Sitting Bull, who was chief of the Sioux at the time of the battle, was shot and killed by tribal police while trying to incite the Ghost Dance on a nearby reservation. Many Native Americans, including Sitting Bull, believed the Ghost Dance had the power to reverse the destruction caused by American expansion. They were wrong.

'Sitting Bull refused to give in,' Adelson explains. 'He resisted to the end, and when he couldn't resist any more militarily, he resisted culturally. He ultimately died for his expression of their right to do what they wanted to do.'

'Those guys on top of that hill –' Adelson points to the mass grave site where Custer's men are buried, '– they were seventeen-, eighteen-, nineteen-year-old guys – some of them have never even seen an Indian before, and now they're out here shoving bullets in their carbines in the last moments of their lives, all on behalf of the United States government and American policy,' he says. 'I want people to come away with the whole idea that this is a human drama. It's not about widgets and grommets . . . behind every one of these military headstones, and Indian headstones, red and white, there's a human life. There's a human life behind every one of them. A story to be told. And don't forget that.'

The Clark Fork River, ice-cold, brimming with trout, runs through the centre of Missoula, Montana, a hard-drinking town seated in the foothills of the northern Rocky Mountains. I check into the Mountain Valley Inn, take a much-needed shower, then head out to the Missoula Veterans of Foreign Wars post.

The VFW is a national fraternal organization, founded by veterans of the Spanish-American War to help take care of wounded vets lacking medical care. It's karaoke night at the Missoula VFW, and the place fills steadily as I sip my beer. A middle-aged woman croons something indistinguishable into the microphone, causing the bartender to wince every so often. She says she knows a few Iraq and Afghanistan veterans but that they only come around for the monthly meeting. They don't typically hang out at the bar, especially not on karaoke night.

I meet Jay, an unemployed cook about my age who could be part Latino or Native American. He tells me his brother has served three tours in Iraq and is now studying at the Massachusetts Institute of Technology on a scholarship. 'I think he came home with a pretty bad taste in his mouth,' Jay says, sipping his Olympia beer. As for Jay, he's mostly concerned with the economic devastation wrought at home by the wars. 'We're broker,' he says. 'We're broker and we're still as angry as we were when we went into the war. It hasn't done anything. It's fanned the flames of anger, hasn't done anything to stop it.'

We talk about the Florida preacher Terry Jones and his Quran-burning stunt, as well as much-publicized attempts to block construction of an Islamic prayer centre a few blocks from Ground Zero in New York City. 'It's very racist!' Jay exclaims. 'We were founded on racism. We stole the land from dark people.' Recalling the squalor of Rosebud and Pine Ridge, I realize that the Sioux really did fight to the death – when it was all over, their warriors and elders were dead, and their culture was damaged beyond repair.

Later that night, I stop to talk to a pair of clean-cut guys who look like they could be military personnel. Aaron Flint – thirty-one, college graduate, National Guard veteran, white middle-class male with deep ties to Montana's ranch country – is pissed off at what he perceives to be a liberal conspiracy to emasculate the nation. 'All these hippies, they don't have a clue what's going on out there,' he says. 'They're happy to sit in their little espresso bars here in Missoula and do nothing, because it was never about a war or a perceived war, it was about politics.'

Aaron is at war with the environmentalists, the anti-war activists, and anyone who drinks fancy coffee; he's a carbon copy of right-wing sloganeers such as Rush Limbaugh and Glenn Beck, but there's a big difference between Aaron and most people I meet who share his opinions, Limbaugh and Beck included: Aaron went to war, twice.

Whatever his beliefs, he didn't merely hold forth from an armchair in Missoula.

'I think we need to finish the job over there,' he says firmly, referring to Afghanistan.

Aaron's template of success is the 2007 'surge' in Iraq, the brainchild of General David Petraeus, former commander of the multinational forces in Iraq. 'We surged not only American forces but Iraqi police and Iraqi Army into Iraqi neighbourhoods,' he explains, 'and then the Iraqis who were afraid before, who said, "Well, they're gonna cut my head off" . . . they finally said, "OK, the Americans are invested."'

'Iraq and Afghanistan are very different countries,' I say.

'It's just like gang warfare in Los Angeles,' he counters. 'The fundamentals don't change. If the locals –'

Before Aaron can finish, his wife pulls up by the sidewalk. She idles patiently while I give him a business card, and as he climbs into the truck, he waves and says, 'I'll google you now.'

Several weeks later, I decide to google him back, and I'm amazed to discover that he's the host of *Voices of Montana*, a conservative radio talk show styled on the divisive model of the right-wing provocateurs like Limbaugh – something he failed to mention. His show caused uproar when it began airing in 2009 on a traditionally liberal Missoula station. 'Call in, be a part of the show,' Aaron jibed in the local newspaper. 'Get out of your Toyota Prius for just a second, just get mad and throw your coffee cup.'

Montana's hills give way to the big skies and tawny ranges of Idaho, where pronghorn antelope graze in twos and threes beside the highway, sharing the land with lumbering Herefords. Around noon, I cross into Washington State, and soon I'm climbing high into the Cascade Mountains. The temperature drops almost to freezing, and the embankments are piled high with dingy snow. Then the highway descends into a foggy canyon toward sea level and the air grows thick with the luxuriant aroma of cedars.

With my windows down, I cruise toward Tacoma, where I plan to stay a couple of days with Daniel Steciak, a former army infantryman I met in Afghanistan. In September 2009, I took a break from my job with a humanitarian organization in Gaza to travel to Afghanistan for the first time, where I embedded as a journalist with Steciak's battalion. Apache Company 2-87 lived in a dusty outpost at the base of a rocky outcrop in the Tangi Valley – no hot showers, rarely a hot meal, and excesses of boredom, machismo and IEDs. On the first patrol I walked, an IED blew a truck off the Tangi's main road near Apache's outpost and Steciak's platoon was ordered to provide over-watch from the rooftop of an abandoned *qalat*. We were chatting, and Steciak said he was from Maryland, and I said I was too. It turned out we had a lot more in common than just our birthplace, and we still do.

As I pull into his neighbourhood, an A-10 Warthog thunders in low over the road for a landing, almost pulling up alongside me. Steciak greets me with a hug in the parking lot of his generic apartment complex. In Afghanistan, he was living on a diet of stress, altitude and cigarettes. In April 2010, after six years of service, including two year-long tours in Afghanistan with the 10th Mountain Division, Steciak got out of the army. He's at least twenty pounds heavier now but he still walks with the upright gait of a former soldier, rigid, eyes straight ahead.

Steciak followed his wife Abby, an army intelligence officer, when she received orders to Fort Lewis, here in Tacoma. They fell in love in high school when they were both cadets in the Civil Air Patrol. Relocating from one active-duty post in upstate New York to another on the other side of the country has not allowed him to leave the army far behind. Reminders are everywhere – his wife going to work every morning at five in her uniform, soldiers in the parking lot.

When I met Steciak, he was an avid reader and seemed more thoughtful and serious than most of the other guys in the platoon. We spent hours smoking and playing guitar, arguing about politics while he patiently taught me to sing and play 'Blackbird'. He was lean back then, his cheeks burned to a ruddy brown by the Afghan sun, his black hair buzzed and dusty. As a baby, Steciak was adopted from Korea by a middle-class American family in Columbia, Maryland. If he had exchanged his filthy uniform for a shalwar kameez, he could've easily passed for a Hazara or an Uzbek.

Abby has prepared a dinner of pulled pork barbecue, baked beans and French fries. We rehash stories over 16oz cans of Bud Light. That night, we stay up late playing guitar. He teaches me another Beatles song, 'Norwegian Wood', and I'm soon obsessed.

It's been tough for Steciak to reconcile the vast gulf between the humdrum life of an ordinary American and the deadly serious, testosterone-addled life of a combat soldier. 'It was great at first, the whole "I don't have to get up and do PT; don't have to shave this morning if I don't feel like it", but it's hard to find that purpose,' he says. 'I look back on my days before the army, and it's like I'm looking at someone else's life. I was expecting after getting out there would be a moment where I was like, "OK, I'm ready to move on now." But I still feel like a soldier. I still think like a soldier, walk like it, talk like it, act like it.'

Steciak didn't join the army out of necessity – he joined out of a true sense of obligation, shaded with middle-class guilt. 'I was sitting there in my upper-middle-class house watching American soldiers on CNN fighting in Afghanistan and Iraq,' he says. 'I mean, obviously there was some 9/11 nationalism going on, but also I figured . . . politics aside, if they're willing to do this for their country then I should be willing to make the same sacrifices. Maybe that's a little naive, but when the country goes to war they're going to send somebody, and it may as well be me.'

On his first deployment, as a twenty-year-old private, Steciak says, 'The world was black and white to me, comfortably so. Good, bad, evil, very definite labels that were easy. I mean, the Taliban, the insurgents we're fighting, they're the bad guys, and Americans, we're the good guys.' His Manichaean world view didn't survive the first few months in Afghanistan. The platoon visited a village in Paktika Province, on the eastern border with Pakistan, and promised to bring humanitarian supplies. When they visited again, they heard that 'the Taliban had come through the village and started beheading people. After that we would get hit every time we ventured out in that direction, and that was the first time I started to wonder, and understand, that maybe there were factors beyond "we're the Americans and we're here to help you". I realized what a difficult position the villagers were placed in.'

By the time Steciak returned to Afghanistan for his second tour in 2009, he had no illusions that America would win the war. IEDs had become the main killer in Afghanistan, and the IEDs in Wardak that year were big enough to blow the army's twenty-tonne mine-resistant vehicles to smithereens. It was a constant battle of one-upmanship – the army bought bigger, multimillion-dollar trucks, and the Taliban responded by packing an extra ten dollars' worth of fertilizer into the plastic jugs they buried beneath the roads. There is no illusion of control in the fight against IEDs; there is no machine-gun position to take out, no bunker to blow. Day after day, Steciak says, 'I was going out and just trying not to get blown up.' His unit, the 2nd Battalion of the 87th Infantry Regiment, lost nineteen men and had over a hundred men wounded that year, almost all due to IEDs.

If I hadn't been there with him, it would be extremely difficult to see the young man sitting in front of me – soft around the middle, wearing jeans and a polo shirt, a picture of suburban normalcy – staring down the scope of an M14 sniper rifle, preparing to take a human life. Sometimes, he says, it's even difficult to imagine himself back in Afghanistan. More than once, he assures me that he does not suffer from post-traumatic stress disorder, or PTSD, but sometimes, he says, 'I wonder if there will be more repercussions for me.'

Two pet rabbits – Margaret Thatcher and Eleanor Rigby – suckle noisily on a water bottle while we talk. The bunnies started as a joke. Abby wanted a pet, but both of them travel too much to have a dog or a cat, so Steciak brought a rabbit home one day and then they decided she needed a companion. 'I keep offering to cook them up,' Steciak dead-pans, 'but she won't let me.'

Before I take off the next morning, Steciak and I practise 'A Day in the Life', my favourite Beatles song. Steciak tells me he's thinking seriously about going back into the army as an infantry officer after college.

'You better start running now,' I tell him.

In March 2005, I came home from Iraq and spent a few months drinking up my savings and travelling the world – making up for lost time – before I began studying at the University of Virginia. The hard part wasn't dealing with the things I'd seen – it was moving amid crowds of civilians who had no idea there was a war going on, and didn't want to be reminded.

Although I was only three or four years older than my classmates in terms of age that first year of school, I felt a hundred years older in terms of experience. I had friends who'd been blown up by a suicide bomber, and there was no good reason it wasn't me. Nothing else seemed remotely serious.

Then sometime around Valentine's Day in 2007, the second alert order came in. We looked around the room at one another in the National Guard armoury, staring at the papers in our hands. We listened to the commander read and mouthed expletives to one another. You could immediately tell who would try to get out of it.

Back at school, my work suffered instantly. I believed the war was an illegal action, a waste of American and Iraqi life, destined for failure. Moreover, my contract was almost up and I was due to get out of the National Guard for good in July, the same month we were due to begin mobilization. If I didn't protest, I'd be 'stop-lossed' – involuntarily extended for the duration of the Iraq deployment. But I was in a predicament: a lot of the guys I served with the previous tour, some of whom I loved like brothers, were still in the unit, and ditching out would mean abandoning them. I'd also been given a fire team – privates whose lives I didn't want to entrust to anyone else.

In a bizarre twist of fate, I had been given a torturous choice. My arm was still broken from a snowboarding injury requiring a steel plate and six screws. The orthopaedist said it would be a year before I fully healed, and that I could seriously re-injure myself if I wasn't careful. If I showed my X-rays to the doctor at the pre-deployment screening there was a chance he'd send me, but probably he wouldn't. So, it was up to me.

In October 2007, my unit arrived in Baghdad without me. Within weeks my squad was hit on a routine patrol. Two soldiers were killed and three were wounded badly enough to get sent home permanently, one of whom, Josh Primm, had been a room-mate of mine in Iraq. The blast from the molten copper charge that penetrated his armoured vehicle burned him badly enough that he's still in outpatient rehab four years later.

Somewhere south of Portland, Oregon, I exit the freeway and head west towards the sea, where I pick up the coast road and cruise along the forested shores of the blue-grey Pacific. In northern California, I sleep atop a cliff by the sea, soaking up the sound of the crashing waves and the wind in the giant redwoods. I stop for a few days in Long Beach, outside Los Angeles, to stay with Ryan Lenhart, my old buddy from basic training. Ryan was a skinny kid when we were trainees, but he's massive now, and quieter. In 2005, Ryan's California National Guard unit served a brutal tour near Sadr City, a Shia slum in greater Baghdad and an epicentre of sectarian fighting.

Despite the relentless frequency of IED attacks and the extremely high casualties his unit was taking, Ryan didn't want to go home. He felt like he had nothing to come back to – his wife had cheated on him while he was overseas, and he had to spend his two weeks of mid-tour leave organizing divorce paperwork. That same year he was called as a character witness for several of his friends who were charged with and eventually convicted of abuse of Iraqi detainees. Ryan eventually came home in 2006 and went back to his job with a police dive squad, where he had a close relationship with his partner. Inexplicably one night, his partner drove to a park near his home and shot himself in the head. When he tells me all of this, I begin to understand the depth of his silence.

Memorial Day finds us at a fancy hotel pool by the beach, where one of Ryan's friends has rented a cabana.

A few of the guys are racked out on pool chairs, their blood alcohol levels catching up to their tans. It's another beautiful day in southern California, and I'm miserable. I feel a sudden urge to jump into the pool and fill my lungs with water. Instead, I sit there in the sun, drinking a beer and feeling guilty for not doing something more appropriately pensive on Memorial Day.

The sparkling lights of the Los Angeles basin recede behind me, and without regret, I aim my car past Riverside and across the Mojave Desert toward Arizona, heading east for the first time in three weeks. At a rest stop, a sign warns of rattlesnakes.

In September 2010, in another harsh desert – in Kandahar Province, southern Afghanistan – I was just logging off from a military computer, preparing to head back to my cot, when I saw a strange message posted on my Facebook page.

The message said, 'Dude, Weaver died.' Certain that it was a mistake, I deleted the message immediately, afraid that Todd Weaver's wife might see it.

Todd Weaver and I were enlisted soldiers together in Iraq. We worked out almost every day and often shared our meals in the chow hall with a tight-knit group of friends. On National Guard drill weekends after we came home, I would stay with him in Williamsburg, where he was studying at the College of William and Mary. When we graduated in 2008, Weaver took a commission as an infantry lieutenant and went off to Ranger School, and I left for the Middle East to study Arabic and to begin working as a journalist. We lost touch for a couple of years, but then somehow we both wound up in the Arghandab District of Kandahar last summer – he as a platoon leader, and I as a reporter covering his battalion.

Weaver's outpost was so close to where I was embedded that I could hear when his platoon was getting attacked. I tried to get out to see him, but there was another journalist there, and the commander didn't want to crowd the unit with press. On 28 August, he emailed, 'It's a blast being down here. I pretty much earn my CIB every day.' The CIB, or Combat Infantry Badge, is the cherished prize of combat soldiers who have engaged the enemy. On 3 September, Weaver wrote, 'This place is a lot different than Iraq huh? Talk about a conventional fight.'

On 9 September, Weaver led his platoon on a patrol into the tangle of steamy pomegranate orchards flanking the Arghandab River. He stepped on a home-made pressure plate, igniting a blast under his feet that killed him instantly. He was twenty-six.

Todd's wife posts pictures online every now and then of Kiley, their daughter, who was born a few months before Todd deployed to Afghanistan. In one of the photographs, she carries a stuffed doll dressed in an army uniform with a clear plastic window for a face. Behind the plastic, a close-up snapshot of Todd stares out at his little girl, forever smiling. ∎

JIHAD REDUX

Declan Walsh

I returned from a long reporting trip in late 2006 to find a letter waiting. It was handwritten, in a spidery script that sloped off the page. 'I read with great interest your articles in the *Guardian* concerning Osama bin Laden and the "war" in the North West Frontier,' it began. 'I spent six years there once.' A flush of black-and-white pictures, dated in the 1930s and 40s, tumbled out. In one, sweaty-faced British officers in pith helmets trudged up a boulder-strewn hill; in another, white tents were arrayed under a line of sawtooth peaks. A turbaned Indian soldier posed on a desert airstrip before a biplane that was, inexplicably, tipped forward on to its nose. Then there was a portrait of a young soldier: tightly shaven in pressed khaki shorts, frowning into the camera, looking rather hot. This, it turned out, was my correspondent.

Charles Burman was ninety-two years old, writing from his home in Shropshire in western England. He was wheelchair-bound, a nurse cooked his meals, and arthritis had rusted his joints, but that didn't stop him following the news from Pakistan. His particular interest was the tribal belt: the mountain citadel nestled against the Afghan border that, since 2001, had become one of the world's most notorious trouble spots, a bubbling cauldron of tribesmen, Taliban and al-Qaeda fugitives. The headlines stirred deep, sometimes disturbing memories in the old man. Seven decades earlier, he explained, in the twilight of the British Empire, he had been dispatched to the tribal belt to fight a war with striking echoes of the present conflagration. 'I stayed two thousand days,' he noted with bitter-sweet precision. 'It was rather dicey then too.'

Burman arrived in 1938, landing in Karachi by steamship before proceeding by train to the North West Frontier province. The son of a Lancashire telegraph operator, he had joined the army for a lick of adventure and 'the fresh-air life'. British India would provide an uncomfortable abundance of both. Crossing the Indus in a rickety taxi, he arrived at the imposing gates of Fort Akalgarh, an ancient Pashtun citadel now occupied by the British. The young soldier was charmed by the fort's exotic trees and chirping parakeets; otherwise he found it hellish. Bats infested the rafters, snakes slithered from the crumbling walls and the heat was suffocating. Huddled under his mosquito net at night, he penned anguished letters to a girlfriend. 'Not an ideal place to be stationed,' he recalled drily. Days later came relief – but of the brief variety, such as the gap between frying pan and fire. He was sent north, along the ancient camel trails, into Waziristan.

The tribal belt had troubled the British for nearly a century. It was a territory of immense strategic value, forming a spiky bulwark on the north-western tip of British India (present-day Pakistan) that protected the Raj against rival imperialists, notably tsarist Russia. The problem was its people. While the Pashtun of the plains had acquiesced to colonial rule, the tribesmen of the mountains proved stubbornly resistant to the charms of the empire. Parties of horse-mounted raiders thundered from the hills, guns blazing, to plunder, kill and snatch hostages from unprotected villages. The British retaliated with 'punitive expeditions' – brutal sallies into the mountains backed by elephants pulling nine-pounder guns and, later, armoured vehicles with machine guns. When that failed, they courted influential elders with bribes and blandishments. But peace was often short-lived, especially in Waziristan, the tribal belt's most indomitable corner. In 1920, the viceroy, Frederic Thesiger, noted regretfully that British forces had conducted an operation in Waziristan on average every four years since 1852. 'A forbidden land,' noted one chastened officer. 'It was impossible to go; and if you did your bones would be left there.'

Burman had arrived in time for the latest revolt. He was posted to Razmak, a highland camp of six thousand troops ringed by jagged peaks and filled with constant danger. Tribal sharpshooters, wedged behind lofty boulders, opened fire on convoys as they twisted through the narrow valleys. Camels pulled down British telegraph poles, severing communications. Soldiers were picked off as they played hockey or snoozed in their tents. Nobody was safe, not even the dead. The camp graveyard had to be closed, Burman recalled, when insurgents started to dig up British corpses at night only to ransom them back the next day.

The force behind this havoc was a charismatic cleric whose name soon burned the lips of every soldier on the frontier: the Faqir of Ipi. Born Mirza Ali Khan, the faqir – the title denotes a Sufi mystic – settled in the village of Ipi among the Daur, the smallest of Waziristan's three tribal clans (the others are the Mehsud and Wazir). He rose to prominence in 1936 on the back of a popular scandal. A teenage Hindu girl had converted to Islam in murky circumstances and married a Muslim, taking the name 'Islam Bibi'. The British, perhaps unwisely, sided with her parents and ordered soldiers to bring the girl home. Outraged cries swept through Waziristan – the infidels had slighted Islam! – and protest snowballed into rebellion with the faqir at its helm, rallying tribesmen under the banner of jihad.

It seemed an uneven contest: tribesmen wielding swords and bolt-action rifles against the world's great military machine. Foreshadowing the pilotless drone strikes of today, the Royal Air Force deployed its latest technology – Audax and Wapiti biplanes – to pulverize rebel villages. 'We would bomb from six thousand feet and three bombs would go down,' one pilot later recalled. 'Then we'd swing around and see how good it really was. That would go on all day.' Yet the Pashtun guerrillas kept one step ahead, leveraging their knowledge of the harsh terrain and networks of tribal spies to deadly advantage. The worst, Burman said, were the attacks on supply convoys – a chain of one hundred or so trucks, crawling through the mountains at a teeth-grinding pace, waiting for the first shot to ring out. It was terrifying. 'You never knew what would happen when you went out on that road.'

At the height of fighting, in 1941, Britain had 40,000 troops in Waziristan, yet the faqir remained infuriatingly elusive. The wily cleric was hiding in a cluster of caves near the Afghan border, insulated from the Audax bombers and cultivating a mythical aura. Devotees believed he could transform sticks into guns and, Jesus-like, feed the masses from a single basket of bread. In London, the papers dubbed him 'the Scarlet Pimpernel of Waziristan'. Other powers also grew intrigued. With the Second World War rumbling in the background, news of the faqir's fabled resistance reached representatives of the Axis powers stationed across the border in Kabul, who scrambled to recruit him. In June 1941, an official at the Italian legation, disguised as a Pashtun, slipped into Waziristan for an audience with the faqir. One month later the German Abwehr intelligence service dispatched its own team – 'leprosy experts' Professor Manfred Oberdörffer and Dr Fred Brandt – who travelled under the cover story of a mission to cure disease and trap rare butterflies. They didn't get far. A mysterious ambush south of Kabul, probably instigated by British intelligence, killed Oberdörffer and wounded Brandt, and the Nazis never made it to Waziristan. But cash and supplies slipped through and, still today, apocryphal stories circulate of the faqir's German printing press – and his Volkswagen Beetle.

In January 2011, Charles Burman's daughter sent me an email: her father had passed away. She sent more pictures – the young signals sergeant fiddling with an ancient radio in Waziristan, the smiling pensioner being pushed through an English garden. I read back over our correspondence. Burman's two thousand days in Waziristan had clearly marked him for life. 'The emptiness of the hills left me with a permanent desire to live in a quiet place,' he wrote. If there was a lesson from it all, he continued, it was the futility of force in the tribal belt. 'It is evident that the Afghan [Pashtun] Moslems prefer to live their own life and let "democracy" take its own course,' he wrote. 'You're never going to change their style of living, that's for sure.'

The British withdrew from Waziristan in 1947, at the birth of Pakistan, with little more than tenuous control and the faqir still at large. He expired peacefully, at home in bed, thirteen years later. Thousands flocked to his funeral; his tomb became a place of pilgrimage. In London, they paid tribute to the adversary who had outlived and outfought the mighty Raj. 'A doughty and honourable opponent,' noted the obituary in *The Times* in 1960. 'A redoubtable organizer of tribal warfare.'

But the British had not been his final foe. In 1955 Christopher Rand, an intrepid correspondent for the *New Yorker*, trekked across the Hindu Kush on horseback in search of the ageing outlaw. He found him sitting calmly outside his caves, in a peach turban and bandolier, still in a state of war. Having vanquished the Raj, the faqir had turned his guns on the fledgling state of Pakistan. 'He was quite motionless as he sat there, his brown eyes gazing somewhere else, but his presence was compelling,' wrote Rand. The faqir said little, he noted, except to make one declaration. From Genghis Khan to the British, Waziristan had never bowed to outsiders. It was not about to start with this newfangled invention called Pakistan.

The first time I saw Waziristan was in 2005. I stared through the porthole window of a clattering Pakistani military helicopter as it swept over the crumpled land, slightly awestruck. The guts of the earth, it seemed, had been torn open, exposing a rippling tide of rock and scree that raced to the horizon. Fortress-style houses clung to vertiginous slopes; a jeep scrambled insect-like across a dry riverbed; and giant shafts of light pierced the clouds, swimming lazily across the majestic landscape.

The Federally Administered Tribal Areas, as the tribal belt is officially known, have long inspired wonderment. 'Wild men in wild country,' wrote one colonial visitor. Perched in the lower reaches of the Hindu Kush, the area is composed of seven tribal agencies – Bajaur, Mohmand, Khyber, Kurram, Orakzai, South and North Waziristan – and six 'frontier regions' (buffer zones within the settled areas) that, in total, cover an area slightly smaller than Belgium and which are home to perhaps four million souls. Each agency has its peculiarity: the marble mines of Bajaur, the smugglers of Khyber, the well-armed Shia population of Kurram. Parts are surprisingly close – the entrance to Mohmand lies a leisurely two-hour drive from my suburban Islamabad home. But in every meaningful sense, the FATA is profoundly disconnected from the rest of Pakistan.

Since 1947, the area has been governed under an archaic system of laws that deprives residents of the most basic rights and protections. Political parties and newspapers are banned, decisions taken through tribal *jirgas* (councils), and order is enforced through collective punishment. Life is particularly dire for women who cannot, by law or custom, inherit property or even prosecute for rape. This woeful situation is largely a consequence of the Frontier Crimes Regulation, a draconian law drafted by British colonists between 1871 and 1901 and which, astonishingly, remains in force today. Under the FCR, legislation passed in Parliament applies on the say-so of the president, which is rarely given. Instead, all power in each agency lies with the Political Agent, a civil servant of extraordinary authority. 'He is our version of a king,' a tribesman once told me, without irony.

In one of my early trips to the FATA, before the situation deteriorated, I went to see one such putative monarch. Tariq Hayat Khan, a former army officer with jet-black hair, sunk into an old leather chair at his office in Miram Shah, the dusty headquarters of North Waziristan agency. A fan turned languidly overhead; on the wall behind him hung a wooden board listing in gold letters his predecessors dating back to 1895. The first fifty years of names were British. 'I am the law around here,' Khan declared. 'I double up as the judge, the chief of police and the head of development. I can grant relief to a man. Or I can come down on him like a ton of bricks.' He paused for dramatic effect. 'You could call me a benevolent despot.'

A faint smile played on Khan's lips; I had the impression he enjoyed the shock of his words. But he was barely exaggerating. Under the FCR, he could jail a man without trial for up to three years, extract fines from his relatives or have his village razed to the ground. There was no avenue of appeal. 'It's basically a cut-price administration,' he said, half modestly. But the PA quickly added that such powers were worthless without local support. He gestured at a slightly rough-cut gang of older men, with sun-worn faces and hennaed beards, clustered on the far side of his desk, listening politely. They were the maliks – government-appointed chieftains who underwrote the entire system. Their titles were inherited from the British era, when colonial officers offered selected elders cash payments – essentially protection money – in exchange for peace. Little had changed; there were 1,300 maliks in North Waziristan alone. They formed an influential if conservative elite. With the PA translating, I asked the maliks if they wished to integrate into mainstream Pakistan. Haji Noor Din, a wizened man of indeterminate age, rubbed his chin thoughtfully. 'No,' he answered firmly. 'Those NGO women from Islamabad, with their jeans and T-shirts, might encourage our women to go out in public. We couldn't have that.'

The FATA's Victorian legal system reflects a deeper neglect. Average incomes are $250 a year – half the national average – and 60 per cent of residents live below the poverty line. Barely 30 per cent of men are literate; among women the figure is 3 per cent. Many women die in childbirth. Industry is virtually impossible – without courts, banks are reluctant to lend – and some 80,000 men are thought to be jobless. Crime takes up the slack: gunrunning, drug smuggling and trading in stolen vehicles. The Tirah Valley produces famously head-spinning hashish; the gunsmiths of Darra Adam Khel produce a mean imitation Kalashnikov. Corrupt officials are on the take too. Tax-exempted goods headed for Afghanistan regularly 'vanish' as they pass through the tribal belt, only to reappear in Pakistani markets at knock-down rates. Last January the government estimated the scam had cost the exchequer $435 million since 2006. This cloudy reputation has become a cultural icon: in Pakistani films, villains dodge the law by roaring past a sign that reads 'Tribal Belt'.

The image of the tribal rascal, however, obscures the more humdrum reality of most lives. The scions of wealthy families, some Western-educated, have become top-flight businessmen, generals and diplomats, while most ordinary folk scrape by on remittances from relatives employed in menial jobs in Pakistani cities, the Gulf or the UK, making the tribal economy globalized as well as remote. But for those left behind, the graft-steeped maliki system limits their chances of self-improvement. A Pashtun friend explained how it worked. The PA has government funds to build a school. He awards the contract to a favoured malik, who pockets the cash and recruits his relatives as teacher and guards, guaranteeing salaries for years. The teachers may not be qualified; in fact the school may not get built. No matter: the PA has the malik in his pocket. 'The system is inherently corrupt; money for nothing,' my friend said, shaking his head regretfully. 'People don't like it.' He knew all this, he added, because his own father was a malik.

The tribesmen's plight excites little sympathy among fellow Pakistanis, who largely view them as gun-toting, God-fearing hillbillies. 'Frankly, those people can kill each other as much as they like,' a senior newspaper editor in Karachi told me some years ago. 'As long as they keep it up there.' Yet this sorry state of affairs is not only a product of casual prejudice – it stems from decades of foolish manipulation. This blemished history is at the core of the present upheaval, in which the FATA has come to occupy a dark place in the Western imagination as a dystopian emirate of chaos, spewing violence in every direction – 'the most dangerous place in the world' according to President Barack Obama.

Pakistan's rulers, taking their cue from the British, have long treated the FATA as a strategic 'asset': a recruitment ground, a proxy battlefield and an ideological laboratory. The army sent tribesmen to fight India during the countries' inaugural war in 1948, dispatching a Waziristan militia to the fight in Kashmir. Then it turned their home into a vast buffer against Afghanistan. From the 1940s until the 1970s, the Kabul government laid aggressive claim to the Pashtun territories inside Pakistan, and covertly aided Pashtun nationalists agitating for 'Pashtunistan'. Pakistan retaliated by sealing the border and, occasionally, sending warplanes to bomb Afghan-backed rebels such as the Faqir of Ipi. But the transformational moment came in the

1980s, with the jihad against Soviet troops occupying Afghanistan. Rebel training camps, funded by US and Saudi intelligence but controlled by Pakistan's Inter-Services Intelligence (ISI) directorate sprang up across the tribal belt. Sophisticated new AK-47 weapons flooded in, replacing the old bolt-action shotguns. So did thousands of angry young men from across the Arab world who yearned for a return to the glories of the Muslim empire. Prominent among their number was the son of a Saudi construction magnate, Osama bin Laden. Most significantly, the jihad brought jolting ideological change. The tribesmen had always been fierce champions of Islam – or rather, the elements of Islam that complemented their Pashtun traditions. The anti-Soviet fight imported a harsher and more political version of that religion. A proliferation of Saudi-funded madrasas churned out guerrilla fighters but also indoctrinated local children. The Americans, funding the fighting, tacitly approved. 'We just said to them: "Go to it, kill the commies,"' one US diplomat stationed in Peshawar in the eighties told me.

The 'commies' withdrew in humiliation in 1989, presaging the wider collapse of the Soviet Union. The CIA station chief in Islamabad sent a note back to headquarters. WE WON it read. A veil of peace fell over the tribal belt. It lasted just over a decade.

Today's tribal belt was forged in the chaotic aftermath of the 11 September 2001 attacks. As the US military swept into Afghanistan with a wounded fury, it had two aims: to topple the Taliban regime and to destroy al-Qaeda. It succeeded in just one of those. Kabul fell quickly, its puny defences pulverized by warplanes and B-1 bombers, but Osama bin Laden and hundreds of followers – Arabs, Uzbeks and a smattering of Europeans – slipped across the border into Pakistan's tribal belt. Most ended up in Waziristan, where sympathizers from the main Mehsud and Wazir tribes swung open their heavy doors, offering bed, board and Kalashnikovs. This warm welcome was dictated by *melmastia,* the Pashtun cultural obligation of hospitality, but also by more earthly considerations: the fugitives paid handsomely for their keep in thick wads of US dollars, and many tribesmen sympathized with their plight. Some were themselves jihadist veterans, having fought alongside the Taliban in Afghanistan; others were simply outraged by the US invasion. And so, protected from the world by rough terrain and rigid bonds of tribal loyalty, al-Qaeda started to rebuild.

In retrospect, this migration was a seismic occurrence, triggering a chain of events that would dangerously destabilize Pakistan. But at the time, Pakistan's president, General Pervez Musharraf, reacted with bluster and denial, insisting that talk of foreign 'miscreants' in the FATA were overblown. By 2004, though, the evidence was unavoidable: rising cross-border attacks into Afghanistan, and persistent speculation that bin Laden was sheltering in the tribal belt. Finally, under intense pressure from Washington, Musharraf sent thousands of troops to Waziristan – the largest deployment since the British departure nearly six decades earlier. It started badly. An intense battle erupted in South Waziristan – the paramilitary Frontier Corps took heavy casualties, and was forced to retreat.

Taking a leaf from the colonial playbook, Musharraf turned to cash, coercion and negotiation as a means of controlling the tribes. A year later, in 2005, I went to see how it was going.

The military convoy bumped down a zigzag road, dust billowing behind. The southern reaches of North West Frontier province* scrolled by: grimy towns and rock-strewn deserts; women hidden under coal-black burkas; trucks painted with scenes from Bollywood movies; the fluttering black-and-white flag of a religious party. Beside me, in the lead jeep, was Major Sarfraz Ahmed, a Kashmiri officer whose balding pate and preacher-style beard make him look older than his thirty-five years. He had spent the best part of an hour delving into a detailed comparison of the Bible and the Quran. 'So many similarities between the great books,' he enthused. Finally, after

---

* In 2009, NWFP was renamed as Khyber Pakhtunkhwa.

ten hours, the convoy rumbled over a low concrete bridge. Off to the side, fingers of rock thrust from the soil at sharp angles, like the stakes of an ancient palisade. Houses with long sand-coloured walls, unbroken save for watchtowers and crenulations, sat on both sides of the road. A man goading a camel sauntered past. 'We have entered Waziristan,' Ahmed announced.

The tribal belt is usually off-limits to foreigners, hidden behind a thicket of red tape and permissions that are never granted. The only way in is the official visit: one-day, propaganda-heavy affairs involving a whistle-stop tour of military bases by helicopter, interviews with carefully coached elders, and regular breaks for tea, samosas and PowerPoint presentations. But in June 2005, the army made an exception for me because they had a story to sell: the 'miscreants' were on the run.

Before leaving Peshawar I had been to see Lieutenant General Safdar Hussain, the brash, chain-smoking commander of the 70,000 security forces in the FATA – Frontier Corps paramilitaries, *khassadar* police, tribal levies and, now, regular army. In his office – a cool, marble-floored room that overlooked a sweeping lawn – Hussain lit a fresh cigarette and tossed a photo album towards me. It was a gallery of scalps: blood-portraits of dozens of fighters, many of them teenagers, killed in a recent military operation. Hussain pointed to a young man with sharp features and blood trickling from his mouth. 'Uzbeks,' he said. 'Terrible fighters. Not even proper Muslims, they weren't circumcised in their vital parts. We checked.' The Uzbeks were loyal to Tahir Yuldashev, a zealous preacher who tried to foment an Islamic revolution in Uzbekistan's Fergana Valley in the 1990s, was ejected and ended up in Afghanistan under the wing of Osama bin Laden. Since 2002, Yuldashev's gang – rough fighters, feared for their cruelty – had taken sanctuary in Waziristan, inducting Pashtun tribesmen into the latest jihad. Producing a map of the 'pacified' tribes, Hussain insisted that, since he had taken command a year earlier, they had swung to his side. 'The locals don't want terrorism; they want jobs,' he declared. Then he excused himself: he had a round of golf to attend. 'When I arrived, the small kids would throw stones at my helicopter,' he said, walking me to the door. 'Now they are waving.'

Pushing into South Waziristan, our convoy passed boys in uniform jaunting along the road, swinging their school bags. They didn't wave, and neither did the old men hunkered by the roadside, fingering their prayer beads and glaring. We paused for tea at the old colonial fort in Jandola, where a plaque recorded that the airman T. E. Lawrence stayed the night in 1930. The road cut through low, rocky hills then swooped into Wana, the agency headquarters: a ragged market town on a wide plain dotted with high-walled apple orchards and, further off, ringed by hills. We passed a dilapidated Shell petrol station, shops with grain stacked outside and a woman in a dark blue burka, squatting beside her children, waiting for a ride. I leaned out to take a photo. Major Ahmed yelled at me to get back in. 'People might mistake you for an American.' If that happened, he explained, they might start shooting.

That night I was billeted in surprising comfort. A new air conditioner hummed gently over my bed in the Wana military camp; there was also a television, microwave oven and plastic flowers that peeked from a vase. The military was flush with cash, much of it American. The Pentagon was funding the entire operation to the tune of $100 million per month, paying for fuel, rations, bullets and, I suspected, the electronics in my room. Tied up by the wars in Iraq and Afghanistan – and realizing that an invasion of nuclear-armed Pakistan was a risky proposition – the US had subcontracted the fight against al-Qaeda to Pakistan. But the army, it turned out, was talking instead of fighting.

The fragile peace had been won through a 'cooperation agreement' with Baitullah Mehsud, a thirty-one-year-old militant commander with a reputation for brutality who was emerging as a powerful tribal warlord thanks to his links with the al-Qaeda fugitives. In some ways he was a modern incarnation of the Faqir of Ipi – albeit one who swapped Pashtun pride for nihilistic Islamist violence. Born into a poor mountain family, Mehsud was a madrasa dropout and one-time bodybuilder who suffered from a debilitating kidney disease. He vaulted out of his straitened circumstances through jihadist violence, and would later found the Pakistani Taliban, declaring himself as emir, or supreme leader. Like his mentor, the Afghan Taliban leader Mullah Omar, Mehsud shunned photographs but demonstrated a keen nose for publicity. He was credibly accused of orchestrating the assassination of Benazir Bhutto in Rawalpindi in December 2007 and, months later, invited the media to a press conference in his mountain hideout. Later, he would be killed in an American drone strike. But for now, Mehsud was a friend of the military.

Five months earlier, in February 2005, General Hussain had flown to meet Mehsud at an old colonial fort in Sararogha, deep in the mountains, to strike a deal. In return for an army withdrawal to base – and a cash consideration of $842,000 – Mehsud promised to expel his foreign charges. It was a controversial tactic. Only a year earlier, in March 2004, Hussain had signed a similar pact with the top troublemaker in the ethnic Wazir areas, a dashing young militant with movie-star good looks named Nek Muhammad. The two men invited the media to a ceremony where they hugged and garlanded each other with flowers. But the smiles didn't last long. Muhammad reneged on his promise to evict al-Qaeda fighters, and three months later the CIA violently ended the 'peace deal'. Late one evening, after he had taken a satellite phone call from a journalist in Peshawar, a Predator drone hovering overhead fired several missiles into Muhammad's living room, killing him instantly. It was popularly believed that the phone call gave his location away. Angry protests erupted across Waziristan, a popular shrine to Muhammad sprang up and the Pakistani military, embarrassed by the American incursion, tried to claim it was responsible for the hit. Years later, this form of remote combat would go on to redefine the idea of war in the tribal belt. For now, though, the army was confident its second 'peace deal' would hold firm. 'The people are friendly towards us thanks to Baitullah Mehsud,' a young Punjabi officer told me in a briefing. 'It has opened the doors to prosperity and development.'

We set off from Wana the next morning, pressing deep into pine-forested mountains. The road vanished and we jerked along at ten miles an hour, splashing through chocolate-coloured streams and passing piles of stacked lumber. There were few signs of life save for flashes of movement from the ramparts of the high-walled houses overhead; we were being watched. Globs of rain started to fall and, wheels spinning, we slithered up a greasy hill. At the top was a roadblock – a length of string manned by two puny Frontier Corps paramilitaries – that marked the entrance to the Shawal Valley, one of Waziristan's most notorious al-Qaeda bolt-holes.

Hundreds of militants, many Uzbek, converged on Shawal in March 2002 following Operation Anaconda, an American military offensive in southern Afghanistan. A year later bin Laden himself, accompanied by a personal guard unit of Arab and Central Asian fighters, was sighted at a meeting in the valley. Looking around, I could see why the Saudi might like it here. Shawal was actually three valleys, carpeted in trees and studded with peaks that soared as high as 9,600 feet. Snowbound for five months of the year, it had no electricity and few roads; the Afghan border was just seven miles away. Now, the brigadier in charge assured me, the government enjoyed '99.5 per cent writ'. To mark its arrival, it was building a road.

We climbed to a mountain-top site where soldiers driving bulldozers were slicing into the rocky soil. The locals were largely cooperating, an engineer said, reeling off a list of development projects like new schools and wells. Those who refused faced an iron rod: the army had just torched a village suspected of harbouring fugitives, and fined them the equivalent of $7,000. Still, he added, gesturing to the sweeping valley, the human landscape was hard to navigate. 'It's difficult to know who is who round here,' he admitted.

Many army officers came from Punjab and seemed to view Waziristan as a virtual foreign posting, a place inhabited by strange tribals best understood through colonial clichés. The locals were 'filled with religious fervour' and 'attach extreme importance to money', the brigadier declared over supper that night. 'Every Pukhtoon is almost an army in himself.' Some were more reflective. After supper the brigade major led me up the slope to an observation post, where we sat on the boundary wall, legs dangling, peering into the shadowy night. The young officer pulled out a pair of American night-vision goggles and suddenly the valley came to life, in blurry shades of green. Smoke drifted from a cluster of compounds; a mangy dog scampered down an empty track. I couldn't see a soul. 'These tribesmen have been out of our control for fifty years,' the brigade major said quietly. 'It will take us a while to get them back.'

I returned to Islamabad a few days later with well-stocked notebooks and a faint sense of unease. The army operation seemed perilously complacent, with many officers in denial about the scale of militant infiltration. Some preferred to blame America and journalists. 'We don't know what this al-Qaeda is,' Major Ahmed snapped at one point. 'We only hear about it in the international media, not on the ground.'

But the fighting was not over; in fact it had barely started. During the following eighteen months the army completely lost control. The Baitullah Mehsud peace deal collapsed, as did a subsequent agreement with other militant leaders in North Waziristan. Mehsud declared himself leader of the Tehrik-e-Taliban Pakistan, and his long-haired fighters swept across the tribal belt, imposing a crude vision of Islamic rule. Sharia courts replaced traditional *jirgas*, accused criminals were hanged in village squares and shops that sold 'blasphemous' foreign movie DVDs were blown up. Suicide bombers flung themselves at army checkposts, while barbers who trimmed men's beards received threats. The old social order, already weakened, came under further strain. Maliks were assassinated or forced to flee – on one army-sponsored trip to Wana, I met a tribal leader who was gunned down the following day – while the Taliban signed up recruits from the poverty-stricken underbelly of tribal society. They were drawn by a heady cocktail of guns, religion and money: the Taliban paid five times more than the Frontier Corps. The army floundered badly. Soldiers retreated into their bases, morale plunged and casualties soared. In the ultimate military humiliation, the Taliban kidnapped two hundred soldiers in August 2007 without firing a single shot.

The rout seemed puzzling: by then the army had over 100,000 troops, heavy artillery and F-16 warplanes in the FATA, not to mention over $1 billion in annual American payments. Their weakness was partly training. Pakistani troops had been readied for battle against India on the plains of Punjab, not for a knotty fight against tribal insurgents in their own backyard. But the greater difficulty lay back at army headquarters in Rawalpindi, where Pakistan's generals were engaged in a complex game of deception.

After the September 2001 attacks, Pakistan had cut its ties with the Afghan Taliban, a movement it previously supported. The break was temporary. While the army openly combated some militant groups – by 2006, half of all inmates at Guantánamo Bay had been captured in Pakistan – it was secretly helping others. Along the length of the 1,600-mile border, the ISI nurtured ties with militants who used Pakistani soil as a rear-base for the war in Afghanistan. They became known as the 'good' Taliban: fighters who zipped across the border on motorbikes and marched through the hills, primed for battle against Western soldiers. The 'good' Taliban were concentrated in the border areas of Waziristan and, further west, in Balochistan, where the Afghan Taliban was staging a dramatic resurgence. Later that year when I attended the funeral of young Pashtun named Aziz Ullah, near Quetta, the capital of Balochistan. He had been killed by American soldiers in Kandahar, his brother told me. 'He always wanted to die like this, as a martyr.' As we spoke, a heartfelt oratory, broadcast from a mosque, echoed across the village. The speaker was the provincial minister of health, a political ally of Musharraf.

If the strategy was complex, the goal was simple: to sway the outcome of the Afghan war, and outfox the old enemy, India. The abiding fear of Pakistan's generals was that an Indian proxy would come to power in Kabul, leaving Pakistan vulnerable to attack on both its borders. As a result, they figured, only the Taliban could guarantee Pakistan's future interests. The problem with this Byzantine strategy, of course, was that it clashed violently with American priorities. The 'good' Taliban killed American soldiers, cost billions in taxpayer dollars, and were helping bin Laden to rebuild his terrorist network.

Inevitably, American patience snapped, and Washington took matters into its own hands.

In the summer of 2007, the *National Intelligence Estimate*, a document produced by America's sixteen intelligence agencies, went public with worrisome news: al-Qaeda had established a new global headquarters in the tribal belt. Numerous plots, successful and failed, could be traced back to Waziristan: the London Underground attacks of July 2005; a plot to kill American soldiers in German discos; a plan to blow up seven transatlantic airliners using liquid explosives. The foreigners had become deeply embedded in local communities; fresh recruits arrived from across the world; wealthy Arab donors provided funding. Most ominously, al-Qaeda was allying with some of Pakistan's most notorious jihadi groups such as Lashkar-e-Jhangvi, whose members were setting up camp in Waziristan. The tribal belt was becoming more dangerous than the sum of its parts. A 2009 email from the US-born jihadist David Headley, later charged with helping to execute the bloody attacks on the Indian city of Mumbai, offered a rare insider's perspective. In Miram Shah, where I had interviewed the Political Agent three years earlier, foreigners constituted one-third of the population, he estimated. 'This bazaar is bustling with Chechens, Uzbeks, Tajiks, Russians, Bosnians, some from EU countries and of course our Arab brothers,' he wrote. 'Any Waziri or Mehsud I spoke to seemed grateful to God for the privilege of being able to host "foreign mujahedin".'

The CIA watched in dismay. The spy agency had been operating in the tribal belt since late 2003, posting agents to small, often two-man spy stations that were hidden inside Pakistani Army bases. Officially, Pakistan's military denied their presence; on the ground, teams of Special Services Group commandos guarded the CIA outposts. It was an uncomfortable alliance, steeped in frustration and mutual mistrust. Now, the CIA turned to its trump card: Predator drones.

The CIA had been using the pilotless aircraft for reconnaissance purposes for years. In 1999, Predators loitering over Taliban-controlled Kandahar beamed back images of a robed man, surrounded by armed bodyguards and strolling through a farm, believed to be Osama bin Laden. But it was initially reluctant to use them to kill. 'It isn't the CIA's job to fly airplanes that shoot missiles,' director George Tenet told Bush administration officials in 2001. That meeting, however, took place on 4 September. A week later the world had changed, and the CIA's qualms vanished.

The Predator is an odd-looking aircraft: an emaciated fuselage with twiggy legs and gangly wings that span forty-nine feet, with an empty cockpit and a twitching robotic eye. In the air it is powered by a snowmobile engine whose maximum speed barely exceeds 130 miles an hour and is a precocious craft to guide, sensitive to vagaries of weather, heat and dust. But in the shadow wars of the tribal belt, it is a stealthy killing machine. They take off from Shamsi airbase, an airstrip hidden deep in the ochre deserts of Balochistan that was originally built by Arab sheikhs on falconry trips. CIA technicians based in Shamsi service the drones, load their weapons and cast them into the sky. But once they leave the tarmac, control passes to an operator clutching a joystick and sitting before a large flat-screen monitor thousands of miles away, at the CIA headquarters in Langley, Virginia. These remote-control pilots, known as 'reachback operators' – a mix of retired intelligence and air-force officers – guide the drone along the 350-mile journey to the southern tip of Waziristan where, thanks to the light airframe and lack of pilot, it can wheel the skies for up to twenty hours. Then the Predator starts to hunt its prey. The pilot guides it using information provided by CIA spies on the ground and technicians from the National Security Agency, which monitors all radio, telephone and Internet traffic from the FATA. Senior CIA officials track progress through a bank of video screens, watching the plains and peaks of Waziristan scroll by, zooming in with cameras powerful enough to read a vehicle licence plate. When the Predator finds its target – a remote farmhouse, a cluster of men in an orchard or a moving vehicle – a CIA lawyer in the room signs a strike authorization. The pilot presses a button. One or several laser-guided Hellfire missiles, travelling at 950 miles an hour, shoot towards the ground. Because the weapons are travelling at supersonic speed, the target doesn't even hear them coming.

At first, the CIA employed Predators cautiously in Pakistan. After the first strike in 2004 – against Nek Muhammad, the Wazir hothead – there were just eight strikes over the next four years. The CIA was restrained by political considerations – President Bush was keen to avoid embarrassing his close ally, General Musharraf – and its own bloody blunders. In January 2006, a Predator attack on a house in Bajaur, at the northern end of the tribal belt, missed its target – bin Laden's deputy Ayman al-Zawahiri – but killed eighteen people including women and children, sending ripples of outrage across Pakistan. On another occasion a drone crashed in the tribal belt, necessitating a secret raid to recover its wreckage by US Special Forces based in Afghanistan – the Americans feared the Pakistani military would 'reverse engineer' the technology. But in 2008, in the dying months of the Bush administration and amid mounting concern about al-Qaeda's new sanctuary, the gloves came off.

The first high-profile target was Abu Khabab al-Masri, the head of al-Qaeda's chemical and biological weapons programme. The Egyptian had instructed militants in the use of ricin, cyanide and other poison gases, conducted ghastly experiments on animals and toyed with building a 'dirty' nuclear bomb. In July 2008, four Predator-fired missiles slammed into a madrasa near Wana, killing al-Masri, two militants and three young boys. The drone hit rate soared: thirty-three in 2008, fifty-three in 2009 and 118 in 2010. It was America's largest targeted assassination programme since the Vietnam War, yet Pakistan had little say. Musharraf had granted the CIA access to the Shamsi airbase for reconnaissance missions but implored the agency to use force sparingly, conscious of the furious reaction attacks provoked in Pakistan. But the momentum was unstoppable: while the Americans employed the ceremony and language of diplomacy in public, behind closed doors their statecraft was much more blunt. 'We made it very clear to the Pakistanis that these targets needed to be prosecuted. And if they weren't willing to do it, there was nothing they could do to stop us taking unilateral action. Zero. Zip,' a US official who had served in Islamabad told me. 'We said, "If you're not going to do it, then get out of our way." And that's what happened.'

The drone campaign had a dramatic impact on Waziristan's al-Qaeda guests. Militants moved higher into the mountains, far from telephone and Internet connections, and started sleeping under trees to avoid the airborne menace that the Pashtun nicknamed *machai* – stinging wasps. Their paranoid Taliban hosts mounted witch-hunts for informants, casting the decapitated bodies of suspected spies on the roadside, usually accompanied by a scrawled note branding them as 'American spy'. A ruthless Taliban counter-espionage outfit calling itself 'Mujahedin I Khorasan' posted propaganda videos of their 'confession' on the Internet; in one tape the militants are seen storming a village, summoning a public meeting to harangue the locals, then blowing up an alleged spy in front of them.

While some victims were innocent, the CIA was certainly redoubling its efforts. American spies stationed in Waziristan, confined to their tiny bases (one was nicknamed 'Shawshank', after the prison), hired a covert network of Pashtun tribesmen to do their work for them. The local informants were paid to identify militant targets, locate their houses and install covert surveillance devices such as cameras and vehicle-tracking beacons. Their CIA handlers sent messages via computer but never physically met them: they were 'cut-outs', spy-speak for operatives hired at one or several removes, in this case through intermediaries elsewhere in Pakistan or in Afghanistan. Pakistan's ISI was kept in the dark about this secret network, whose dimensions remain unknown – a source of frequent tensions between the two agencies.

Pakistani cooperation increased, however, through 2008 and 2009 as Taliban violence exploded across the country. Graduates from Waziristan's bustling suicide-bomber academies spilled out of the tribal belt, attacking five-star hotels, police-training centres and buses full of ISI employees. To win the army's trust, the CIA widened its target list to include the Pakistani Taliban, scoring its most spectacular success on a warm night in August 2009. Baitullah Mehsud was reclining on a rope bed on the roof of his father-in-law's house in Zangara, a hamlet in South Waziristan, hooked up to an intravenous drip for his kidney illness, and tended to by his wife and a doctor. Without warning, a flurry of Hellfire missiles flashed from the night sky, killing Mehsud, his wife, the medic, his parents-in-law and seven others.

Two months later the Pakistani Army followed up with a ground assault on Mehsud's South Waziristan stronghold; three weeks into the operation I flew to the front line with a group of journalists, where we found evidence that suggested Waziristan had become the headquarters of global jihad. It was an area of scrub-covered hills and deserted houses. The air boomed and the ground shuddered as soldiers lobbed artillery shells into the distance; Cobra helicopter gunships swarmed overhead, their guns tilted menacingly. A two-star general clutching a bamboo cane led the way to a hilltop, from where smoke could be seen rising from a neighbouring village. 'The miscreants are sitting over there,' he said. Further along, in the debris of a bomb-shattered house, the soldiers had laid out the possessions of fleeing jihadis on a table – weapons, smashed computers and a stack of passports. One of them, showing a dour-looking German with curly hair, identified its holder as Said Bahaji, a member of the team that facilitated the September 2001 attacks.

By September 2010, the drones touched a blood-soaked crescendo: twenty-two strikes in thirty days that killed as many as 157 people – the deadliest period yet. The Obama administration, which boasts that drones have killed half the al-Qaeda leadership, has warmly embraced them. Predators have been supplanted by larger Reaper drones, which fly faster and higher; their arsenal has been expanded to include sinister-sounding 'thermobaric' warheads,

195

with crushing pressure waves that, the spies claim, can penetrate the deepest bunkers and caves. US officials brush aside questions about legality – a UN expert has warned of 'PlayStation Warfare' syndrome – while the president cracks questionable 'drone jokes' at dinners for journalists. As the CIA director Leon Panetta put it, the drones are 'the only game in town'.

The view from Pakistan is very different. TV talk shows simmer with righteous condemnation while nationalist politicians, such as the former cricketer Imran Khan, organize street rallies. But the debate is highly confused. Innocents have certainly died as a result of the strikes, although accurate figures are impossible to ascertain due to lack of access to bomb sites. Meanwhile, Pakistan's leaders, who publicly fulminate against the strikes yet privately support them, have deliberately clouded the furore over sovereignty. According to the WikiLeaks diplomatic cables, Yousaf Raza Gilani, the prime minister, told a US diplomat that he didn't 'care if they do it as long as they get the right people. We'll protest in the National Assembly and then ignore it.' The army chief, General Ashfaq Kayani, is engaged in similar dissembling, other cables show.

The Americans are conflicted too. Some worry the drones are mutating from a good tactic into a poor strategy – one that could ultimately create as many militants as it kills. Faisal Shahzad, the thirty-year-old Pakistani who tried to explode his car in New York's Times Square, said the plot was payback for the drones swarming over his homeland. 'They don't see children, they don't see anybody. They kill women, children, they kill everybody,' he told a judge in May 2010. Before leaving Pakistan, the former US ambassador to Islamabad, Anne Patterson, warned her superiors that drones were unlikely to purge al-Qaeda from the tribal belt, and ran the greater risk of 'destabilizing the Pakistani state, alienating both the civilian government and military leadership and provoking a broader governance crisis without finally achieving the goal'.

And by the end of 2010 the hovering robot hunters had failed to catch the most wanted fugitive of all. The decade-long hunt for

Osama bin Laden, involving thousands of American spies and soldiers, and costing billions of dollars, had fizzled from view. Like the Faqir of Ipi, the elusive Saudi had become the subject of myth and wild speculation. Various reports had him sheltering in China, Iran or Kashmir; dead from kidney failure; or, as one Afghan told me in Kandahar, living under CIA protection in the White House basement. 'If the Americans can find a mountain goat from a satellite,' he insisted, 'then it's the only thing that makes sense.' In Washington, though, bin Laden had become an embarrassment, seldom mentioned by politicians who disliked having to explain the failure to capture him; some spies called him 'Elvis', for the flood of false reported sightings.

So where was he? The smart money pointed to the tribal belt. In March of 2010, Panetta, the CIA director, told a reporter that his spies hadn't had a good lead in seven years. Asked to hazard a guess, he pointed to the colour-coded map of the FATA on his office wall. Bin Laden and al-Zawahiri were, he said, most likely to be 'either in the northern tribal areas or in North Waziristan'.

Soon, Panetta would prove himself wrong.

Outside powers have always favoured force as a means of doing business in the tribal belt. Just over a century ago, shortly after British troops had quelled an extensive uprising in the mountains of north-western India, the viceroy, Lord Curzon, offered his solution to the great conundrum. 'Not until the military steamroller has passed over the country from end to end will there be peace,' he concluded. Yet, as every campaign since has demonstrated, violence seldom works, at least not for long. Today, Pakistan's military is bogged down in conflicts in all seven of the agencies. And the drones, for all their futuristic killing prowess, feel like the latest expedient of an impatient power – more effective, certainly, than the crude biplane bombers of Charles Burman's war, but with little guarantee that they will ultimately be more successful.

There's a temptation to see this as an old cycle, looping endlessly.

197

But if history repeats itself, it does so imperfectly. Over the years, comparisons have been drawn between bin Laden and the Faqir of Ipi. There were striking similarities – both guerrilla jihadis hunkered (or thought to be hunkered) in caves, hunted by the latest Western warplanes and surrounded by fanatical followers. Some even nicknamed bin Laden the 'Scarlet Pimpernel of Waziristan'. But, as events have shown, such comparisons can be misleading. In the end, bin Laden did not die in the caves of Waziristan, but in a three-storey suburban house in the garrison town of Abbottabad, surprised by American soldiers who leaped from a helicopter to shoot him in the head. And, ultimately, the differences between the two men were more instructive.

The faqir was a Pashtun warrior, dedicated to the centuries-old pursuit of autonomy and defending his mountain redoubt, oblivious to the outside world. Islam was his creed but not the driving force. Bin Laden, on the other hand, was a megalomaniac of global ambition – the creation of a pan-Islamic caliphate and the destruction of America. And the dark forces he harnessed drew from the tumultuous changes of the past thirty years in tribal society: the corruption and neglect of the Pakistani state and the irresponsible state promotion of a cancerous ideology that conflates religious faith with violence. The 'great game', as the British once called it, has rarely been so complicated.

Bin Laden's demise had little immediate impact on the tribal belt. The drones resumed work four days after the Abbottabad raid, with three strikes in quick succession; then came the gruesome response. A pair of Taliban suicide bombers on motorbikes struck at the gates of a Frontier Constabulary training centre north of Peshawar, killing over a hundred young Pashtun recruits as they boarded buses to return home. Hours later I found myself standing amid the wreckage. Soldiers towed away charred minibuses crushed by the explosion; shopkeepers swept debris from buildings pocked with a thousand ballbearings; and I did my best to avoid stepping in the ubiquitous pools of sticky blood. ■

Resistance Movements Through History

Evacuations frequently prioritize the rescue of larger animals;
smaller zoo mammals are rumoured to be left behind in fires.

Wailing and trapped, the way we came is the way we will go.
Lichen form tufts to resist the pressure of arctic snow

but no finger can stop the groundwater and its relentless swell,
mole rats gasping upwards for air, the gag of liquid in lung.

Platoons of ants interlock legs to form floating balls
of panicked bodies. The child who sees another child fall, cries.

But who will look after the nocturnal bumblebee bat,
when firemen tap at his glass and move on, thinking no one home?

I wonder each day who will save me, and if it's a question
for a deity or city government. 'Dear councilperson,' I begin.

'Upholstered chairs seem luxurious, but lay traps for the health.'
Strategies can be improved by studying the appetites of every beast:

lichen comprise the bulk of the caribou diet. Stooping, they sniff it
hidden under snow and gouge out craters with a sharp front hoof.

The way of the world is attack by surprise: the bear hovers
behind the hive, the next-door neighbours are named as spies.

A cocooned moth tugs open a tiny hole. Sometimes I mix up fear
with hissed instructions. As another silk thread snaps, whispers rise.

THEATRE

LAIKAS I

Kathryn Kuitenbrouwer

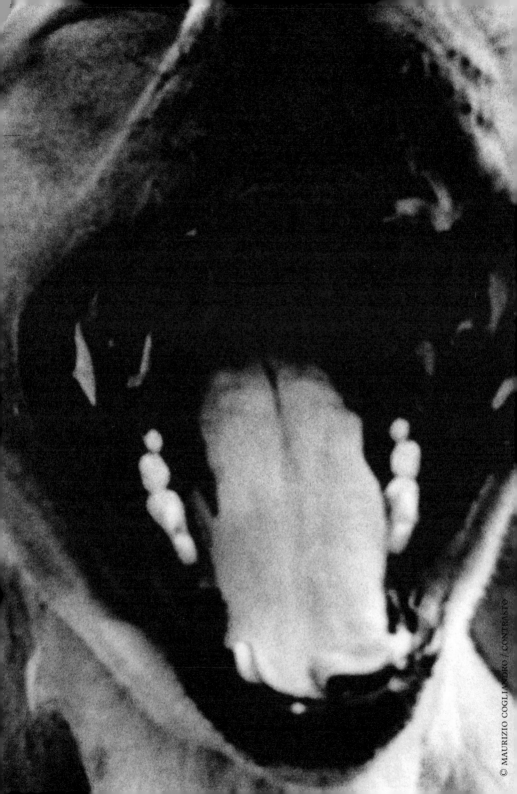

'Trevor?' Hilary called through the mail slot, having pushed open its tarnished little door. When he opened up to let her in there were so many strays jostling that he didn't see her crouched there among them at first. But he knew it was her by her voice and the crazy magnetic pull on his heartstrings. The dogs continued to lay claim until she whistled and growled, 'Laikas, sit!' Then they all lowered, panting, some cocking their heads, some not.

Laika was the Russian dog that went up in a space rocket and Hilary had named the pack collectively in memoriam. To some of them she had given individual names but as a group they were always Laikas. Now, Monday, at 7.15 a.m., seventeen strays stared at Trevor. And there was Hilary in sweet profile.

'Smoke?' Trevor handed her the thin cigar he had already lit.

'I was in the neighbourhood,' she said, smiling, turning her face to him.

In fact, Trevor had texted, called and finally begged her to stop by. He was slumming at this present address on Fairview. He'd moved out of home to share an apartment with three delinquent acquaintances, something his wealthy parents lauded as potentially character-building. But because the room-mates were usually out and/or stoned, Trevor was often lonely. Plus, he was experiencing lovesickness. Now that Hilary had finally arrived, he knew the jealous dog pack would give them an hour – maybe – and then she'd be laughing at his fabulous attempts to keep her there.

'I don't know why you tolerate them,' he said. Hilary had scars where she'd been bitten and an oozing wound that she wouldn't let Trevor tend. 'Those dogs are feral, Hilary!' They were tucked to the hips under an old red velvet curtain on the sofa. An ashtray he'd liberated from his parents' place was nestled into the concave of his belly.

'I don't tolerate them,' she argued. The ashtray, Hilary saw, was one of those Greek black-figure-vase replicas. She leaned over and twisted her cigarette softly on Orpheus's leg, watched his skin peel off. 'I have no idea about them, at all,' she said. 'They like me. They lick and nip. It's just *play* that goes too far.'

Trevor could hear the dogs outside, whimpering, beckoning. He flexed his pectoral muscles tight and tried to look naturally hot. He pouted elegantly, desperately. He proffered more Cuban cigarillos. He exhaled earthen smoke into her ears, her mouth, whatever opening he could think of.

When he went too far, Hilary giggled and pushed his face away from down there. Then, getting serious, she said, 'In the old stories there is always a door through which the hero must never pass.' She was thinking specifically about Orpheus leading Eurydice out of Hades, and how he had looked back, and lost her forever.

'Death's door?'

'It's a portal to this truly marvellous place.'

She drew on the cigarillo so deeply it almost disappeared, then jabbed the stub in a strange random way into the air. He tried to make sense of the action but couldn't – she was sometimes so mysterious to him, he felt undone.

'Sometimes,' she continued, 'it can be a real door, or a closet, or just an abstraction – you know, the threshold of maturity. It can be a willingness to acknowledge and live with your fears. Yeah?'

He mulled over what she might mean by threshold. He had thought they were talking about her body. Well, he had been talking about her body. God, it sounded as if the dogs were mauling the porch screen. A howling set up in response to a siren off in the Junction. *Threshold of maturity*, he thought, and grabbed Hilary's ankle; he noticed a long scratch, like on torn nylons, only raw, fresh skin.

'Damn dogs,' he moaned. 'They'll eat you one of these days.'

'It's something stupid *I* did,' she said, holding his ashtray in one hand now. She could see he wouldn't dare ask what stupid thing she might have done.

The dogs began jumping on to the windowsill, drooling on and worrying the glass pane.

'I have to go,' she said. 'I have a new job.'

'Job?'

'Well, I have to pay for school somehow.'

'But Hilary – '

He stood in the doorway – damned threshold – while she left. The dogs were whirling outside, anticipating her. They worried and nibbled one another's ears, and showed their gums in undeniable grins. Trevor counted them as they followed her receding sway. There were now twenty-nine strays.

She walked away from Trevor's place along Fairview Avenue, and into the Sunny Cafe for some sour keys. Sucking, then chewing the candy, she headed down to the subway at High Park. The dogs trailed politely behind.

N o pets below in peak hours,' said the ticket guy. Hilary could hear 'Bohemian Rhapsody' seeping out of his earbuds and felt herself moved by the arguably manipulative orchestration.

'They're not mine.' She smiled at the guy and walked through the turnstile. 'And they certainly aren't pets.'

A few of the dogs sat, then lay down, possibly to await her return, but the rest went under the bars, or over (the dog she called Snot took pride in her immense leap), and Hilary pretended like she didn't know, or see, or even sense them. 'Bohemian Rhapsody' was looping in her mind now, the best part of the song.

The ticket guy whimpered, 'Hey,' but what could he do, and did he get paid well enough for this shit? A queue of folks wanting tokens and passes and information was forming, so he finally gestured something between goodbye and whatever, and hoped for the sake of his job that no one was videotaping him.

Chick had awesome babe swagger, he thought. His eyes followed her until she turned the corner. He would like a chick so hot the dogs followed her ass down the subway and . . . where? Heading east. Heading downtown. 'Hey, scram,' he said to the strays that had stayed behind. 'Get outta here. Out!'

He looked up and saw the terrorist dude who ran the concession stand staring right the fuck at him, and barked, 'Jesus!' as he realized he would have to leave his booth – which he did – in order to lunge at the dogs until they took the hint and skulked back up the escalator.

The car was pretty full but there were seats, so Hilary sat down, the dogs finding space among the legs and backpacks of commuters, one leaping up and nestling in between two men, both of whom appeared to be examining something invisible in the mid-distance. Perhaps they did not notice the basset hound sprawled out there.

During the difficult economic years, things had gone from merely bad to an almost clichéd worse. Thousands of dogs had lost their owners and many people were appalled by the feral packs. Still, sympathetic media *had* reported dogs with routes – clever dogs who maximized their panhandling, who had figured out where to find kind humans, places to crash on cold nights. These reports had resulted in a sort of rebranding of the animals, making the dogs seem intelligent in ways humans could relate to. There were now stray-dog activists.

Hilary was not one of them.

She was heading to her new job – a half-time position at a downtown recreational facility. Snot and Mangy were taking turns licking her wound. When she noticed, she leaned over, whispered, 'That's enough, you two.'

Once out of the subway, she decided she would walk down Dovercourt. The dogs kept pace, only stopping here and there to nuzzle the pavement or urinate on spindly trees they passed. At Dewson, she halted and had them sit and stay, then headed in for day one.

The front desk had no knowledge of a new hire. Hilary put more weight on one leg and raised her eyebrows. 'I dunno,' she said. 'Today is supposed to be my first day. A guy named Danny hired me last week. To wipe down machines.'

'Oh, yeah. I overheard something, now you mention it. Hi, I'm Judy,' Judy said, extending her hand to shake. Judy pulled her hair

GRANTA 116: TEN YEARS LATER

YOUR PASSPORT TO THE BEST STORIES FROM AROUND THE WORLD

Have *Granta* delivered to your door four times a year and save up to 42% on the cover price.

'PROVIDES ENOUGH TO SATISFY THE MOST RABID APPETITE FOR GOOD WRITING AND HARD THINKING' – *WASHINGTON POST*

USA
$45.99

CANADA
$57.99

LATIN AMERICA
$65.99

Subscribe now by completing the form overleaf, visiting **granta.com** or calling toll-free 1-866-438-6150 (quoting ref: US116)

GRANTA
THE MAGAZINE OF NEW WRITING

SUBSCRIPTION FORM FOR USA, CANADA AND LATIN AMERICA

Yes, I would like to take out a subscription to *Granta*.

GUARANTEE: If I am ever dissatisfied with my *Granta* subscription, I will simply notify you, and you will send me a complete refund or credit my credit card, as applicable, for all un-mailed issues.

YOUR DETAILS

MR / MISS / MRS / DR ....

NAME ....

ADDRESS ....

CITY .... STATE ....

ZIP CODE .... COUNTRY ....

EMAIL ....

(Only provide your email if you are happy for Granta to communicate with you this way)

☐ Please check this box if you do not wish to receive special offers from *Granta*

☐ Please check this box if you do not wish to receive offers from organizations selected by *Granta*

YOUR PAYMENT DETAILS

1 year subscription: ☐ USA: $45.99 ☐ Canada: $57.99 ☐ Latin America: $65.99

3 year subscription: ☐ USA: $112.50 ☐ Canada: $148.50 ☐ Latin America: $172.50

Enclosed is my check for $_____ made payable to *Granta*.

Please charge my: ☐ Visa ☐ Mastercard ☐ Amex

Card No. ☐☐☐☐☐☐☐☐☐☐☐☐☐☐☐☐

Exp. ☐☐☐☐

Security Code ☐☐☐

SIGNATURE .... DATE ....

Please mail this order form with your payment instructions to:

Granta Publications
PO Box 359
Congers NY 10920-0359

Or call toll free 1-866-438-6150
Or visit GRANTA.COM for details

Source code: BUS116PM

back and Hilary saw she had a tattoo behind her ear. It was one of those tats done with white ink so they look like scar tissue build-up.

'Is that a mongoose?'

'No. But that's funny. I've heard it looks like one from a few people.'

'What is it?'

'It's actually the word "strife" shaped like a fish. Do you like it? It's my favourite word.'

'Yeah, it's awesome.'

'Mongeese are cool, too,' Judy said. 'I buzzed for Danny. He should be a minute.'

Hilary rolled *mongeese* around all day after that. The job was a cinch. She only had to wipe down machines with a spray bottle and cloth, recalibrate resistance trainers, replace the weights in the right order and smile at people. Twice that day she cleaned out the ladies' toilets and checked the shower, steam and whirlpool area, and reported back to the main janitor. Easy minimum wage plus she got a free membership, so after work, she used the facility to clean herself up. She smiled and waved at Judy on the way out the door, 5.30 sharp, and Judy waved back. 'Hey,' Judy called, 'how'd it go?' Hilary gave her the thumbs up.

The dogs were waiting in different places along the route and had attracted more strays. It was hard to count them as they jockeyed for position, smelling her crotch, jumping on one another. Eventually Hilary gave up. Back to the subway, through to High Park, Hilary detoured to Sunny Cafe for a slice of pizza and another sour key or two. She loved the way the candy chemical gave over to sweet just too late, so that right when her mouth puckered, it began to soften.

Trevor called just as she got inside her apartment. She had a hard time concentrating with the dogs anxious in the small space, vying for her attention. 'No,' she said, into the phone, then 'Hi, yeah!' then 'No, I don't think so,' and 'Well, I'm really sorry.' Snot had her paws on Hilary's feet and was stretching, bum up, tail wagging wildly. Mangy and Perk were into the garbage already. Hilary needed to get better at sealing that. 'OK, but don't expect conversation,' she was saying. 'I'm a working girl now.'

By the time he got there she was asleep; the dogs tumbled in and around her, using her face and neck and legs as pillows. Trevor had a key. Seven dogs came in with him, having scented Hilary out from High Park once dusk reminded their stomachs of her.

She was a curl of pink, a half-moon face partially obstructed by the scruff of a labradoodle. Trevor gasped. He'd never seen anything as breathtakingly beautiful. It reminded him of those baby portraits with the newborn in a flower or a bunny suit, and he wanted to cry or, alternatively, make love.

He got down on all fours and pushed the dogs out of the way until he was snuggled in with her. He tried to wake her with a few loud sighs but she wouldn't move. 'Honey?' he said, right into her ear. 'Honey? Can I?' Already he had his hand rotating around her nipple but as he pleaded with her to wake up, he slid his fingers down her tracksuit pants and into that damn portal.

'Let me ravage you in your sleep, baby.'

He took the faint grimace that crept on her face, and the tiniest shift towards him in body language, to mean yes. Snot and Perk looked on while he pulled her pants down, gently turned and mounted her.

'Fuck off,' he muttered guiltily, but the dogs only edged in closer and looked up at him. It turned out OK, though, because Hilary woke up and got into it. He was exonerated! It was the first time they'd done it all the way since this dog manifestation started the week before and Trevor had been increasingly jealous and temperamental about it – not at all philosophical as she'd suggested he be.

Now he was actually enjoying the proximity of the pack, their hot breath around him, the encroachment, the *wildness* of it. A pugbeagle licked their toes metronomically through the entire lovemaking. Trevor had never been to an orgy and wondered if this counted.

'Hilary?'

'So tired –'

'It's coming up to the end of the month.'

'Trevor, can this not wait?'

'I've been thinking of moving in, actually.'

'What?'

'Yeah, well, I'm pretty much here all the time, anyway.'

D ay two went reasonably well. The TTC guy managed to stop most of the dogs from entering the system. But then they refused to leave the main area, and hounded the Sikh who sold chips and newspapers, essentially ruining his morning, until he finally grabbed a Mr Big, tore the wrapper down, waved it out at the pack and then turned and ran screaming up the escalator, the dogs giving chase.

'Hey, dude,' said the ticket guy when the Sikh returned, and then when he got no response, 'Dude! Osama!'

The seller only shook his head in disbelief, or mock disbelief, and went on looking at the floor of his booth, trying to catch breath.

'Dude. Osama! Yo!'

That finally elicited a glare.

'What? Wha'd I do?' The ticket guy looked over to make sure his booth was locked. He'd recently bought a Kevlar vest and was wearing it now. Dude had been freaking him out since he'd won the concession. Dude could be from, like, anywhere. No one could expect to feel safe any more. 'Why don't you never talk? For Christ sakes. Dude never talks to no one.'

'I talk.'

'You never talk.'

'I am talking with you right this second. And why do you call me Osama? My name is Yusef. Call me Yusef.'

'It's no big deal, dude.'

'Yusef! It's a deal. No big deal. My name is Yusef.'

'It's friggin' slang.' People had become too soft-skinned. 'It's a joke. You don't have humour where you come from?'

'Yusef!' And here Yusef raised his right arm high above his head and pointed to the roof of his kiosk. He did not know the word slang.

'I come from Brampton.' He added, 'We have humour.'

'Yusef,' the ticket guy said. Jesus, with all the conversation and the Kevlar, he had started sweating.

'Exactly.'

'Thanks for getting rid of those dogs.'

'You're welcome. Now shut up.'

'Hey, pal!' He really wanted to make this good. He unlocked the booth and waddled out to find Yusef's line of vision. 'Yusef,' he said, then smiled. 'I am Mike. You can call me Mike.' Yusef nodded and Mike waddled back towards the booth. He didn't get paid for this, so he muttered, 'I don't get paid for this, Yusef. Maybe you do, but I don't.' Then he turned back, fumbled in his trouser pocket for change, asked for and received a Coke and a Kit Kat. 'Here,' Mike said, 'keep the change.' Which he thought was hilarious, since he was actually short a couple of pennies.

There were thirty-five dogs by day's end and Hilary, exhausted, found them sitting alert in the small park opposite the station at High Park. There was a new cur lounging on the park bench and another huge emaciated dog off behind the main grouping. It was tawny and scraggly and fierce – *cold*-looking. Wow, she thought, and then: Kinda wolfish, though she'd never seen a wolf. But then she brushed the thought out of her mind, since it made no sense. Anyway, the new dog or whatever it was didn't bother following her home when the rest did.

The next day, after work, Mike called out, 'Hey, lady,' as she pushed through the turnstile. 'Hey, dog-lady. I see that wolf down here again and I'm calling the cops.' She didn't look his way at all, which left him with something to think about, but she *had* heard, he was pretty sure.

Hilary hadn't wanted to acknowledge A: herself as dog-lady; B: any problems re wolves or whatever; C: Mike, period.

There were three 'big dogs' in the pack when she got out the door.

'Well, holy fuck,' she whispered.

She could hardly hear above their clamour but she was pretty freaked about the pack coming in now there were these creatures amid them, so she bolted them outside the door and called Trevor.

'Probably not wolves, honey.'

'The TTC guy thinks they are.'

'Fat Mike? He grew up in Scarborough. He wouldn't know a wolf from a – Hey, I bet that's what you are dealing with.'

'Dealing with?'

'Yeah, Irish wolfhounds or else some mixture.'

'Really?'

'Yeah. Totally. Tawny? Wiry hair? Big?'

'Yeah!'

'Totally wolfhounds.'

Hilary unbolted the door and let the dogs stream in. They appreciated this and let her know it by snuffling her and by smiling their lips back, showing their teeth without growling. This always made her laugh and it did now. These wolfhounds were the noblest dogs she had ever seen. They hung back and circled one another, yipped quietly, then sat on their haunches and watched the other dogs hump each other and rise up nipping and ear-chewing in gorgeous faux battles.

Every once in a while, for fairness, Hilary pulled the playing dogs apart and made them sit, and let other small groups of dogs clash together in these strange, seemingly ritualistic fights that she thought she might never tire of watching. Play-fighting dogs *were* beautiful. Even the wolfhounds seemed to be enjoying the arena.

But then, when she made space for two miniature schnauzers to play, things went awry. She wasn't aware of the shift but in retrospect she would allow that there had been a stiffening in the posture of some of the dogs on the group periphery. Initially the schnauzers circled and turned, almost dancing, noses to asses, one licking, the other avoiding by curling its butt toward the ground and twirling away. And then, here, what she loved to watch, they rose on their hind legs and batted with front paws and teeth, swiped at one another. Oh, such verve and joy.

'Nice one!' Hilary clapped. 'Yes! Clever!'

They looked like puppets of dogs to her, and she laughed at this thought, and while she was laughing, very suddenly, the Irish wolfhounds pounced upon the schnauzers, seizing them and flinging them to and fro, letting them free only to bite through their small backs. She could do nothing.

The schnauzers were shrieking. And then not shrieking.

The energy in the apartment was suddenly so clenched down that there was nothing to hear but the silky manoeuvring of the wolfhounds, and when it was over, such a baying and a yipping, as they hunkered and called out to the other dogs, warning of *their* territory and *their* kill, the meal they then set to licking and tearing apart.

Hilary was paralysed with fear.

And the blood, so quiet in its redistribution, splashed out across the kitchen, so that Hilary pressed up against the fridge in the far corner, suddenly shocked back to herself, and screamed.

'Ah, jeez.' It was Trevor, who had come in too late to do anything. 'Coyotes.'

Coyotes had had a presence in High Park for some time. The animal services entry, found through the obvious search engine, though dated, read:

> Coyotes are extremely intelligent and they adapt and learn very quickly. Every encounter that isn't scary may encourage the coyote to get closer next time. Ideally, park users would actively scare a coyote away at every sighting (suggestions on how to do this are attached).

The attached PDF pamphlet gave helpful hints like being mean, large, loud, etc. It also had directions for a coyote shaker, which Hilary promptly made by recycling an aluminium diced-tomatoes can and filling it with coins. The pennies made a loud but not unpleasant susurrus when she shook the shaker. The can didn't have much of an effect on the coyotes, though. They just looked at her and seemed, in between yips, to snicker.

There were more and more each day. So, she took to dropping meat at the small park so they'd stay behind, which worked, but only sort of; it caused a lot of jealousy and consternation among the main pack of strays, and once they'd done ripping apart the meat and devouring it, the coyotes followed her scent back to the apartment anyway. Every dog in the city seemed to know how to intimidate or charm someone into opening the doors of buildings, and likewise, the coyotes would make their way up and bay and scratch at Hilary's sixth-floor apartment door. But she wouldn't let them in the apartment any more.

They'd burned their bridge on that account.

Judy locked eyes with Danny until he finally said, 'What?'
'Don't you think she's the tiniest bit weird?'
'She's a hard worker.'
In strained baritone, Judy said, 'When asked by the police whether he had ever seen any unusual behaviour from the suspect, her boss, Daniel Grainger, declared, "She's a hard worker."'
'So what? She is.'
'Have you noticed the fur smell?'

On the morning of day six, there were three mismatched puppies prodding at Snot's belly when Hilary and Trevor woke up. Trevor gleefully hugged Hilary and they stood there ogling the creatures so long that Hilary had to skip breakfast. While she showered, Trevor packed her a tuna fish wrap and a pickle. It was *his* favourite lunch.

'Nature is wondrous,' he exclaimed. 'Oh my God, look at how cute they are.' Snot looked so loving, and no one would deny the puppies were – well, anyone's heart would be shattered at the sight.

Hilary made her eyes big and smiled. 'Yeah!' Then, 'I better get going or I'll be late.' She had to press herself to the wall and edge through the door to keep the coyotes out. Two of them had managed to get past the building security and there were a few – five, actually – just outside the main door. An elderly woman with a walker was coming up the street scolding them.

'In my day,' she said, 'there weren't all these animals.'

'Shoo,' said Hilary, and scattered them to let the woman by.

'They're so BOLD!' said the woman.

Hilary thought about the schnauzers and nodded.

Judy was sick with a head cold so Danny spent ten minutes teaching Hilary the front desk and then left her to it. The job involved making people membership cards and taking their money and saying, 'Of course,' as politely as a person can that many times a day. As in, 'Of course, I'll call the manager for you.' Or, 'Of course, you are right. Let me take your phone number and I'll have someone get back to you.'

And this wouldn't have been brain surgery if she hadn't looked through the front windows mid-afternoon to see the pack pressing up to the glass, licking it, pawing it, jumping upon or curling around one another so that it was difficult for patrons to get their frumpy bodies in on time for yoga chant class.

'There are these dogs trying to get into the foyer.'

One woman shrieked; it turned out she was 'pathologically afraid of canines'. Hilary wondered if that pathology was terminal, but did not ask. She was finding herself increasingly anxious with all the dog attention. Why her? It felt metaphoric but she couldn't fathom of what.

At 3.35, Trevor showed up sweaty and half naked from jogging over, and pranced in showing off his abs. He was wearing suspenders – over nothing.

'*Scaramouche!*' He struck a Freddie Mercury pose, lunging his hips out exactly right.

'All right, then. Wow.'

'What? You've been humming it all week.'

'I have?'

'*Oh, Oh, Oh, Oh!*' he sang.

'Weird.' She shook her head, in a way Trevor interpreted as *you awesome thing*, and then she said, 'How are the pups?'

'The whole pack is taking care of them.' Trevor looked back and acknowledged the dogs outside the window and added, 'Well, except for those ones. The ones who stayed when I opened the door to leave are really great parents. I mean truly awesome.'

'And these guys?'

When they got back to the apartment, the door was ajar and one of the puppies was – well – no longer whole. Several of the dogs were still whimpering. Trevor let out a shrill 'Nooo!' Then, 'How the hell did the door get opened, for Christ's sake?'

'You must have accidentally left it open.'

'No,' Trevor said. 'No fucking way was it left open.'

'Are you sure?'

'I'm getting a goddamned gun. No one should be coming into the apartment like that.'

'You think someone did this?'

'I mean those animals did this.'

Hilary cleaned the mess up and Trevor couldn't even help, he was so angry. He just sat up on the kitchen counter and lit a smoke and shook his head, trying with his foot to keep Snot from licking the blood off the rug. 'Oh, man! Oh, MAN!' Eventually he got down and went to Hilary's computer and typed 'Guns' and 'Toronto' and came up with Al Flaherty's Outdoor Store, the last remaining gun shop in the city, and said, 'Honey, I'm going for a walk.'

'Should I come?'

'Sure you can.'

'Forget it, I'm too tired from all this,' meaning the coyotes, the dead puppy, and all the YMCA front-desk generosity. But mostly it was the wanton cruelty that had made her tired.

While Trevor was gone she wondered whether she could care, really care, for a guy who had a gun, and she decided that any guy who was so infantile as to think that a gun would solve any of the world's problems was not the kind of guy she would be able to see herself with long-term. But when he arrived some hours later, and woke her up by turning the lights on and standing Rambo-style with the wooden-handled, single-shot BB rifle, she saw him in a new light. He looked like the pissed-off cowboy of her dreams, and where before he had seemed a little effete and fey, now he seemed effete and fey in a sexy way. And Hilary thought, maybe.

They went outside the apartment building and Trevor levelled the gun toward the pack of coyotes circling an abandoned shopping cart and squinted to line up the sites, then pulled the trigger and screamed so loud a few lights went on and they had to make a run for it. His elbow was bleeding and, from the look of it, the BB had ricocheted off the shopping cart right back at him. They turned in time to see the coyotes scatter into the shadows. It was as if they were phantoms, as if they never existed except in the imaginations of Hilary and Trevor. But the elbow wound was real.

Trevor later joked, 'You should have seen the other guy.'

On day seven, Yusef arrived early at his concession stand to have some quiet time before the morning rush. The subway was usually dead until around 6.30 and so he could sit and think and read the newspaper and eat the lunch his wife had packed for him before she went to bed. Often, eating the dhal and chapatti or egg salad sandwich was the first thing he did in the morning, right after he ate his breakfast.

Now, Yusef looked up and saw Mike on the other side also looking up, and between them were many, many, bristling, huge and possibly starving coyotes.

'What the fuck?' Mike was thinking how the Kevlar wouldn't do dick in this situation and then regretted thinking dick.

'I'm dialling 911,' replied Yusef.

'Don't you carry a piece?'
'What's a piece?'
'A gun, yahoo.'
'Yahoo? My name is–'
'–Yusef.'
'Why would I carry a gun?'
'I thought all you guys carried weapons.'
'Shopkeepers?' Yusef felt the sandwich pressing up against his oesophagus, and regretted his indulgence. 'It's illegal,' he managed. 'Jesus wept,' said Mike.

The cops and the fire department showed up and made such an unholy racket running down the stairs that the animals jumped the turnstile and hid underground. The authorities shut the system down for two hours while they pretended to find and evacuate them. Fact: they never saw one coyote. This delay was especially annoying to Hilary who was one hour and twenty-six minutes late for work. Note: through the entire event Mike had 'Bohemian Rhapsody' wailing into his left ear. He needed to hear the lyric in looping glory, so he'd put the song on continual repeat. How could one song carry so much truth?

When the cops and the press had finally dispersed, Mike looked over at Yusef, and said, 'Sheesh! Yusef!'

'I know,' said Yusef. 'We made the news.'

It was funny what let you really know a person, Mike thought. It was weird and uncanny and funny. He crossed the floor to give props to Yusef.

'Buddy!'

'Yusef,' Yusef reminded him again.

'Oh, yeah!' Mike hadn't really smiled – really truly smiled – in years, and now he *beamed*.

Judy raised her eyebrows when Hilary recounted the subway debacle, but Danny took it in his stride. Hilary got busy wiping down the ellipticals. If she looked closely some of them seemed to have flakes of skin on them, so she tried not to look closely. As soon as she had the opportunity, she sidled into the change room, sat herself down where she wouldn't have to witness the parade of denuded privates, took out her device, texted: *Alleged coyotes in TTC.*

Reply: *OMG.*

Alleged! Trevor put his cellphone down and danced around with the dogs. He loved that woman. Tonight, he thought, tonight would be the night.

'No pets,' said Mike. He had pushed the booth open and was coming out to stop Hilary. 'You hear me? I don't wanna tell you this again. I don't wanna have to call the police again. Did you read the newspaper? We covered for you here. Me and Yusef over there – we covered for you.'

There were scores of dogs following Hilary from Dovercourt station, and these were the ones who had managed to break through the security at that end. The rest were probably on their way to her apartment door or waiting in the park. There were no coyotes as far as she could tell but if she was honest with herself there had been shadows and rank odours – wild rancid smells she could not account for. She stopped for Mike and asserted, 'They aren't mine. I'm telling you.'

'They come with you. They go with you. I've seen you feed them. I've seen them lick you. They're yours. And they can't come down any more.' Mike looked over at Yusef in the hope of getting some basic support and was pissed to see Yusef look away. 'Yo, Yusef!' he said. 'Support!' and then Yusef lifted his eyes and damned if he didn't look scared before he dropped them again.

'They aren't mine,' said Hilary. 'I don't even own a leash. These are city dogs. I can't help it if they follow me. I can't do anything about anything.' And Hilary pushed past Mike.

Mike held on to the sleeve of her jacket. 'Admit you don't like this,' he said.

'I have no opinion whatever.' Hilary pursed her lips, glared. 'Call the city. Or the police.'

'Yeah, we've seen how well that works.'

'Open your eyes,' she quipped, and Mike thought he recognized something and shut up. She added, 'Let me go.'

Mike gasped. Queen, he thought. No way. He let go of the fabric of her jacket, his eyes widened and he tilted his head like a dog for a bone. 'Oh,' he said. 'Oh!'

Hilary smiled, sang a few bars of the 'Scaramouche' section until Mike nodded. She got him. Really got him. Cool. Nobody had ever got him.

Trevor led Hilary down Annette, through Baby Point – the swank houses had old money ivying around them – and then down an old rotten stairwell to the thin green belt along the Humber River. It smelled like mould and earth down there, and fish. The dogs followed, as did car horns honking, for the animals did not wait for lights.

'I thought you meant a walk in High Park.'

'The dogs know it so well, I thought I'd bring you all here.'

The sun was pressing the horizon when Trevor finally stopped in a treed dip in the landscape, the dogs edging them, their coats aflame with sunset and Hilary's face turned up wondering.

'You're stopping.'

He was standing very close to her, the dogs getting jealous, nuzzling her legs and pushing the two of them apart as well as they could. Mangy jumped up and tore a superficial line down Hilary's cheek. 'Down, Mangy. Laikas, sit!'

Then, briefly, except for the monkey jabber of squirrels, it was as quiet as it ever got in an urban park.

Trevor put something into her hand, too shy to even look at her, and when she saw it was a box – that famous Birk's blue and velveteen that every girl but Hilary knew to yearn for and to covet – she opened it, and there nestled in a little pink velvet cleave was the prettiest ring she had ever seen.

'Trevor?'

'Gosh,' he said. 'Gosh.' From now on, it would be this: Hilary, the dogs and him. He was so nervous! Trevor flung his arms up, in celebration, and asked, 'What do you say?' He could hear the soft moaning of the coyotes, a kind of gorgeous, primal soundtrack to this moment.

She had the ring on and was marvelling at the way the diamonds glittered in the waning light. 'I say thank you!'

His smile had dwindled; he'd never felt more serious. He said, 'But will you marry me?'

'What?'

He raised his eyebrows, nodded. They would later walk out of this park, and either way, he thought, he would not look back. It was a promise he made to himself. Either way, she was his girl and he would not look back. So beautiful, she was; he only had to look at her . . .

Hilary hadn't thought about marriage before. She had neither considered what a wonderful covenant it might be, nor what an immense commitment and responsibility. She felt something dark and sober pressing in on her, and then she looked to the dully glinting precious stones encircling her finger. The sun was a smear of matte orange on the horizon, and the night air began to chill her to the bone.

The dogs, tired, or perhaps sensing her concern emptying out into the waning light, had all sat or lain down and were arranged around her, sentinels, panting, watching. From time to time they whined, or turned their heads toward the coyotes just outside the sight lines, lurking in shadows, their yips now accelerating toward strangled, deformed howls. Hilary looked around and down several times, the ring, the dogs, the ring, the dogs, and then she bit her bottom lip, looked up at Trevor and said, 'OK, sure, why not?' ∎

THE AMERICAN
AGE, IRAQ

Anthony Shadid

B AGHDAD COLLAGE WELCOME YOU, the sign reads along a street that is ordinary, but only if you live in Baghdad. Nothing really escapes the detritus of death in this wreck of a city. Certainly not the cement barriers along this wayward street, painted yellow and white but more distinguished by the chisel of wear, tear and bombings. The date trees are unharvested, fruit shrivelled by the sun falling into a pyre of overgrown weeds. A dusty black banner mourning two Iraqi soldiers killed 'in the line of duty' stretches along its kerb ploughed with bottles of Tuborg beer, plastic bags – some of them snared in barbed wire – and empty packages of Foster Clark's Corn Flour.

Unlike Beirut or, closer to home, Fallujah, Baghdad was never destroyed by its war. The city here feels more like an eclipsed imperial capital, abandoned, neglected and dominated by the ageing fortifications of its futile defence against the forces that had overwhelmed it. Think of medieval Rome. An acquaintance once described all this refuse of war as *athar,* Arabic for artefacts, and I thought of the word as I drove down the road to Baghdad College, past piles of charred trash, to see a teacher there.

It was a sweltering day. Alaa Hussein welcomed me with coffee and we sat in the high school's dusty Internet room, next to computers that had no Internet. The red trash can was full, even though there were no students during summer to fill it. He squinted his grey eyes, magnified by thick lenses, and delivered a judgement that I have heard often in Baghdad. 'A jungle,' he called it all, wearily looking around. He meant the school and its disorderly decline. But his terminology felt elastic to me, as if something unruly had encroached on what was here long ago.

No more than a footnote in the histories of the civil wars, invasions, defeats and revolutions that have shaped the Middle East, Hussein's school – run for thirty-seven years by New England Jesuits with precise haircuts and names like McCarthy, Connolly, Donohue,

McDermott, McGuinness and O'Connor – once represented
something more. 'The gem of Baghdad,' one of the 143 Jesuits who
taught in its tan-brick citadel told me, with the ardour of someone
who could still smell the jasmine outside his door fifty years ago. 'A
piece of heaven,' recalled Father Solomon Sara, who had studied at
Baghdad College before going on to a seminary in Massachusetts and
returning to teach at his alma mater after graduation. 'For America, it
was something that people could point to that was noble.' Even now,
memories of the school, sepia-tinted as they might be, are seldom
short of superlatives, recalling a simpler age it inhabited that may
be forever lost. 'A special relationship' was the way it was described
by Laith Kubba, a long-time activist and former Iraqi official who
lives in Washington and credits the Jesuit priests with making him a
more devout Muslim. 'Of course, there is no comparison today. Of
course, of course.'

More than eight years after it invaded, the United States has begun
leaving Baghdad and the rest of Iraq. The American military, at least.
This last summer, in a date more symbolic than practical, it reduced
its number of troops to 50,000, a fraction of the 170,000 who once
roamed the country and helped write perhaps the most traumatic
chapter in America's relationship with the Arab world. The rest are
supposed to leave by year's end. 'Our uncles', Iraqis now call the
Americans, a term that suggests both intimacy and bitterness in a
once-occupied country where names like Abu Ghraib and Haditha
have become more idea than geography. Yet the Obama administration
wants civilians to stay, and it has pledged the dawn of a new era in ties
between the two countries. With a suggestion of hope, and maybe
a current of naivety, American officials now speak of soft power –
the stuff of culture, education, trade and so on – that the barrel of a
gun rarely projects. 'Partnership' is the word they like to use. As one
embassy official puts it, 'a strong civilian partnership with a lot of
Americans of a variety of stripes involved in every sector of Iraq'.

Down the undulating street, Baghdad College, filled with the
remnants of American trajectories blunted a generation ago, is a

lesson or perhaps a lament about that ambition. The *athar* of the last real intersection between America and Iraq are still here, fragments of memory at Hussein's school. From the window, you glimpse the cemetery where five Americans are buried under white marble, one of whom taught at Baghdad College for thirty-five years, returning home just once. In the library, cards are catalogued for books that long ago disappeared: *An American Engineer in Afghanistan* and *America's Tragedy*, telling the history of another war. The groves of date palms, once nurtured by Father Charles Loeffler, have thinned. And the octogenarian priests in Boston who taught here grasp from the haze of memory at words they spoke before they were expelled in September 1969: *mudeer*, principal; *shwaya*, a little; and Arabized equivalents of Americana like *Bebsi* and *besbol*. America, at least Father Sara's nobler notion of it, left a long time ago, though. Gone with it is the Iraq that those men idealized, when identities were still inchoate enough to mingle, blend and, occasionally, merge. On the high school's walls these days, English is inflected differently. THUG LIFE, reads graffiti rendered as machine-gun fire. BAGHDAD, reads another, with barbed wire coiled along its top. Someone else has drawn a penis and a flower, or something approximating it.

I once asked Ryan Crocker, the former US ambassador to Iraq who has served in the Arab world during some of its greatest tumult, whether America, and the Obama administration in particular, could fulfil that promise of a new era here. Or, more to the point, could America and Iraq reclaim that nobler sense of each other that Father Sara recalled? Crocker paused, careful not to share the pessimism that is so often heard.

'It really is too early to tell,' he said finally.

With a history of saints and martyrs, Jesuits often mention the notion of heroism, not to mention suffering and endurance, and only a few minutes into our conversation at the Campion Renewal Center, a sylvan Jesuit retreat outside Boston, Father Myles Sheehan, the Provincial, and Father Michael Linden brought it up. 'To go to Baghdad, for a group of guys from Boston and New England, really is as far out there as people could have imagined,' Father Sheehan said, a hint of admiration still in his voice.

It was 1932, and the school began, officially at least, with a telegram dated 5 March, from Abdul Hussein Chalabi, the minister of education, perhaps best known today as the grandfather of one Ahmed Chalabi, present-day politician, provocateur and former exile. 'We take this opportunity to wish you complete success,' he told them. It wasn't the Jesuits' first trip to Baghdad. Two of them had gone in 1850, but were robbed twice as their caravan crossed the Syrian Desert. Invited by the local Chaldean patriarch, they were received better this time, as they sailed from Boston to Beirut, then overland by bus to Baghdad. 'A lifetime assignment,' Father Linden called it, and indeed some would spend more than twenty years there, regardless of deaths in their families, bouts of hepatitis and, in the case of Father John Owens, cancer.

The four founders included Father John Mifsud, whose Maltese name translated poorly into Arabic ('corrupter', it could be rendered). He became Father Miff. They lived in what Father Linden called 'relative austerity', and contemporary accounts of the school's temporary quarters were similarly understated. 'Not gems of the builder's craft,' wrote Father Edward Madaras, one of the five Jesuits buried there.

Yet amid the date palms on Baghdad's outskirts, the school soon flourished. Its enrolment grew from 107 students and four Jesuits in one building to more than 1,100 students (a fifth of them on scholarship) and a faculty of thirty-three Jesuits and thirty-one Iraqi laymen on a campus of ten buildings designed by Father Leo Guay, who consciously borrowed from Iraqi styles. 'An Iraqi school for Iraqi boys' was the motto, and it mirrored an era before 1958 in Baghdad and elsewhere in the Arab world when Britain and France were still the imperial powers, reviled for their deceptive agreements in World War I that indelibly shaped the modern Middle East and resented for their colonial ambitions in North Africa, the Levant and Iraq.

The United States, seen as a beacon of modernity, progress and prosperity, was perhaps known better for education, thanks in part to flourishing schools American missionaries had set up throughout the region. (Across town was the American School for Girls, which had opened in 1925.) Crocker called it 'an age of innocence', and although Iranians with memories of the 1953 American-backed coup against the democratically elected Mohammed Mossaddegh might disagree, the era did lack the traumas that war, invasion and occupation have left the present generation.

No project like Baghdad College could probably escape at least a notion of the white man's burden, but those Jesuits, many of them fluent in Arabic, dressed in pith helmets that shielded them from the sun and cassocks of khaki that hid the dust, were at least conscious of its implications. Over time, they managed to embrace – and to be embraced by – their environs as scholars and residents. Even now, Father Charles Healey, a ruddy-cheeked, seventy-seven-year-old Jesuit in Boston and former teacher at the high school, retains a sense of awe for the intellects that spent time there. Some, like Robert Campbell, went on to get doctorates in Arabic studies. Men like Richard McCarthy and John Donohue became formidable scholars of Islam; McCarthy completed a two-volume work on the spoken Arabic of Baghdad, published a collection of his sermons in Arabic and, after suffering a stroke that paralysed his left side, completed a translation of the classic autobiography of al-Ghazali, a medieval thinker.

In an Iraq of Green Zones and barricades, concrete and barbed wire, the Jesuits' ability to knot themselves into the society's fabric was remarkable. So was their determination. 'This mission has to be the biggest waste of money and manpower in the history of the Church – not a single convert from Islam!' Richard Cushing, the former archbishop of Boston, was quoted as saying in an unofficial account of the college. He was right, and therein lay a fulcrum of the Jesuits' success over those years. The student body was eventually half Christian, half Muslim; unlike the practice for a time at the

American University in Beirut, Muslims at Baghdad College were not required to attend chapel services, and proselytizing was forbidden. The priests set up a school to teach themselves Arabic – with mixed success, in the case of Father Joseph MacDonnell. He had accepted an invitation to visit the house of an Armenian student, only to find the student was out on an errand. Father MacDonnell tried small talk with the student's mother, who didn't speak English. He uttered the three phrases of Arabic he had learned in his five months in Iraq: 'The winter is cold, the river is deep and the brown cows are eating the green grass on the high meadow.' After finishing his tea, he said goodbye to a puzzled host. The following Monday, he learned that the student's mother spoke no Arabic either, only Armenian.

Those social calls, often conducted more fluently, were part of the Jesuits' staple. They were welcomed to wakes and funerals. Many of them visited parishes around town, learning to deliver Mass in Arabic and even Aramaic. Father Robert Farrell, now eighty, remembers teaching Shakespeare to his students, sleeping on the roofs in the summertime and, like his neighbours, often waking up to crows perched on top of the support for the mosquito nets. They rode public buses. Their students, themselves elderly these days, still remark on how comfortable the Americans were with the Iraqis. 'They were part of the society. They ate with us, they ate like us, they learned our customs and they were respectful to our parents,' said Waiel Hindo, the son of a Christian general and one of five brothers who attended the school. When his father was arrested after a coup in 1958, a Jesuit visited their home every day. 'What struck me at the time, and struck a lot of students, Muslim and Christian, was this idea: why would an intelligent, handsome, young, educated American give up all the luxuries of the United States – there was a perception that the US was the land of plenty – and come and serve in a high school with no pay, no wife, having to learn another language, having to learn a new culture? These guys must either be crazy or eccentric or dedicated to an ideal that we don't understand, so what is it?' Dave Nona, a graduate in 1964, told me.

Fatheria was what the students called the Jesuits, an Arabized plural of Father. It was probably their most distinct identity. 'They did see us as Americans, but I think they saw us first as *Fatheria*, Jesuits, you know,' Father Healey told me. Father Linden and Father Sheehan, the Jesuits I met at the Campion Center, too young to have taught at Baghdad College, said they suspected the same. 'They were innocent of what came after and the meanings connected to them, the loss of American innocence from, say, Vietnam forward,' Father Linden said.

Both men visited Iraq in May 2010; it was Father Linden's fifth visit. 'To just be part of their world temporarily' was the way he described his travels to me. They stayed in friends' homes, drove around town in an old black sports-utility vehicle, its windscreen broken, and as Father Linden put it, 'stayed clear of the Green Zone'. In time, they made it to Baghdad College. 'So we get out, and I guess it was the headmaster who said, "Who are you and can I help you?"' Father Sheehan recounted. 'I said, "I understand we built this school and could we see it?" All of a sudden, he clapped his hands. "Coffee! Would you like to smoke?" "No, thank you." And we sat there, and they showed us the yearbooks.'

The volumes of Baghdad College yearbooks are stored – tossed, might be a better word – on two shelves at the back of the library. As I thumbed through them on a sun-soaked morning, with the rattle of gunshots in the distance, the same *athar* kept coming to mind. They were the artefacts of a bygone Iraq, as unfamiliar as an America that, in more than twenty years, I had never encountered in the Arab world. They suggested a notion of an inclusive future that bound two countries unencumbered by their pasts, still – as Father Linden put it – innocent in each other's eyes. The first yearbook, handsomely done, was dated 1945.

'The flames of global war have ruined our world; our books were written on the model of the happy, peaceful, pre-war days,' read the farewell, printed as an editorial on a glossy page 23 of *Al Iraqi*, or

The Iraqi. 'We know too well that ahead of us lies a thorny path until the stabilization of the peace is a reality.' That notion of a great, even climactic conflict, punctuated the yearbooks in those years. So did a determination – you might call it hope – that its end meant a new chapter for Iraq, America and the world. 'There remains the task for men of goodwill to bring the world from physical and spiritual devastation to law and order, if we are to have peace, real peace,' another essay read.

As I turned the pages, another war still echoed outside. Two American helicopters rumbled overhead a little after 10 a.m., and the staccato bursts of more gunfire ricocheted through the library windows a half-hour later. Hope remains an elusive sentiment these days in Iraq; triumphalism and expressions of loss, threats, condemnations and vows of vengeance are far more common. The present made the pages feel so earnest as to be naive, until I realized I was probably too cynical. Or, perhaps more accurately, they had the advantage of being written before the revolutions, civil wars and onset of decisive American power in the Middle East, when two cultures still occupied a common space or, at least, a shared American and Arab idea of what progress represented. Each still had a sense of the other's goodness; in some ways, the Jesuits were the right people at the right time. One of the yearbooks at the American School for Girls volunteered its mission this way: 'The path of learning leads to . . . exploration in science . . . explanation in Arabic . . . expression in English . . . expansion in mathematics . . . expectation in art.'

American optimism pervades the yearbooks. So does American culture. Students are compared to Charles Atlas. Hairstyles are American, as is the cut of Tawfiq al-Sabunji's suit. The dedication for Claire Shlomo, a graduate of the girls' school in 1949, captures the mood: 'One word will tell what Claire reads, dreams and talks about – America.' One Jesuit dispatched his students with this homework: 'The Roxy Cinema tonight, boys!', where they were tasked to watch Orson Welles's version of *Macbeth*. COME AND CHEER THE GOLD AND MAROON ON TO VICTORY, reads a poster from 1955, announcing the finals in basketball against the top government school.

Not that the students had abandoned their roots. The yearbooks are filled with essays like 'Chemistry and the Arabs' and 'Kurdish Tribes in Iraq'. (A sample: 'The Kurdish people are so skilful in fighting that one might think they are born to fight.') Students often listed their hobby as Arabic poetry. ('Oh, the Arabic poems that we had to memorize!' others complained.) The identities simply seemed less defined, with fewer assumptions, at a time that American influences were perhaps more pliable. 'We learn foreign languages in order to be able to benefit from what foreign people have said and written, and also to make these people understand what we wish to communicate,' Dhia Sharif wrote in another yearbook. More light-heartedly, students in 1947 noted that 'without flinching, we can spell "jaw-breakers" like *contemptuously* or *equilibrium*'. The favourite expression of Antwan Shirinian, a graduate in 1950, was 'my golly'.

Many of the students in the yearbooks from the 1950s and 1960s are familiar today. Ayad Allawi, a former prime minister and leading politician, has the same burly build as in his youth. 'He was a fighter,' remembered a contemporary, Waiel Hindo. Ahmed Chalabi is recognizable by his eyes. 'So smart,' Hindo called him. Vice President Adel Abdul-Mahdi had a reputation as a bully. Chalabi's brother, Talal, was 'one of the best swimmers in the school'. Another brother, Hazim, 'studied French in his spare moments'. Kanaan Makiyya, a writer and academic, was on the honour roll in 1965.

'The prospect of progress' was how Ahmed Chalabi described the school's ambience to me. Like so many other graduates, he still spoke reverently about what the college represented as an American institution and, perhaps more poignantly, what America represented in an age imbued with the faint echoes of Wilsonian idealism and a notion that America and its success were the model to emulate. 'Hope, progress, enlightenment, prosperity, education.' In a phrase, he seemed to capture the era's ethos. In 1957, the year before American Marines landed in Lebanon, the school's debating society offered this resolution: 'That the United Nations be revised now into a federal world government.' 'This is the space age!' one essay declared. 'An atomic age,' another insisted. 'We may yet see the day,' wrote Tariq Dib in 1953, 'when we shall travel in these rockets for a picnic on the moon, that is, if the moon can be used for such a delightful purpose.'

An advertisement at the end of the 1949 yearbook caught my eye. It was for Levant Express Transport. Based in Beirut, it had branch offices in fifteen cities in Jordan, Syria, Iraq and Iran, along with a car service running between Baghdad and Tehran. (Until the 1948 war, it had offices in Tel Aviv and Haifa, too.) An essay around that time noted that seven airlines offered flights from Baghdad to Calcutta, Sydney, Kabul and all of Europe and the Middle East. Pilots from France, Britain, Italy and Egypt often overnighted. These days, there are regular flights on Iraqi Airways to only two cities – Stockholm and Istanbul – beyond the Middle East.

The history of the past century in Iraq and the region is, in many ways, a story of borders. There is the simple notion of them, frontiers demarcated by war and imperial impetuosity that transformed the eclectic expanse of the Ottoman Empire after World War I into the jigsaw puzzle of the modern Middle East. No less far-reaching, though, are the barriers that narrower notions of identity have created over the past generation. These have served to re-engineer a region, always more diverse than its reputation, that had long represented a remarkable entrepôt of languages, traditions and customs across boundaries gracefully ill-defined. The names in the yearbooks of Baghdad College and the American School for Girls testify to that earlier age: Suham Jack, Haifa Ashoo, Anita Papazian, Nellie Aslan, Vartan Garabetian, Varujan Khalil, Surin Zawin, Victor Rowland and so on. In faith, they represented Jews, Christians and Muslims, though a secular sense of self often held sway. Their nationalities were as diverse: Egyptians, Armenians, Syrians, Iranians, Palestinians and, of course, Iraqis all mingled together under an American rubric.

Today, in a claustrophobic city, where you always know where you are – neighbourhoods precisely demarcated by the colour, flag, portrait or symbol of its Sunni or Shia inhabitants, cauterized by the memories of carnage often visited there – the yearbook pictures of classrooms, basketball games, graduations and picnics are geographically indeterminate. You could be in Spain or Italy, the Greek Club in Cairo or, say, a Lebanese wedding in Sayre, Oklahoma, circa 1952. You never know where you are. Only the number 7 rendered as an Arabic numeral on the jersey of a basketball player leaping for a jump shot on an open-air court tells you the Middle East.

'There were few institutions in Iraq that created national identity and, believe it or not, Baghdad College was one of them,' Laith Kubba, the former official, told me. It was a theme often reiterated by others when we talked about the school's legacy. The time itself was still difficult, nostalgia notwithstanding – Baathists and Communists fought bloody battles in those years, and even today, people recall the televised show trials of Fadhil Mahdawi's *People's Court*, as sordid as it was carnivalesque – but there was a sense of a broader identity shaped by the idea Ahmed Chalabi mentioned of a progressive future. 'In that melting pot, where merit was the essence of competition, it wasn't who your parents were,' Kubba said. 'The essence of differentiation was merit. Everybody accepted and respected that. Those other essences of belonging became secondary. They didn't teach us nationalism as such, but by creating that atmosphere where we were all Iraqis by default, and the values we had were based on the ability to compete and learn and not who you belonged to and where you came from, it was implicit. At the end of the day, where can you find institutions that link Iraqis of different backgrounds? Those graduates of Baghdad College all over Iraq created a fabric; they were part of the fabric that pulled Iraq together. They related to each other irrespective of the things that pulled them apart.'

What Kubba and others were talking about, in the end, was a notion of cosmopolitanism, defined foremost by an absence of fear. Father Linden and Father Sheehan, the Jesuits who visited Baghdad in the spring, mentioned it. So did Father Farrell, who taught there long ago. Chalabi eventually went to the Massachusetts Institute of Technology, where, he says, 'I did not feel alien at all. I did not feel homesick, nothing. There were no surprises for me.' Kubba remembered the same feeling. 'I knew America before I came here,' he told me by telephone from Washington. 'I was comfortable with it. I'm an Arab, I'm Muslim, I had my political views, I had many things I would differ with, but in essence, I knew how Americans think. In essence, I knew American culture.'

Many people still debate the year that might be described as the moment that changed America in the Arab world. President Wilson's failure to follow through with his promises of self-determination could be one date, but it seems too early. The year 1948 is as good as any. It was then that America, over the vociferous, even bewildered objections of Arabs, lent crucial support to the creation of Israel. Some point to 1952 and the revolution that brought Gamal Abdel Nasser to power in Egypt, the Arab world's most populous country. Crocker, the former ambassador, sees it as 1958, when the Iraqi monarchy was overthrown, the Marines landed in Lebanon and Syria and Egypt, led by Nasser, declared their union. 'Before that, the United States was mainly known not for political engagement or military conflict or boots on the ground but for education and culture,' he said. Soon, he added, 'that became overshadowed by everything else'.

Everything else was the Cold War, which the United States fought in part in the Middle East, wedded to a paradigm of 'us against them' that still echoes today. Likewise wedded was America's growing alliance with Israel, which soon confined to memory the goodwill generated by President Eisenhower's shining moment, when he forced Israel, Britain and France to withdraw from Egypt's Sinai Peninsula in the 1956 Arab-Israeli war and, by default, declared America – not fading European powers – the pre-eminent Western actor in the Middle East. The climax was 1967, when Israel, supported by America, scored a victory so decisive, so complete, that its legacy still reverberates a generation and more later. Ideologies crumbled, most notably a secular nationalism that spoke a language far more familiar to America than the political Islam of today. Coups followed, and yet more borders in a region full of them were drawn; no longer could Ramiz Ghazzul visit Bethlehem. Neither America nor Iraq and the Arab world would be the same again. Within a year of the war, the Jesuits themselves, still teaching in Baghdad, were adrift in the trajectories of a new Arab-American era dominated by the interests of a global power: securing oil, breaking the opposition of secular Arab nationalism and ensuring the supremacy of its allies, namely Israel.

On 4 July 1968, in a modest ceremony, Father McCarthy, the formidable scholar who translated al-Ghazali, laid the corner stone for the Oriental Institute, to be built by Father Guay. It was his dream. He had planned every detail and conceived its mission, a bridge between East and West, where two cultures would meet in mutual respect. But just weeks after the ceremony, the Baath Party returned to power in Iraq in a bloodless coup. 'The handwriting was on the wall,' Father Linden said. Father McDermott, who had returned to Iraq that year for research on his dissertation, remembered the mood. 'They had no illusions,' he said of his fellow Jesuits. 'They knew we were in trouble.'

In September 1968, the Baathist government took over the administration of al-Hikma, a small university the Jesuits had opened in Baghdad in 1956. 'The whole matter is confined to the fact of their being foreigners,' the new president, Saad Abdul Baqi al-Rawi, told an Iraqi weekly the following month. 'Because of this they are unable to understand the stage at which our nation is living, nor can they comprehend our national problems and our struggle with imperialism and Zionism, nor are they favourable to our strivings and aspirations.' The Jesuits continued to teach at al-Hikma and Baghdad College but tensions grew. In a letter he wrote in Arabic to the Revolutionary Command Council, Father McCarthy pleaded their case. 'The Fathers, from the day of their coming to Iraq to this very day, have never meddled in political party or sectarian matters. Moreover they have always been supporters of just Arab causes, and in particular, they have defended, and continue to defend, the Arabs' position and rights regarding the question of Palestine.' There was no reply. Four days later, the Jesuits decided to go on strike at al-Hikma, a move undoubtedly viewed as a provocation by a party that prided itself on its toughness. Within a month, the government expelled them from the country.

Baghdad College remained open, still run by the Jesuits, but it became a target of anger and frustration, themselves an epitaph to an older sense of American charity. An article in the newspaper *Al-Thawra* read: 'Baghdad College still stands in the way of the immortal revolution as a stumbling block and an imperialistic foothold in which minds that try to thwart the course of this revolution and call for the return of imperialism have made nests for themselves.' They were some of the last Americans left in the country, and on 24 August 1969, the thirty-three Jesuits of Baghdad College were ordered to leave, ending their nearly four decades of work in Baghdad.

The crucifixes in the classrooms came down. Fridays, not Sundays, became the day off. There was no more baseball. Nor was there an edition of *Al Iraqi* in 1969. When the yearbooks resumed, they were more modest. The 1970 edition was dedicated to the minister of higher education. The following year, the foreword declared that Baghdad College was once 'established in a strange, closed world and never experiencing the bitter realities, nor taking pride in a glorious past. Its world was as foreign as those foreigners who administered it and who were quite indifferent to this country and its aspirations.' In each successive year, the argument was reiterated, sometimes shrilly, in the bluster of people desperate to convince someone of something not even they believe. 'Feelings of isolation and lostness' were swept away. Another edition read,'by the colossal Revolution of July'. At the former American School for Girls, the principal sponsored a burning of books in English. A xenophobia not unfamiliar to wartime America became grounded in the official discourse. The yearbooks lost their flair. Essays that once waxed eloquently about the Kurdish spring, 'when the land turns into a sea of green grass waving in the winds like angry waves of a roaring sea', became impenetrable agitprop. The 1975 yearbook offered this Gordian knot of prose: the situation, it said, 'required theoretical stands and positive process inter-reacting with the objective circumstances and tangible reality dialectically and creatively, preserving the strategical revolutionary horizon in accordance with the aims of unity, liberty and socialism'.

It would be the last yearbook. It was dedicated once again to Ahmed Hassan al-Bakr, president of the Republic of Iraq. But he shared the honour with a newcomer to the yearbook's pages, Saddam Hussein, vice chairman of the Revolutionary Command Council. 'Long live the Leader Party, the Arab Baath Socialist Party,' the foreword read.

Just as the date of America's new incarnation abroad is debated, so is the moment that marked a new watershed for the Arab world, when older, more secular sensibilities, the kinds that made it possible for Jews, Christians and Muslims to study amicably together at Baghdad College, gave way to narrower identities. The Baathism of the 1968 coup descended into an instrument of power and oppression, as brutal as it was crass, wielded by an empowered Sunni minority from the countryside, then Saddam Hussein's own family. War with Iran would ensue, a chapter that traumatized and brutalized Iraq like no other conflict; it was to Iraq what World War I was to Europe. A tenth of Iraq's population became soldiers, many of them schooled in violence. A quarter of a million would die. 'Soldiers lying like matches on the ground,' as one Iraqi general would describe them.

Across the region, Islamic movements ascended, seizing the language of their eclipsed secular and nationalist rivals and soon making a mockery of a common Arab and American notion of progress. Conflicts were redefined as West and East, Muslim and Christian, currents that once intersected deflected by the absolutism of Manichaean and messianic paradigms. In Iraq, the battles were no longer between Baathists and Communists – at least nominally adhering to an idea of universalism. Gone was a notion of citizenship – if it ever existed – in Iraq or other Arab countries. Primordial identities, exclusive as they are, became the sole axis around which politics revolved.

The Iraq that the Americans inherited after invading in 2003 bore as much resemblance to the one the Jesuits knew as the America they represented stood true to Iraqis. As the Jesuits in Boston mentioned, neither was really recognizable to them. Iraq had suffered Saddam's tyranny, the murderous war with Iran and sanctions that destroyed a middle class that once watched Orson Welles's *Macbeth* at the Roxy. America was, in the best reading, a country of unimaginable power bent on achieving its interests in Egypt, Iraq and the Persian Gulf. A worse reading, uttered by a taxi driver in Baghdad, is that it had become merely a warmonger. The memories of another age often reside in exile, where many of Baghdad College's graduates have sought refuge. 'The United States is no longer the America that people knew in the 1950s,' said one of them, Faruq Ziada, who has moved to London. A classmate had the same lament for his own country, bereft of its cosmopolitanism. 'The sectarian flame has been kindled everywhere,' said Muwaffaq Tikriti, who now lives in Montreal, Canada. 'I'm not sure who is who. We don't have an identity. Sunnism, Shiism, these are not Iraqi identities. These are separations, these are isolations. These are chauvinistic and fanatic approaches to life and to politics.'

The American Embassy in Baghdad is a severe place, architecturally at least, full of sharp angles, thick glass and reinforced concrete. You might call it American realism, the fortified style of diplomatic outposts these days that altogether lacks the grace of Father Guay's syncretism, his arches and domes evoking another age. It is a garrison in a place where cultures, visions and identities are now contested.

I had an appointment there with Martin Quinn, whose portfolio includes education and cultural affairs, and David Ranz, the embassy's spokesman. Quinn, sixty-five, is a garrulous, gracious type, with an impressive record of time in the Middle East. He taught in Iran before the revolution, then at Cairo's storeyed Al-Azhar University, before becoming a diplomat and serving in Saudi Arabia, Qatar, Syria, the United Arab Emirates, Israel and elsewhere. 'Complicated' was the way he described America's relationship with the Arab world over his time, which barely missed intersecting with the Jesuits' departure from Baghdad. Part of his job these days is to try to make it less so.

Billions of dollars have been spent on 'public diplomacy', a diplomatic term for trying to make people like us more. American radio and television stations broadcast to Iraq and the rest of the Arab world, with mixed success. President Obama, at Cairo University in 2009, called for 'a new beginning' between two cultures that, in a phrase that could have come from an etiolated edition of *Al Iraqi*, 'share common principles – principles of justice and progress, tolerance and the dignity of all human beings'. The American Embassy in Baghdad, and diplomats like Quinn, have the formidable task of making that a reality – or, more bluntly, trying to recapture what America (its missionaries, diplomats and graduates of its schools) managed to do in a gentler era.

In the offing is a potpourri of acronyms and good intentions – exchange programmes, training initiatives, English instruction and, with an investment of $7.5 million, partnerships between Iraqi and American universities that will bring to Basra the oil expertise of Oklahoma State University, and to Najaf the University of Kentucky's approach to learning English. Quinn spoke of a process that, while gradual, 'is going to happen'. Ranz spoke about treating the 'many, many years of isolation'. The American government wanted to build what he called 'a long-term relationship', Ranz told me, one that would begin to flourish as the American military withdrew the rest of its troops by 2012. 'In a year from now, roughly, they're all going to be gone and what's going to be left behind, we hope, is a strong civilian partnership with a lot of Americans of a variety of stripes involved in every sector of Iraq, whether it's agriculture, whether it's education, culture, energy, all those things,' he said. 'Over the course of time, those are the impressions that are going to be, I think, burned into the minds of Iraqis.'

Diplomats, especially in Baghdad, have a way of speaking with authority that is often infectious. It is earnest and righteous, like a graduate-school seminar. Ranz and Quinn sounded committed – no doubt, they are, serving in one of the grimmest assignments in the history of American diplomacy – but as I listened, I felt that most Iraqis I had met only rarely shared their assumptions, that their contexts were too often different. Both diplomats were newcomers to Iraq, and their comparisons to experiences in Egypt, Morocco, the United Arab Emirates and Saudi Arabia, while sometimes insightful, still felt, in Iraq at least, as thin as dry pitta bread. And while they spoke about ending isolation, I wondered how you would go about treating Iraq's near destruction – 100,000 and probably many more dead, millions having fled the carnage, a society's fabric tattered in wars, the last one so seminal to today's image of America abroad. It is hard to have a flourishing exchange when the same mission issues warnings like this every so often: 'The US Embassy has learned that Westerners travelling in Southern Iraq, including those using Personal Security Detachments (PSDs), are at increased risk of being targeted for kidnapping operations.'

Most diplomats spend a year or so in Iraq, and they tend to treat the country as a tabula rasa. They espouse benevolence when many Iraqis see arrogance. They still talk in blacks and whites, when most Iraqis are stranded in the greys of a new era. Eight years on, fundamental mistakes about Iraq's recent past are still routinely committed. In the meeting at the embassy, reference was made repeatedly to Iraq's isolation beginning in the 1970s, as Saddam Hussein ascended to power. For many Iraqis, the 1970s were an oil-propelled golden age; the society was devastated in the 1990s by sanctions the United States crucially supported. For the Americans, the problem is still Saddam and his immiserating legacy inflicted on a generation. For Iraqis, the problem was always Saddam *and* the

America that this generation has come to know. Often the harshest indictment is from those Baghdad College alumni who knew an older America most intimately. 'Arrogance and hubris,' Dave Nona told me. 'It's a hubris and arrogance that comes with power, that we know best, that we have the mightiest army, the money, the psychology. That we know best, even if events have shown otherwise.'

I asked Ranz and Quinn what the goals of their initiatives were, of public diplomacy itself, in an age where America is burdened by the memories of its past. 'We want their views to be broadened about the United States so they can understand what the United States really is about, as a culture and as a society,' Quinn told me. I suggested that in my time in the Middle East I had never really found all that much antipathy for Americans themselves, but rather for their policies, the agenda of a superpower – be it wars of their choosing, support for Arab dictators or double standards in, say, the respective right of Iran and Israel to possess nuclear weapons. Only zealots denounce American-celebrated liberties and rights; virtually every Arab disagrees with America's lavish support for Israel. Wounds have become scars, though, and the scars remain. 'Even if there isn't antipathy,' Ranz answered, 'what there is is a broad lack of understanding about what the United States is really about.'

I wasn't so sure. Nona and Tikriti, schooled by Americans, living in North America, certainly understood America. In fact, I thought, the problem the embassy faces might not be a lack of understanding, but rather too much of it.

Of the names the Iraqis have given the Americans, none is more popular than *khawalna*, our uncles. The word suggests intimacy, the intonation bitterness, like a family joined by marriage, but riven by the grudges and slights of too much time too close together. Alaa Saadoun, a young sculptor whom I met at the Fine Arts College, smiled at the mention of the name. 'Even someone who hates them will call them that,' he confessed.

I met Saadoun and his friends a few days after visiting the

embassy. Their campus felt a little like a harbour, offering rare shelter.

At least here, no one seemed to notice the blast walls and barbed wire outside the college's entrances, barricaded by tree trunks and barrels filled with cement. (The fortifications are as utilitarian as they are ugly. Across the street, in the old British cemetery, built to bury occupiers of another age, blast after blast has toppled scores of tombstones with names like P. Riley, J. A. Grant and F. F. Marshall.) Conversations are often hurried in Baghdad – no one wants to stay somewhere too long – but the talk here was idle, as I asked them about the legacy of *our uncles*. 'There is no question the Americans are going to leave behind *athar*,' Ali Zaid, a twenty-three-year-old film-maker, told me.

There are still the *athar* of another American age in Iraq. At the Campion Center in Boston, Father Linden showed me pictures of Baghdad still hanging in the hallway, a sort of memorial. 'Fred Kelly's BB team', one caption read. 'Leo Guay's church', another said. At the former American School for Girls, around the corner from Chalabi's house, the Honor Board remains after all these years, alongside clocks no longer keeping time. Nearly all of the forty shelves in the Baghdad College library are empty, save the remnants of an older education – *The Oxford Companion to English Literature* and *The World Almanac, 1965*. Plumes of dust billow from the yellowed pages of *Anna Karenina* when opened. The library at the girls' school is similarly frozen in time, books turned upside down, dust on the shelves undisturbed by fingertips. *The Adventures of Tom Sawyer* was last checked out in 1991. No one has read *Charlotte's Web* since 1985. *They Live in Bible Lands* was checked out all of once, by Mae Abdel-Karim in 1978. 'Are you wondering what happened to Babylon and the other great cities of Bible times?' the book asks. 'Through the centuries, their walls were broken down and the sands of the desert drifted over the cities.'

Today's *athar* are a more crass sort, the stuff of a collision. It only takes a little while of living in Baghdad to see how the city has been transformed by the forces that are the very antithesis of Jesuit-inspired cosmopolitanism. Like other great Arab capitals, Cairo and Beirut among them, Baghdad has lost its tolerance, receding behind those walls – the abundance of concrete here deprives the phrase of any metaphor – that demarcate now-familiar sect, ethnicity and class. Identity has become less malleable, life far less convivial. The Green Zone has become a lesson that even in democracy, or some notion of it, a divide, yawning and unbridgeable, remains between ruler and ruled. The old have a nostalgia for the past, circa Baghdad College – the imagined grace and civility of a black-and-white Egyptian movie. The younger bear the stamp of forces the invasion unleashed in 2003, the dawn of a new American militarism, and the civil war that extinguished the last ethos of that bygone era.

The *athar* of this American age are tattoos and piercings, frosted facial hair and Skoal tobacco, diffused by soldiers and what Iraqis call the *infitah*, or opening, which has brought the Internet, satellite television and cellphones. There is a martial bent to the imported words. 'Hummer' means armoured jeeps; 'mister' is an American soldier. A popular haircut is called 'Marines'. Grandmothers warn their children that if they misbehave: 'I'll tell the Americans to come and get you.' Fittingly, the Iraqi Army bears the most indelible stamp of this modern conjecture of America. Iraqi soldiers don sunglasses once deemed effeminate, gloves, suede-coloured boots, flak jackets and the khaki camouflage of the decade's wars.

As I stood with the students, they offered their own examples, from haircuts ('spiky' and 'cut') to fashion, from words (*terps* for interpreters) to obscene gestures. Even a child can belt out a string of English expletives worthy of an audition for a Tarantino movie. 'My opinion?' asked Baqr Jassem, film-maker (and part-time barber). 'What people say? We saw the Americans only by war, of war, and what they left us were the remnants from war.'

I thought back to a conversation I had with Ahmed Chalabi, who enjoyed talking about that notion of estranged intimacy. 'It's alien,' he said in describing America today. 'How many Americans have been in Iraq in the past seven years? Two million? Iraqis don't know Americans now. Can you believe it? They just don't know! They don't know!' His aide, Entifadh Qanbar, put it another way. 'All boots, dogs and tattoos,' he said. Estranged, though, never felt like the right word to me, and comparisons between yesterday's Jesuits and today's soldiers are unfair. This was rather the intimacy between a new America and new Iraq, so bound by the miseries of conflicts, breeding fear and cynicism as they do, that each can no longer idealize the other. Each has become anonymous and menacing to the other, like a clichéd enemy in a straight-to-DVD action movie. Reeling from wars, adrift in the most painful nostalgia, Iraq had changed far more than Americans ever realized. In these days, America seems only to lend the crass commercialism of its globalized self.

Other than the embassy, the only other locale that carries America's name in Baghdad is the American Market, a rough-and-tumble souk that has grown like a tree's roots around the concrete barriers originally meant to protect it. Under tarps and umbrellas, Massari blasts from three-foot-high speakers, which sometimes share space with the soundtrack to Sylvester Stallone's *The Expendables*, a mercenary flick offering a character named Hale Caesar. (Another movie on sale: *A-plus College Girls*.) Mannequins adorned in bandanas, camouflage shorts and parachute pants wear goatees. Shirts are emblazoned with Snoop Dogg. 'Paid the Cost to Be Da Boss', one reads. The fashion is *banki*, perhaps a derivation of the word Yankee, though no one seems to know for sure. 'It's the American style,' one of the vendors, Thaer Abdullah, told me simply.

Perhaps all of it – Dave Batista and Tupac, Motörhead and Metallica – is a fad, the equivalent of Aram Gabriel's comparison to Charles Atlas in the Baghdad College yearbook all those years ago. It felt more entrenched, though. These are the artefacts of war, and war is America's legacy today, the intimacy of violence. I asked the students – one of whom lost five relatives to the conflict, another whose friend had his left hand severed – when they thought their generation might forget.

THE AMERICAN AGE, IRAQ

'We can't forget,' Osama Amer, a painter with a faint beard, told me.
'We haven't forgotten the British yet,' Jassem, the part-time
barber, said.

'It's history, our history, and it has to be remembered,' Amer went
on. He smiled at me as he smoked, but there was an edge in his voice.
'Iraqis don't forget anything.'

At 10.53 a.m., the detonation of a car bomb cracked about a
hundred yards away. Staccato bursts of gunfire followed, in an attack
that would leave twelve people dead that day. I flinched. No one else
moved. They may have blinked, but I didn't see it.

In September, I finally talked to Father Solomon Sara, who was
inspired by his education at Baghdad College to become a Jesuit.
For weeks, I had tried to reach him at Georgetown University, where
he has taught for more than four decades, but calls from Baghdad to
anywhere are not all that easy. When we finally did talk, the phone felt
fitting to me, as we spoke between two worlds over a bad line on the
verge of disconnecting.

'We gave a different image not only to their society, but to our
society,' he told me. The words struck me. The college did not
represent simply an intersection, I thought, but perhaps something
more, what Father Sara would describe to me as noble. It incarnated
an age when all the rhetoric and the promises – those pledges that
Iraqis have heard since 19 March 1917, the date Major General Sir
Stanley Maude defeated the Ottomans, marched into Baghdad and
declared his troops liberators – were made possible.

I asked Father Sara if that kind of intersection would ever be
realized again. He paused, but only for a moment. 'It will take time,
of course, because everything has become toxic there. Ethnicity has
become toxic, religion has become toxic, even geography has become
toxic. Everything is negative. Nobody says we're just Iraqis – and
that was our attitude, that everybody is Iraqi, that everybody is on
an equal basis.' Father Sara mixed the first-person plural; for a while,
we were the Iraqis of his birth; at other times, the Americans of his

home. 'We divided the country into three pieces. We're telling them in practice the country is not one. It's the foundation for American policy: the north is Kurdish, the south is Shiite and the centre is a government that is not representative. We emphasize the differences and identities. Can you imagine doing that here, in the States? I can't imagine doing that and surviving. But that's exactly what we did there. Even before the war, ten years of an embargo. To succeed you have to have allies, and to have allies, you have to divide. To conquer, you have to fragment. The more you divide, the more you control. There's confusion, therefore you control.' Father Sara's voice was too gentle and weary to be angry, but I could hear the hurt as he listed the chapters of America's engagement, from American troops occupying Saddam Hussein's palaces as they conquered Baghdad to the war crimes of Abu Ghraib. 'Do they think that is noble?' he asked me. 'My goodness.' He stopped. 'What happened to us?' He repeated the question again. 'Somebody like me lost two countries at the same time. Who do you cheer for, America or Iraq? The two countries I love best, I love most, and here they are, tearing each other apart.'

Not so long ago, I rebuilt my family's ancestral home in Lebanon. It paled before the stately villa it once was, perched in a backwater no longer at the intersection of trade, languages and culture. Still, I had managed to make sure it would be more than an archaeological footnote, abandoned and crumbling like so many other stone mansions in the town. That didn't matter to my cousin, who told me he would never visit the house again. Why would he want to see it, he asked me, when he could remember it as it was? Father Sara was of the same idea. The country is in shambles, he said, 'and I don't want to see that'. Chalabi echoed this sentiment. He never wanted to go back to see Baghdad College, its walls now scrawled with swastikas and graffiti that read GANGSTER and THE PLAYER. 'I don't want to see the shit they did to it,' he told me. Memories would be their *athar,* those fragments of an older American legacy that manages to perhaps live on abroad, in exile, among that diaspora that no longer recognizes America or, more painfully, Iraq. Nor does it want to. 'I know the old Baghdad, I know the old Iraq. We have gone through three wars and Iraq is not Iraq any more,' said Muwaffaq Tikriti, speaking to me from Montreal. 'It's . . .' He paused. 'To go back to what Iraq was would take a miracle.' Father Sara's words were the most haunting I heard, though. 'Baghdad is dead for most of us.'

'The atmosphere is so poisonous that if you opened Baghdad College today, you wouldn't survive. We wouldn't survive.' I could hear his voice quiver, then tremble, his *we* still interchangeable. 'The symbiosis was perfect, we loved them, and they loved us. They welcomed us, and we welcomed them. It was completely mutual.'

'When we entered the gate,' he told me, 'we entered a new world.'

And, as he put it, those worlds are gone. Even the Jesuits, as Father Sara himself acknowledged, would fail today. Hardly any common ground is left.

Before I hung up the phone, I promised to have coffee with him when I visited Washington. Soon after, I tucked away a page I had copied from one of the yearbooks to bring with me when I saw him. It might not mean that much, but the words felt right to me. The passage was written by Aram Seropian in 1945, the year Father Sara entered Baghdad College. 'Baghdad changes with the time of the time,' it went.

Her people march with the tempos of civilization. She weeps when the Tigris is stained with the blood of her sons, when her hearths are smouldering in chaos. Yet she smiles when the Tigris is rippling with joy and her halls are echoing with laughter. Destiny may change her emotions, but her classic beauty, her historical pride always remains the same. She is a gem that may lose her brilliance under the dust of time . . . ∎

The Society of Authors

The K Blundell Trust
Grants for Authors under 40

Grants are offered to writers under the age of 40 who have already published at least one book and who require funding for important research, travel or other expenditure relating to their next book, which must contribute to the greater understanding of existing social and economic organization.

Closing dates for all applications are 30 September 2011 and 30 April 2012

Full details from www.societyofauthors.org or send sae to Paula Johnson, The Society of Authors, 84 Drayton Gardens, London SW10 9SB

The Royal Society of Literature Jerwood Awards for Non-Fiction

The Royal Society of Literature and Jerwood Charitable Foundation are again offering three joint awards – one of £10,000, and two of £5,000.

These awards are open to writers engaged on their first commissioned works of non-fiction. UK and Irish citizens and those who have been resident in the UK for three years are all eligible.

Applications must be submitted by Monday 3 October 2011.

For entry form see www.rslit.org or email Paula Johnson for further details at paula@rslit.org

---

The Society of Authors
Grants for Authors

Within the Authors' Foundation, which offers grants to writers of fiction, non-fiction and poetry, the following specific awards are also available:

The Great Britain Sasakawa Grant (fiction or non-fiction about any aspect of Japanese culture or society)
Roger Deakin Awards (writing about the environment)
John Heygate Awards (travel writing)
John C Laurence Awards (promoting understanding between races)
Elizabeth Longford Grants (historical biography)
Michael Meyer Awards (theatre)
Arthur Welton Awards (poetry)

Closing dates for all applications are 30 September 2011 and 30 April 2012.
Full details from www.societyofauthors.org or send sae to:
Paula Johnson, The Society of Authors,
84 Drayton Gardens, London SW10 9SB

CONTRIBUTORS

Nadeem Aslam was born in Gujranwala, Pakistan, and now lives in England. He is the author of the novels *Season of the Rainbirds, Maps for Lost Lovers* and *The Wasted Vigil*.

Tahar Ben Jelloun is a Moroccan novelist, short-story writer, essayist and poet. In 1987 he was awarded the Prix Goncourt for his novel *The Sacred Night*. His recent books include *Rising of the Ashes, Leaving Tangier, Yemma, This Blinding Absence of Light* and *Racism Explained to My Daughter*.

Nadia Shira Cohen has worked as a photographer for the Associated Press and Sipa Press. She has served as director of the New York office, and then as special project director, for the photo agency VII. She lives in Rome, Italy.

Linda Coverdale has translated over sixty books. A Chevalier de l'Ordre des Arts et des Lettres, she won the French-American Foundation Translation Prize twice, the Scott Moncrieff Prize and the International IMPAC Dublin Literary Award, for Tahar Ben Jelloun's novel *This Blinding Absence of Light*.

Janine di Giovanni is the author of five books, including *Madness Visible* and *Place at the End of the World: Essays from the Edge*. Her latest book is *Ghosts by Daylight: A Memoir of War and Love*.

Ahmed Errachidi was held in extrajudicial detention in the US Guantánamo Bay detainment camps in Cuba for five years until his release in 2007. His memoir, *A Handful of Walnuts*, will be published by Chatto & Windus in 2012.

Nuruddin Farah's works include three trilogies, plays and a non-fiction book, *Yesterday, Tomorrow*. 'Crossbones' is an excerpt from his most recent novel, *Crossbones*, to be published in the US in September 2011 by Riverhead. He lives in Cape Town, South Africa.

Pico Iyer is the author of two novels and seven works of non-fiction and writes regularly for the *New York Review of Books, Harper's*, the *New York Times* and others. His most recent book is *The Open Road: The Global Journey of the Fourteenth Dalai Lama*. His next book, out in January 2012 from Knopf, is *The Man Within My Head*.

Adam Johnson is the author of *Parasites Like Us* and *Emporium*. His stories have appeared in *Esquire, Harper's, Tin House* and the *Paris Review*, as well as in *The Best American Short Stories*. 'The Third Mate' is an extract from his new novel, *The Orphan Master's Son*, forthcoming in 2012 from Random House in the US and Transworld in the UK.

Lawrence Joseph is the author of five books of poems, most recently *Into It* and *Codes, Precepts, Biases, and Taboos: Poems 1973–1993*, and two books of prose, *Lawyerland* and *The Game Changed: Essays and Other Prose*. He lives in Manhattan.

Phil Klay is a veteran of the US Marine Corps and served in Iraq. His essay 'Death and Memory' was featured in the *New York Times*. This is his first published story.

Nicole Krauss was named one of *Granta*'s Best Young American Novelists in 2007. She is the author of the novels *Man Walks Into a Room, The History of Love* and, most recently, *Great House*, which was shortlisted for the 2011 Orange Prize and was a finalist for the National Book Award.

Kathryn Kuitenbrouwer is the author of the novels *Perfecting* and *The Nettle Spinner* and the story collection *Way Up*. She lives in Toronto.

Jynne Martin's poetry has appeared in the *Kenyon Review, Ploughshares, Boston Review, New England Review, TriQuarterly* and elsewhere, and has been read on PBS's *NewsHour with Jim Lehrer*. She lives in Brooklyn and is Associate Director of Publicity at Random House.

Anthony Shadid is a foreign correspondent for the *New York Times* based in Beirut. He is the author of *Night Draws Near: Iraq's People in the Shadow of America's War* and *Legacy of the Prophet: Despots, Democrats, and the New Politics of Islam*. He won the Pulitzer Prize for International Reporting in 2004 and 2010.

Clive Stafford Smith is founder and director of the human rights organization Reprieve. Since 2002, he has volunteered his services to detainees at Guantánamo Bay. He is the author of *Bad Men: Guantánamo Bay and the Secret Prisons*.

Declan Walsh is the *Guardian*'s correspondent for Pakistan and Afghanistan. His forthcoming book is titled *Insh'Allah Nation: A Journey Through Modern Pakistan*.

Elliott Woods is the writer and photographer behind *Assignment Afghanistan*, an award-winning project in collaboration with the *Virginia Quarterly Review*. He served six years in the Army National Guard, including a one-year tour in Iraq.

Contributing Editors
Daniel Alarcón, Diana Athill, Peter Carey, Sophie Harrison, Isabel Hilton, Blake Morrison, John Ryle, Lucretia Stewart and Edmund White.

GRANTA 116: SUMMER 2011 | EVENTS

LONDON

The Global Citizen and 9/11: Adventures in Travel and Security
5 September, 6.45 p.m., Asia House, 63 New Cavendish Street, London W1G 7LP
Pico Iyer in conversation with Ellah Allfrey. For ticket information, please visit www.asiahouse.org or call 020 7307 5454.

Ten Years Later, London Launch
6 September, 6.30 p.m., Foyles Bookstore, 113–119 Charing Cross Road, London WC2H 0EB
Readings, discussion and drinks with authors from the issue. Free.

Lost Liberty and Silence
8 September, 6.30 p.m., Free Word Centre, 60 Farringdon Road, London EC1R 3GA
A discussion with *Granta* and English PEN on what is given up in the wake of terror. Free.

9/11: How Remembering Tells Our Future
9 September, 7 p.m., Frontline Club, 13 Norfolk Place, London W2 1QJ
A discussion with Tony Curzon-Price, Isabel Hilton and other *Granta* contributors on media, memory and 9/11. In association with openDemocracy. Please visit www.frontlineclub.com/events for ticket prices and bookings.

9/11: Ten Years On
11 September, 11 a.m., Hampstead and Highgate Literary Festival, London Jewish Cultural Centre, Ivy House, 94–96 North End Road, London NW11 7SX
David Aaronovitch, Gavin Ensler, Frank Ledwidge and John Freeman in discussion. For ticket prices and information, visit www.hamhighlitfest.com.

The Terminal Check
12 September, 6.30 p.m., Paradise Row, 74 Newman Street, London W1T 3DB
An interactive literary salon about travel, security and global living post-9/11. Free.

CHICAGO

Ten Years Later, Chicago Launch
8 September 7 p.m., Barbara's Bookstore, 1218 S. Halsted Street, Chicago, IL 60607
Granta 116 contributors Nuruddin Farah and Anthony Shadid join Aleksandar Hemon and Nami Mun to explore themes in the recent issue. Free.

NEW YORK

The Fireman's Family and the Soldier
6 September, 7 p.m., Barnes and Noble, 150 East 86th Street, New York 10028
Peter Carey introduces Phil Klay and Samantha Smith, writers from Hunter College who are contributors to *Granta* 116.

Islamophobia, the Media and Echoes of 9/11
7 September, Venue TBC
John Freeman, Todd Gitlin, Lawrence Joseph and Alia Malek discuss key issues that arose post-9/11. In association with the South Asian Journalists Association and Voice of Witness.

Ten Years Later, Manhattan Launch
8 September, 7 p.m., McNally Jackson, 52 Prince Street, New York 10012
Celebrate the launch of *Granta* 116 with discussion and drinks with contributors. Free.

Ten Years Later, Brooklyn Launch
9 September, 7 p.m., BookCourt, 163 Court Street, Brooklyn 11201
Join Nicole Krauss, Jynne Martin and Lawrence Joseph for readings and discussion. Free.

TORONTO

Ten Years Later, Toronto Launch
7 September, 6 p.m., Type Books, 883 Queen Street West, Toronto M6J 1G3
Readings and conversation with Jared Bland, Sadaf Halai and Kathryn Kuitenbrouwer. Free.

WASHINGTON DC

Ten Years Later, Washington DC Launch
13 September, 7 p.m., Politics and Prose,
5015 Connecticut Avenue NW, Washington,
DC 20008
Steve Coll discusses Ten Years Later with Olga
Grushin, *Granta* 116 contributor Elliott Woods
and Robin Wright. Free.

GRANTA ACROSS AMERICA

We're taking *Granta* 116 across America,
starting 6 September in various cities and
ending with San Francisco's Litquake on
11 October. Please check granta.com/events
for participating authors and details. Here is
a list of venues that will be hosting events. All
are open to the public.

ANN ARBOR, MI
Nicola's Books
2513 Jackson Avenue
Ann Arbor, MI 48103
www.nicolasbooks.com

BOSTON, MA
Porter Square Books
25 White Street
Cambridge, MA 02140
www.portersquarebooks.com

BOULDER, CO
Boulder Bookstore
1107 Pearl Street
Boulder, CO 80302
www.boulderbookstore.indiebound.com

BUFFALO, NY
Talking Leaves Books
3158 Main Street
Buffalo, NY 14214
www.tleavesbooks.com

CORTE MADERA, CA
Book Passage
51 Tamal Vista Boulevard
Corte Madera, CA 94925
www.bookpassage.com

HOUSTON, TX
Brazos Bookstore
2421 Bissonnet Street
Houston, TX 77005
www.brazosbookstore.com

IOWA CITY, IA
Prairie Lights Bookstore
15 South Dubuque Street
Iowa City, IA 52240
www.prairielights.com

MADISON, CT
R.J. Julia Booksellers
768 Boston Post Road
Madison, CT 06443
www.rjjulia.com

MINNEAPOLIS, MN
Target Performance Hall
The Loft Literary Center, Open Book
1011 Washington Avenue South
Minneapolis, MN 55415
www.loft.org

OAKLAND, CA
Diesel Bookstore
5433 College Avenue
Oakland, CA 94618
www.dieselbookstore.com

PASADENA, CA
Vroman's Bookstore
695 E. Colorado Boulevard
Pasadena, CA 91101
www.vromansbookstore.com

PHILADELPHIA, PA
Robin's Bookstore and Moonstone
Arts Center
110 A S. Thirteenth Street
Philadelphia, PA 19107
www.robinsbookstore.com

RALEIGH, NC
Quail Ridge Books & Music
3522 Wade Avenue
Raleigh, NC 27607
www.quailridgebooks.com

RICHMOND, VA
Fountain Bookstore
1312 East Cary Street
Richmond, VA 23219
www.fountainbookstore.com

SANTA FE, NM
Collected Works Bookstore & Coffeehouse
202 Galisteo Street
Santa Fe, NM 87501
www.collectedworksbookstore.com

SEATTLE, WA
Elliott Bay Book Company
1521 Tenth Avenue
Seattle, WA 98122
www.elliottbaybook.com

ST LOUIS, MO
Left Bank Books
321 N. Tenth Street
St Louis, MO 63101
www.left-bank.com

TEMPE, AZ
Changing Hands
6428 S. McClintock Drive
Tempe, AZ 85283
www.changinghands.com

LITERARY FESTIVALS

Granta will also be participating in the
following international literary festivals.
Please check granta.com or the festival
websites for details.

BERLIN, GERMANY
Internationales Literaturfestival Berlin
7–17 September
www.literaturfestival.com

NEW YORK, NY
Litcrawl
10 September
www.litcrawl.org

BROOKLYN, NY
Brooklyn Book Festival
15–18 September
www.brooklynbookfestival.org

CHARLESTON, ENGLAND
Small Wonder: The Short Story Festival
23–26 September
www.charleston.org.uk/smallwonder

PORTLAND, OR
Wordstock
6–9 October
www.wordstockfestival.com

SAN FRANCISCO, CA
Litquake
7–15 October
www.litquake.org

LONDON AND THE UK
DSC South Asian Literature Festival
8–23 October
www.southasianlitfest.com